THE Ninth Sphere

THE Ninth Sphere

JOSEPH SCIUTO

IGUANA

Published by Iguana Books
720 Bathurst Street, Suite 303
Toronto, ON M5S 2R4

Publisher: Meghan Behse
Editor: Lee Parpart
Front cover design: Ruth Dwight, designplayground.ca

ISBN 978-1-77180-494-3 (paperback)
ISBN 978-1-77180-495-0 (epub)

This is an original print edition of *The Ninth Sphere*.

Dedicated to my Uncle Tony.

Prologue

The first of two epiphanies hit me right after I finished watching the New York Knicks go down to another defeat as they edged ever closer to another losing season. The last time my Knicks won a championship was back in 1974. It's hard to believe it has been almost forty years since that victory. But through all of the pain and suffering and yelling at the TV, I have stood by my team. That's more than I can say for a lot of my fellow expatriates out here in Los Angeles. After living here for over thirty years, most of the other New Yorkers I know have switched to the Lakers — a team that has won about fifteen championships since my team won their last one.

Watching my team suffer defeat after defeat is made a little easier with the generous application of ice-cold Budweiser beer. In truth, my Knicks are usually out of the game by halftime, but the pain persists, so I continue drinking until the final buzzer goes off.

After my final beer on this particular night, I extracted myself from the comfy L-shaped couch that sits in front of my big-screen TV, went into my bedroom, and started getting ready for bed. I remember standing there in my boxers, looking around my room, and thinking that I had done okay. I live in a beautiful section of Los Angeles called Studio City, and the house I bought twenty-five years ago is all paid off. Pushing myself to take care of the mortgage early was one of the smartest financial decisions I ever made. Of course, it helped that I have never been married. Actually, I have never even had a steady girlfriend. I have known plenty of girls … just none willing to commit to being exclusive.

I shut the night-light off — a little glowing basketball that I bought about twenty years ago — and lay down on my bed. I fell asleep quickly, and suddenly I was stark naked, on my back, at center court in Madison Square Garden, home of my beloved team. My arms were stretched out, as were my legs. The arena was dark and empty, devoid of fans or players, and a single spotlight moved around until it picked me out like a clown in a circus. I sprang to my feet, covering my crotch with one hand and my eyes with the other, and moved to the edge of the light. I had this desperate feeling that I wanted to step out of the light and into the darkness, but at the same time I was worried that this could be bad for me in some way. As I crouched over and hovered between the cone of light and the darkness beyond, I looked down at center court and there, on the floor, where I had been, was a figure that looked exactly like Leonardo da Vinci's famous drawing, *Vitruvian Man*. Long, wavy hair framing a strong jaw and good cheekbones. Sculpted muscles. Arms and legs in perfect proportion to the rest of his body. The living image of da Vinci's idea of the human form as a microcosm of the universe.

I stared at this unmoving figure and thought, *Maybe my losing Knicks are just out of balance.*

As if being naked at center court wasn't enough, what happened next blew my mind. Vitruvian Man raised himself off the floor and started circling me as though he was studying a deformed alien. He was tall — so tall that for a minute I wondered if he might make a good basketball player. He must have realized that I was sizing him up, because he put his hand to his chin, never taking his penetrating eyes off of me, and started laughing hysterically.

I asked, "What are you laughing about?"

He put his hands close together, as though making fun of my size. Then he reached out one long index finger and tapped my forehead and said in Italian, "Niente dentro." Knowing a bit of Italian, I translated it to mean, "Nothing inside your head."

You arrogant bastard, I thought, but as though proving his point, my mouth and brain couldn't seem to form words.

He kept laughing and laughing, and the sound echoed off the rafters so powerfully that I wondered if the arena would collapse. For once I was happy the Knicks didn't have many championship banners because I was fairly sure that at any moment, they would all have fallen on my head.

I woke up in a cold sweat. The idea of standing stark naked at center court at the world's most famous arena was bad enough. I mean, I didn't start taking off my shirt at the beach until I was almost thirty years old, and at that time I was in great physical shape. But to be fully exposed like that, and to be laughed at in such a humiliating way, was enough for me to go into hiding.

I climbed out of bed, relieved to discover that I was still wearing boxers, and walked into the bathroom. There, under the harsh fluorescent lights, I leaned into the mirror and looked closely at my reflection. It's not like I was ever stupid enough to think that I looked like Clark Gable, or Errol Flynn, or Gregory Peck or George Clooney, but now, for the first time, I saw myself for what I really was: a relatively short guy, somewhat muscular, but with a face that bordered on ugly and with kinky, unmanageable hair. As simple and unflattering as it was, that was the first of my two epiphanies.

Chapter One

Midway upon the journey of our life
I found myself within a forest dark
For the straightforward pathway had been lost.
— Dante (Inferno, Canto 1)

It had become part of my daily routine, sitting on a bench at Moorpark Recreation Center in Studio City, California, watching youngsters play basketball on two full-length courts. It was summertime, which in lovely Southern California simply meant that the kids were off from school. I would arrive at 10:30 a.m. and stay for about an hour and a half. The youngsters, mostly teenagers, were nimble and athletic, and as I watched them it was hard to believe that at one time I was just as agile as any of them.

I was more or less raised on a basketball court, just outside our apartment in the Bronx, in a building complex called Parkchester, in what is loosely known as the projects. My friends nicknamed me "Basketball Jones," because I would play day and night, all year round, come rain, snow, hail or humidity. It wasn't the world's wittiest nickname, but my friends said it with a smile and sometimes shortened it to Jonesy.

For all the hours I put into playing and practicing, I never got very good. On a scale of one to ten, I was probably a three. During lucky stretches, maybe a four. I played with some great ballplayers, including some with talent and smarts that I could never come close to achieving, but I loved the game as much as anyone, and the time I spent on that court was the happiest time of my life.

Decades later, I was reduced to spectating, but it was better than nothing. I would sit there with my iPod as I watched the kids play ball, and just before leaving I would crank up the sound and play Queen's "We Are the Champions." It was what they played on a newscast, while showing highlights of the New York Knicks' last championship win, way back in 1974. I have never forgotten that moment. The Moorpark kids would smirk at me like I was the corniest guy in the world, but I think they secretly enjoyed having a cheering section.

While I was broadcasting their victory song one day, I felt someone sit down beside me. I didn't bother to look until they tapped me on the shoulder. At that point I turned around and found myself face to face with a young girl, maybe six or seven years old, who looked and smelled like she had just crawled up out of a sewer. She was absolutely filthy. The smell made me recoil instantly, and as I looked at her, I could see that she was covered in dirt from the top of her greasy head to the blown-out toes of her ratty sneakers.

I stared at this wretched creature and she stared back. She seemed to be totally unconscious of the layer of filth covering her face, hair and body, including the tattered scraps of cloth that passed for her clothing. When she finally spoke, I was shocked by her soft and melodious voice. I'll always remember her first words: "Do you come to this park often to watch them play ball?"

"Yes, I do," I said, then asked her, "Where in God's name have you been, child, that you could get so filthy?"

"I escaped from over the border and have been on the run."

I eyed her suspiciously. "And what side of the border did you come from, the Mexican or American side? Because you speak perfect English."

"I'm sorry, I lied. I ran away from my foster parents because they were beating me, and that is the truth. My name is Bee."

"I'm Joe."

We stared at each other for another few moments until I felt a lump in my throat.

"Did you really have to run away from your foster parents?"

"I really did."

"Because they were … beating you?"

The urchin nodded.

"Have you talked to the police or children's aid?"

"It wouldn't do any good."

"Why not?"

She eyed me like I was a bit slow. "Do you really not know how any of this works?"

"I suppose I don't."

"Well," she said, "I can't go to the authorities because they would just send me back to the same foster home, and after a few days they'll start beating on me again."

I looked at her and couldn't think of a thing to say. She threw a smile on her face and filled in the silence.

"People tell me I am real pretty, and in a couple of years I could probably make you really good money working as a prostitute."

I couldn't believe what I was hearing. I stared at her and finally said, "Is that your ambition in life, to become a child prostitute?"

"Not really, but it is one way for me to make money. So, what do you think?"

"Are you insane? You're asking me to be your pimp. You're a child and that is totally disgusting and illegal."

"I'm sorry, Joe."

I got up and started walking away. She followed me and asked, "Where are you going?"

"To the bar up the street, and at your age, and as dirty as you are, they won't let you in."

"What are you going to drink?"

"Beer. I love beer."

We came to the entrance to the bar and I looked down at her and said, "Well, Bee, it was nice meeting you."

"It was nice meeting you, Joe. I'll wait for you out here."

I simply shook my head and entered the bar. Hours later, and with a dozen beers under my belt, I walked out of the bar and started walking in the direction of my house.

That's when I heard a voice from over near a dumpster. "So how many beers did you have? You were gone a long time."

I whipped around and there was the dirty little cherub, sitting on a curb next to the bin. I had to squint to be sure she was really there.

"What are you still doing here, Bee?"

"I told you I would wait."

I dug my hands into my pockets and began searching. "What do you want from me? Is it money? A hundred ... two hundred dollars ... will that do?"

She looked up at me and through her dirt-covered face I could see tears roll down her cheeks. "I don't want your money, Joe. I just want to be able to take a shower and not have to sleep on the streets tonight like I have for the last few nights."

It could have been the beer, but as I stood there staring at her, it was like the child shot an arrow through my heart and wiped out whatever logical reasoning I still possessed. The standoff was won, and Bee was my ward for the night.

"Okay, I guess you'd better follow me," I said, and she jumped to attention.

I walked as she skipped and meandered beside me, and within a few minutes I was letting her into my home.

"You can go straight to the shower," I said.

She nodded, and I escorted her to the guest bedroom, and then gave her a tour of the bathroom that was attached to it. As we stood under the bright light, I reached into a cabinet that I had not opened in a few years and took out a clean towel, a washcloth, a fresh bar of soap, and a bottle of shampoo, and handed them all to her.

"Thank you, Joe."

She stared up at me with her arms full, and I looked at her, and I didn't know who was more confused in that moment. Suddenly, a part of my brain started working again and I said, "I can give you some clean clothes, but they're going to be really big on you. Is that okay?"

"That would be wonderful, Joe," she said.

"Wait right here," I said. "Don't get undressed yet."

I went into my bedroom and opened the closet and took out a pair of sweatpants, a sweatshirt and socks. I didn't know what to do about underwear because all I had were men's boxers, so I skipped that part. I brought her the clothes and a plastic bag to put her dirty outfit in, and told her to throw the bag outside the bathroom door so I could wash everything she was wearing.

"Sneakers, too," I said.

She closed the door and a few moments later it opened a crack and the bag with the dirty clothes in it came flying out, followed by her sneakers. I picked everything up and held it all out in front of me. Then I yelled, "Do you like pizza?"

"Yes, Joe, I love pizza," she called back from behind the door.

"Great, I'll order us a couple of pies."

That's when the little wiseass asked me, "Oh, Joe, do you have anything to drink in your refrigerator besides beer?" After a long silence, she said, "That's what I thought. Can you please order me a soda?"

"Of course," I replied. Unfriggin' believable, I thought. The dirty little tramp has been in my house for ten minutes and already she is giving me orders.

"Thank you, Joe," she said just before I heard water running. Her voice was so sweet and soothing that I suddenly felt guilty for thinking of her as a dirty little tramp.

I carried her bag of clothes to the laundry room with my arm extended and my other hand covering my nose. I dumped her clothes straight into the washing machine and threw the sneakers in there too. I didn't want to take any chances touching any of her belongings. God only knew what type of creatures might be living inside them. I put in the maximum amount of detergent, added some stain and odor remover, and chose the hottest, longest setting my machine offered.

While Bee showered and her sneakers banged around in the washing machine, I ordered two pizza pies, garlic bread, and a six-pack of soda. I then took a beer out of the refrigerator and sat down at the kitchen table and started thinking about the possible mess I might be getting into by taking this child into my house, even for one night. I thought about calling child welfare, or the foster care hotline, or even the police, and then decided it could all wait until tomorrow. If they came to get her there would be interviews and a trip to the police station and a long wait until a new foster family could be found, if one was even available. Or maybe Bee was right, and the police would send her right back to the same foster family.

The bell rang and it was the delivery guy. I paid him, left him a nice tip, and took the pizza pies and soda and shut the door with my foot. Then I turned around and nearly dropped the boxes in my own front hall when I saw a kid there that I had never seen before.

"Who the hell are you?" I asked.

"It's me, Joe."

"Me who?"

"Bee!"

"The dirt-encrusted child I met at the park?"

"Ugh, Joe, yes, it's me," she groaned, laughing a little. "Can we please eat the pizza? I am so hungry."

"Sure," I said, not taking my eye off her. "I suppose I have to believe you since you are wearing my sweatpants and one of my shirts. How many times did you have to roll up the pant cuffs?"

"Five."

I put the pizza pies on the table and opened the top box and before I had a chance to ask if she wanted a plate, she was already on her second slice.

I stared at her as she ate. I still couldn't get over the transformation. The child before me looked nothing like the filthy urchin who entered my house an hour earlier. This one had long, straight, light-brown hair that was still a little wet, tied in a ponytail. Her face was a near-perfect oval, and her skin seemed to be glowing, like the layers of an oil painting shining through the translucent surface. She looked like she could have been a mixture of Scandinavian and northern Italian heritage, with her eyelashes, hair, and eyes all various shades of lighter and darker brown.

I sat down across from her and she said, "The pizza is delicious, Joe. Thank you so much." Her mouth was only a little full of pizza when she said it.

"You're very welcome. I guess you were pretty hungry, weren't you?"

She nodded and continued to eat. I couldn't take my eyes off of her. I finally said, "Did you know that you are absolutely beautiful?" She smiled at me with full cheeks that sprouted adorable dimples.

"Thank you," she said. "People always tell me that I'm pretty. That's why I told you I could make money for us in a few years…"

I put my pizza slice down and drilled my eyes into hers. "I swear, if I ever hear you bring up that idea again, I will kick your little butt right the hell out of here and back onto the streets."

She put her pizza slice down too and looked at me like she was about to cry. "I'm sorry, Joe. I didn't mean to upset you. I will never bring it up again. I promise."

I shook my head in silence and walked to the refrigerator, where I took out another beer. I pulled back the tab, took a long swig, and sat down again.

"You really like your beer, don't you Joe?"

"I've been drinking beer since I was your age."

"I didn't know it was legal to drink beer at nine years old way back then."

"Well, it really wasn't legal, and I probably didn't start to really drink until I was fifteen."

"It was legal at fifteen?"

"In the Bronx, it was."

"What's the Bronx?" she asked as she munched away on her fourth slice of pizza. The child was apparently starving.

"It's one of the five boroughs that make up New York City, along with Staten Island, Brooklyn, Queens, and Manhattan."

"Is it very nice there, in the Bronx?"

"It was when I was growing up. I loved the Bronx."

"It's not nice anymore?"

"It's changed a lot, and I haven't been back in quite a while."

"Are you married, Joe?"

"No, never have been."

"You never wanted to get married?"

"I would have gladly got married but none of the girls I liked were interested in me. Just too ugly, I guess."

"I don't think so. You might not look like Justin Bieber, but I bet at his age you were just as cute."

"Thank you. I guess the girls I liked back then just didn't think the Justin Bieber type was very attractive. Tastes change."

"I don't think that's the reason."

"And what do you think is the reason?"

"I think you were just too shy to ask them," she replied.

"Maybe," I said, happy to be given the benefit of the doubt. Then I asked, "What happened to your biological parents? Are they still alive?"

I saw her shift in her seat, but I wasn't expecting what came next.

"They were killed in a car accident three months ago. It happened not that far from here."

"Oh, my God, I'm so sorry," I said. "You weren't in the car, were you?"

"I was," she said. I put down my beer and stared at her in mute amazement. She finally spoke.

"My father was drunk and arguing with my mother and he drove through a red light and a big car hit our car and they were killed. I was in the back seat, but I had my seat belt on and nothing serious happened to me."

"Thank God."

This girl had lived through more in nine years than anybody I had ever met, and she sounded so calm about it.

"If you have a computer, I'm sure we can look it up," she said. "They had a picture of them on TV and a picture of me."

"Did the authorities try to get in touch with any of your other relatives to see if they wanted to take you in?"

"I only have a grandma, but she is very old and living in a home, and she doesn't remember much."

I got up and walked into my bedroom and picked up my laptop computer and put it on the table. "Is it okay if we look it up, or would you rather wait?"

"No, I want you to see it," she said as she walked over to my side of the table, eating her sixth slice of pizza, and sat down next to me. "If you like, I can probably get to it quickly." I slid the computer next to her and watched as she typed into the search engine, "Eve and Adam Roberts killed in auto accident in Los Angeles, CA."

Articles and pictures of her parents and of her came up immediately. It was just as she said. They jumped a stop sign and an SUV smashed into them. I read through a few of the articles, and looked at the pictures of Bee and the wreckage and said, "My God, Bee, thank goodness you were smart enough to wear your seat belt."

"I wish I didn't and that I had been killed also. Then I wouldn't be forced to live with people who beat me and force me to run away and sleep on the streets."

She suddenly stood up and pulled down her oversized sweatpants to reveal a series of gruesome bruises covering her entire backside. I stared at her without touching the blue and purple welts, then asked her to pull her pants up and said, "I need to take you to a doctor right now."

"No, Joe, it doesn't hurt and it will heal on its own. Please, I don't want to go see any doctors. Please!"

I looked into her dark brown eyes and I saw fear, and whereas I thought she should certainly see a doctor I did not have the heart to push the issue. It is one thing to see fear in an adult, but it is a completely different thing to see it in a child. I stared ahead and folded my hands together on the table while I thought.

"Okay," I said. "No doctors for now. But we're going to monitor this. Do you hear me?"

"Yes, Joe," she said, and returned hesitantly to her pizza.

I sat there boiling with silent rage. What kind of animals would do this to a child? I had no children of my own, but I had always believed that hitting children was wrong. I never bought into that old-school bullshit that "a good spanking" was the best remedy for improper behavior. There are countless other ways to teach a child a lesson. You can take away their TV rights, or their computer, or their phone. If I was caught misbehaving, my parents wouldn't allow me out of the house for a week. That was the worst of all possible scenarios. It meant that I wasn't able to play basketball, and it had more of an impact on my behavior than any spanking.

Bee picked up her seventh slice of pizza. I didn't even want to know the last time this child ate. She asked, "So have you been living in this house a long time?"

"Nearly thirty years. I bought it when home prices in this area were a lot lower. Today, I would never be able to afford a house in this neighborhood."

"It's a very nice home," she said. She smiled, and the sight of her dimples helped to relieve the rage that was still churning inside me.

I asked, "What are some of the things that you like doing, Bee?"

"I like looking at movies," she replied.

"What type? Action adventure? Super hero movies?"

"Not so much, I like mysteries and love stories that end happily."

"Yeah," I said softly, as though I understood. "What else?"

"I like going to the beach and watching the seagulls."

"Do you know how to swim?"

"Yes, but it is hard for me to swim in the ocean. The waves knock me over."

"I have a swimming pool out back. If you like, you can go swimming in it."

"Really?" she said, with obvious enthusiasm.

"Sure. Not right now, because you would sink right to the bottom after eating all that pizza and I would have to jump in and pull you out. But you could try it tomorrow."

She laughed at that and I said, "Come on, I'll show you the pool." I got up and I took her little hand and led her out behind the house. She looked out over my rectangular pool for a long time before saying, "It's beautiful."

"As long as I can watch over you, you can go swimming anytime you like."

She smiled and then shook her head and I asked, "What's wrong?"

"I can't go swimming. I don't have a bathing suit." Then, just as suddenly as she said that, she started crying, and I leaned down and asked her what was wrong.

She was sobbing now. Not playing, not acting. Really crying. "I have nothing. Joe, I left without packing a suitcase. I ran out the door and down the street and slept in an alley and ate from a dumpster. I don't have a bathing suit. I have nothing and no one." Her breathing was suddenly strained and she began to hiccup from crying.

I sat her down on one of my lawn chairs and held onto her shoulders. "You have me, Bee. I'm someone."

She looked at me and said, "You're not going to turn me into child services and have them take me back to my foster parents?"

"I'll tell you what I'm going to do. I'm going to get in touch with a lawyer friend and have him get in touch with the local Foster Parent Chapter in Los Angeles. I'll let him handle your case and I will become your foster parent. I think we will have a very convincing case. I will never let them take you back to your foster parents. Never!"

"You would do that for me?" she asked suspiciously.

"Yes, Bee, I can't think of anything I would like to do more," I replied as I looked across at the child. Tears were still flowing down her cheeks and I reached over to wipe them away with the sleeve of my shirt.

She was tiny, and only then did I realize just how tiny she was. The dirt and grime covering her entire body had seemed to obscure her size, and seeing her in my clothes would naturally make her look small. She was wearing sweatpants and a shirt ten sizes too big for her, and when she had pulled down her pants to show me the bruises, I had averted my eyes and simply concentrated on the contusions and welts. But bending down beside her, and putting my hands on both her arms, it became apparent that she was a pint-sized little cherub.

As I rubbed her skinny arms and listened to her hiccups and watched her crying slowly subside, the reality of what I had just promised to do hit me all at once. The world had dropped Bee in my lap, and I was going to have to answer the call.

Chapter Two

We walked back into the house, and I put the one pizza pie that we hadn't touched in the refrigerator. Then I brought the empty box out to the recycling and left Bee inside on the couch, flipping through my dog-eared copy of the *Complete Illustrated History of the New York Knicks*.

The sun had just set, and as I stood there watching the last of a purple sunset slip beyond the horizon, I thought about the day's events. It was pretty clear that I was not thinking rationally. Here I was, sixty-one years old, never married, no children, and now I was thinking about becoming a foster parent to a child that I had met less than a day earlier. The upside was that she was nine, and so there would be no diapers. The downside was that in a couple of years every boy in the neighborhood would want to date her, and I could suddenly be the father of a teenage hellion. I had seen some of my friends' daughters transform overnight from angels into demons, and it frankly scared me.

I went back inside the house and sat on the couch not far from Bee, who looked up and smiled and then went back to my Knicks book. I kept looking at her as I drank my beer. Yes, little girls of five and six had faces that one could easily describe as angelic — that word kept popping into my head — but it was somewhat unusual to see a nine-year-old girl whose face conjured the word so completely. Maybe it was just that I'd had too many beers that day, or maybe I was having an LSD flashback from college ... sure, a little late in life, but it's not as if my brain was ever ahead of the curve. If anything, I seemed to be way behind the curve. I had aced college and gone on to do a master's degree, and all I had to show for my post-graduate education was a spotty career as a busboy, waiter, part-time bartender, and manager at the same restaurant for nearly a quarter of a century. Sure, I made great money — as much as US Senators, not counting the dark money they made on the side from lobbyists, corporations, and Mafia kingpins — but worldly wealth was never the yardstick I wanted to measure my life by.

Before I went to work for the restaurant, I really thought I could make a difference in people's lives. More to the point, I *wanted* to help people. The spark that lit that fire went back to my teen years in the Bronx. I would be playing basketball, practicing when no one else was on the court, and occasionally a mother would pass by wheeling her disabled son. He was about my age — fourteen or fifteen — and he would look at me playing with an eagerness and a desire in his eyes that made me want to do something, anything, to give him the same chance at playing basketball that I and my friends took for granted. I imagined taking all of the passion and energy I was putting into basketball and redirecting it into helping and healing kids like him.

Little did I know how far my life would veer from that original wish. I wasn't even sure anymore if I had made life better for one person on the planet. At sixty-one, I was no longer sure of anything.

The great Hall of Famer Ernie Banks, shortstop for the Chicago Cubs, once said, "When you stop dreaming, you stop living." At times, I felt like I had stopped living a long time ago. I had met Mr. Banks many years earlier, at the restaurant where I would go on to spend my whole career. He was as sweet and generous as a human being could be. The night I met him I went home with a smile on my face, knowing that a man I had idolized as a kid was not only a great ballplayer, but more importantly, a wonderful human being.

I was thinking about all of this when I realized that Bee had put the book down and was watching me with a concerned look on her face.

"Are you having second thoughts about becoming a foster parent?"

"No, sweetheart, that is the last thing I am thinking of, and I can promise you that. I was remembering a great baseball player I met at the restaurant I worked at many years ago. His name was Ernie Banks, and he was so nice. He played way back before you were born."

"I could look him up on the computer and read about him."

"Yes, you could, and he would be the type of person I'm sure you would love."

Bee looked unsure, and I suddenly felt like I might have crossed a line. It was a subtle transgression, but what did I know about her preferences for anything? We had just met. I shrugged and looked down. "I mean, you *might* love him. You would have to see."

Bee's eyes brightened and I saw her return to the way she had been before. Easy and natural. Curious. She smiled and asked, "Do you love baseball the way you love basketball?"

I hid my relief. How strange to be sitting here talking to this precocious child who I hardly knew and to already be so concerned about her opinion of me. I resolved to speak simply and from the heart. I would not make assumptions about her, and I would not try to get her to like me. I would be myself.

"It's a different type of love for me," I said. "In the Bronx, where I came from, there were very few baseball fields and certainly none close to where I lived, but I always looked at the games on TV and listened to them on the radio, and my parents and grandparents used to tell me stories about the game all the time, and especially about the New York Yankees."

"I've heard of the Yankees. They're famous."

"Yes, they are," I said, smiling to myself at the understatement. "We can watch some of their games on television. Would you like that?"

"I would love that," she said. Then she added cautiously, "And maybe you can tell me some of the stories your parents and grandparents told you."

"I would love to do that."

"Did Ernie Banks play for the Yankees?"

"No, he played for the Chicago Cubs. But I was always taught that you had to respect and admire all players, even if they didn't play for the Yankees."

"That is so nice. So, tell me, Joe, how is your love for baseball different from your love of basketball?"

I blinked at her and smiled. "You are like a novelist interviewing someone for a character. I've never heard of a kid nine years old asking such great questions."

Bee just shrugged her shoulders and smiled.

"Okay. Well, there was a basketball court right outside the apartment we lived in, and for the longest time I would play with my friends, night and day, through rainstorms and snowstorms, and I always wanted to play for the New York Knicks, who were and always will be my favorite team. But even though I played all the time, I never got good enough. And as you can see, I'm not very big. It was a dream that would never come true, but it was the happiest time of my life. I loved playing basketball and looking at basketball on TV, whereas I never played baseball and never even thought of becoming a baseball player. That's the difference."

"That's very sad, Joe. I'm sorry you never got to play for your favorite team."

"But I did get to play with my friends, and there are many children who never get that chance. Some are born with disabilities or ailments and others just never get the opportunity to play. I was very lucky."

"I guess you really were lucky," she said. "My parents never put me in sports. I had to figure out ways to bring in money from the time I was six. My dad taught me how to pick pockets on the bus and both of them once got me to rob a Red Cross Christmas donations box outside the grocery store."

"Oh no," I said. "Really?"

"Cross my heart," she said. "I remember they picked out a nice grocery store in Beverly Hills because they thought there would be more money in the collection box. They dressed me up in a hat and sunglasses and told me when to run through and how to grab the box and where they would meet me after I ran around the corner. I did everything they said, but then the strangest thing happened. Just as I was running away with the donation box, I looked up for a second and I saw this beautiful blond woman who looked exactly like that actress … Reese …"

"Witherspoon?"

"Yes. Reese Witherspoon, from *Legally Blonde*."

"And a lot of other movies."

"Maybe it was her and maybe it wasn't. I just remember catching a glimpse of this beautiful blond woman who looked like a movie star and thinking, 'What am I doing here.' That was just last year. I was eight."

"Wow," I said. "Did she see you?"

"I think she did. I felt like she looked into my eyes. But we were both wearing sunglasses, so who really knows."

The stories Bee told about her upbringing had a way of tilting me sideways. I hardly knew what to say. What insight or advice could I, who had had such a happy childhood, possibly offer to a child who had lived on the margins and known so much tragedy in her short life so far? I stammered and flailed until Bee rescued me from my own consternation by changing the topic by asking another of her famous probing questions.

"Did you meet a lot of famous people at the restaurant?"

"Yes, it was a very famous restaurant where a lot of movie people and musicians and ballplayers came to eat or just hang out."

"And were they all nice like Mr. Banks?"

"Yes, they were nice, but not many of them were as nice as Mr. Banks. He was so friendly and gracious that he made you feel important."

As I watched her take this in, I thought about the many times Muhammad Ali came into the restaurant. He was not only "The Greatest" in the ring, but a great human being outside the ring. He would have waiters and busboys sit down at his table with his family and show them card tricks and joke with them. He was a sweet, funny, friendly person with a heart as big as the moon, and whereas Parkinson's disease might have slowed down his motor skills, his mind was as quick as ever. I cried when I heard he died.

When Bee suppressed a yawn I quickly said, "Looks like it might be time for bed."

"But I like hearing the stories," she said as she yawned again.

"And I will gladly tell you more stories tomorrow, and listen to more of yours, but right now you have a nice clean bed to climb into."

We stood up, and I walked her to her bedroom. As she hovered outside the bathroom, I said, "You know, I have plenty of extra toothbrushes they give me every time I go have my teeth cleaned. Would you like one with some toothpaste?"

"Yes, please, and some floss if you have some."

"I have plenty of that, too," I replied, as I walked into my bathroom and picked up a new toothbrush, toothpaste, and dental floss. I thought children always tried to get out of brushing their teeth, never mind flossing them, but apparently not this child. I handed everything to her and said, "It's good to see that you take care of your teeth."

"I really have no choice because my parents had no money to send me to a dentist, and I didn't want to get a toothache because I heard they really hurt." She opened her mouth and showed me her teeth. Even with blots of pizza sauce covering some of them, they positively sparkled, and they were as straight as the teeth one would see on a movie star. Why this surprised me, I don't know. I already had her pegged for an angel. It only makes sense that her teeth would gleam.

I waited for her to finish flossing and brushing her teeth, and then I tucked her into bed and asked if she needed anything else, but she shook her head. I kissed my two fingers and touched them to her forehead and said, "Goodnight, Bee. Sweet dreams." She smiled and as I started walking out of the room she said, "Thank you, Joe."

I turned and looked at her and said, "You're welcome, Bee. And don't you worry, everything is going to turn out great."

"I know. G'night."

I left the door to her room open just a crack, and as I walked into my bedroom it was all I could do to sit on the edge of my bed and stare into space and marvel at the wild joy that was fluttering in my chest. I hadn't felt that way since I was a teenager playing basketball in the Bronx with my friends. It was also the first time in sixty-one years that I had tucked in a child or felt any sense of responsibility for a young person. I was already shocked at how much I wanted this wild, unexpected ride to continue.

One thing I noticed about Bee was how often she said my name. I hadn't heard my name spoken so often since I left the restaurant over a year earlier. Back when I was working the floor, customers and employees would constantly say, "Can you get this for me, Joe?" and "Thank you, Joe," and "What's good on the menu today, Joe?" I had begun to really miss those daily reminders of my own existence, and Bee brought them back, and then some. With her soothing, mellifluous voice, she made my name sound like the sound of waves coming out of a conch shell. She imbued it with magic.

I suddenly remembered the laundry and got up to check on Bee's clothes. Her pants and top and sneakers had been so filthy, and now as I pulled them out of the dryer, I couldn't believe that after one washing in hot water they had come out so clean. I looked at the labels inside her clothes and they were all marked x-small, which was no surprise, because she was tiny. For a moment, I entertained the possibility that she might be an oversized fairy, and the thought made me smile.

I walked into my bathroom, and flossed and brushed my own teeth, adding a little time to my usual routine in an effort to rise to Bee's high standards. I thought about the head start she had in the area of dental care. Unlike this clever girl (or fairy), I had neglected my teeth for the first thirty years of my life, until I finally listened to a girl — someone who I still thought of as the most beautiful girl in the world — and went to see her dentist, Dr. Jacobs. After extensive work that included braces, bridges, drilling, drilling and little more drilling, I was able to proudly show off my teeth and smile and not get any negative feedback.

In addition to working miracles on my teeth, Dr. Jacobs was also a huge sports fan, and despite rooting for different teams we had lively and informed discussions about basketball, baseball, and football. Moreover, his assistant, Belinda, was as sweet and considerate and knowledgeable as any assistant I have ever met…

As I noticed how my mind was wandering down all of these old byways, I laughed out loud at my own train of thought. Something about having Bee in the house was sparking all kinds of memories of wonderful people who I hadn't thought of in years. Thanks to Bee, I was bursting with gratitude.

I got into bed and picked up Don DeLillo's novel, *Libra*, about the Kennedy assassination, but after reading a few pages I fell asleep, and for the first time in ages I slept through the entire night, and woke up at my usual time of five-thirty feeling totally refreshed.

Chapter Three

I put on my exercise gear and walked out of my bedroom and immediately noticed that Bee's door was wide open and that her bed was already made. I walked into the kitchen, and Bee, still in my clothes from the night before, was standing on a high footstool, scrambling eggs over the gas stove.

"What are you doing, sweetheart?" I asked as she looked at me and said, "I'm cooking you breakfast. I hope you like scrambled eggs."

The only type of eggs I like are those that are scrambled. "How did you even know I get up at this time?" I asked.

She pointed to the refrigerator door where I had attached my schedule for when I was still working. Apparently, I never took it down. The only thing on the schedule that remained the same as before was the time I got up. She asked for a plate to put my eggs on, and I picked her up off the footstool and placed her down.

"I don't want you standing over the stove like that. God Forbid you slip and fall. You could get seriously burned."

"I have been cooking like that since I was seven and nothing has ever happened. I have been very careful."

"I'm sure you have, but I want to make sure that nothing happens in the future. When you grow to where you are taller than the stove, then you can start cooking again."

"But I may never get that tall. My parents were very small."

"Well then, you will be one lucky lady as long as you live with me because I will not ask you to cook. A lot of young girls would love that."

"But I like to cook, and I want to help out."

"Oh, don't you worry, I will find things for you to do."

"Promise?"

"Yes, I promise," I said as I took the pan and scooped the scrambled eggs onto a plate.

"And what are you having for breakfast?"

"I already ate. I had a slice of cold pizza, which I love."

"Only one slice?"

"Yes, only one slice, Joe. Last night I was hungry, I couldn't help myself. I never ate that much in my entire life."

"How long did you go without food?"

"Almost two days," she replied. "How are the eggs?"

"Absolutely wonderful. You did great."

"Thank you, Joe."

There was my name again, sprinkled with fairy dust.

"How did you sleep?" I asked.

"Wonderful! It's so nice to sleep in a clean bed. It was like I was in heaven."

"I am going to go for a long walk in a few minutes. Would you like to go?"

"Yes, Joe, I would love to go."

"I cleaned the clothes you were wearing yesterday, and I left them on top of the dryer in the laundry room. Why don't you go change, and then we can go, and afterward we will go to the mall and buy you a bunch of neat clothes and shoes."

"I don't want…"

"What did I tell you yesterday about bringing up money?"

"I'm sorry Joe, I forgot. Do you forgive me?"

"Of course, I forgive you." She smiled and kissed me on the cheek and then ran off to change, leaving me touching the side of my face.

A few minutes later she came running back, dressed in her old clothes that were now shiny clean. The average nine-year-old girl is between four and four-and-a-half feet tall, and Bee was probably around three-and-a-half feet tall. She could easily pass for six or seven, but I was acutely aware that children can have growth spurts at any time, and one day I might wake up and realize that she was suddenly a foot taller. I was hoping not, at least not for a while. She seemed so perfect at the height she was now that I almost wished she never had to grow up.

I went back into my bedroom and took out a hoodie that I suggested she put on. It was about ten sizes too big for her, but at this time in the morning it was still chilly out and it wasn't like she needed to make a fashion statement.

We walked out of the house, and started on my long, regular trek, through lovely Studio City.

As we walked, Bee looked up at me and asked, "Why did you stop running?" I was pretty sure I hadn't said one word to her about being a runner.

"How did you know I used to run?"

It turned out that she had studied my calendar and noticed that I scheduled a run at six every morning. I told her about my hip replacement from ten months earlier, and about how the doctors had reassured me that after a month or two I would be running longer and faster than ever.

"So, it didn't get better?" she asked.

"No, it feels great."

"But you don't feel like running?"

"No, I guess not."

"Did you love running like you loved basketball and baseball?"

I had to think about that. "Not exactly. I loved the feeling it gave me. I felt a lot better when I was running six miles a day."

"Six miles!" she exclaimed. "You must really miss it."

I shrugged.

"And you're sure your hip doesn't hurt?"

"No, the doctors did a great job. It feels as good as new."

Bee sat on that information for a little while and we walked side by side without saying much. I was thinking about how good it felt to talk to someone, and about how little of that I'd done in the past year. Since leaving the restaurant, most of my days were spent alone, except for the couple of hours at the bar drinking. While working at the restaurant I would deal with hundreds of people a day, and I used to dream of the day when I could be alone with my books, and maybe start that novel I had always dreamed of writing. But when I finally had all the time in the world to read and write, I wound up doing less than ever. I would watch TV for hours, and I drank more than ever. I never wrote a word.

Bee looked around at the houses and waved to a man who was out watering his lawn. He just stared at us as we walked past.

"What a friendly chap," she said, as soon as we were out of earshot. I laughed out loud and asked her where she'd heard that expression.

"My dad used to say stuff like that. He would do accents, like a British accent or a German one. He could be funny when he wasn't drinking."

"Oh."

The memory of her dad seemed to deflate her, and she didn't speak for a few moments. Finally, she asked, "Do you know a lot of the people in your neighborhood?"

"Some," I said. "Not many."

"What about the people you worked with? Do you still see them?"

"Not so much," I said. "They're still working and they're all pretty busy."

The truth was, I had tried to keep in touch with my friends from the restaurant, but most of them didn't return my calls or emails, or made excuses when I asked to see them. At first, it really hurt. Many of these people had been my friends for years, and I doubt there was a single employee in that restaurant that I did not go out of my way to help at one point or another. But that's life, and like a billion other employees that left their jobs, I learned that it was "out of sight, out of mind."

Bee started to weave up onto the curb and back down again as she walked and continued to interrogate me about my social life. "What about the customers? Do you keep up with any of them?"

"Actually, yes," I said, suddenly feeling slightly less pathetic. It was true that although many of my fellow employees were quick to forget me, some of my favorite customers kept in touch. We occasionally went out to dinner or lunch or met up for beers. A lot of them were smart, creative people, and loved to shoot the shit about sports and politics. Of course, I didn't put it that way to Bee.

As our conversation meandered all over the place, so did the new little girl in my life. By mile two, Bee was jumping and walking every which way but straight, like a grasshopper. Occasionally she passed right in front of me and I had to detour or stop suddenly to avoid running her over. She was so busy firing questions at me and listening to my answers and pointing out interesting houses that she barely noticed how close she came to being underfoot. She waved to a few other people who came out onto their driveways to pick up newspapers — there were still some of those in this neighborhood — and we dodged a few of the sprinklers that were keeping every lawn and perennial bed and hedge in pristine condition.

Bee smiled and waved at another neighbor, who I didn't know, and said, "You live in a nice neighborhood, Joe."

"Yes, I guess I do," I said, thinking happily that if all went well, this would be her neighborhood, too.

"It's so quiet," she added. "It feels more like the country than the city."

"That's what I always say," I said. "Did your parents ever take you to the country?"

"Sometimes. We would go see my grandparents up north. They're gone now too."

"Where was your foster home?" I asked, surprised that I hadn't thought to inquire about this sooner.

She gave an address in Los Angeles that I knew to be one of the dodgiest parts of downtown.

"How did you get out to Studio City?"

"I scraped together some change and got on a northbound bus and kept going until I saw a park with kids in it. I went back and forth between Woodbridge Park and Moorpark Park for days."

"Did you talk to many other people?"

"A few, but nobody wanted to help. One mom thought she was helping me by calling the police. As soon as I found out what she had done, I ran. I knew I would be back in that foster home that day, with no questions asked."

"Well, I'm glad you found me."

"Me too, Joe."

We talked about some of the different places I had lived, and I told her about how much I love Studio City — how, for me, it has always seemed like a beautiful oasis nestled within the overpopulated jungle that comprised the rest of LA.

After we had walked about a mile, or in Bee's case two miles because of all the jumping around, she asked me if I felt like running. Just like that. "Wanna run?" she said, and I shot her a look of mock contempt that made her laugh.

"Oh, come on," she said. "One block."

"No, I don't think so."

"Joe, please just run with me for a little bit. Please."

I looked at her, which was my first mistake, because her face was like an orb of majestic light that you simply had to follow. My second mistake was listening to her voice, which was like a babbling brook that carried you downstream and made you want to do anything for that kid.

"Okay, but just one block."

She jumped up and down and clapped her hands and squealed with delight. I gave a little groan, and we started jogging side by side.

As we loped along, I was so conscious of her needing to be on the inside to avoid bikes and cars that I didn't even think about my hip. We stopped after the one block because she was out of breath, having never run before. We walked a few more blocks, and after catching her breath she said, "Let's run another block."

We ran another block, stopped, walked a few more blocks so she could catch her breath, and then ran another block and repeated this ritual for a whole six miles, and my hip felt wonderful.

Chapter Four

Back at the house, we took a few minutes to cool down and drink some water, and then I grabbed my wallet and car keys and took Bee by the hand.

"Come on," I said. "We're going shopping."

I let Bee into my 2008 Volvo and got into the driver's seat.

"I like your car," she said. "Is it new?"

"Oh, gosh no," I said. "It just looks new because I hardly ever drive it."

Twelve years after buying the car new, I had gone a total of twenty-one thousand miles. Many citizens of Los Angeles drive twenty-one thousand miles every six months or so. The first eleven years I drove the car back and forth to work, which put about one hundred and fifty miles on the car every week. The last year or so, I don't know if I averaged more than twenty-five miles a week.

I did not like driving, and ever since my mental breakdown and severe and debilitating bouts of depression, I tried to stay off the road as much as possible. Killing myself would have been fine, but I did not want to kill or harm innocent people just because I couldn't control my emotions behind the wheel. After about ten years of trying different types of medication, my psychiatrist came up with a cocktail of psychotropics that finally helped me, and when Bee found me, I was starting to have days when I would go five or six hours feeling pretty normal. That might not sound like much, but after going months at a time feeling like I was living in a fog and contemplating suicide constantly, I considered that real progress. I didn't tell Bee any of this, but I was thinking about it as we were getting ready to go to the mall.

I checked to make sure Bee had her seat belt on and she did, and then I drove down the driveway and headed toward the Sherman Oaks Galleria and shopping mall. I didn't want to alarm Bee but I had to ask, "Do you think the authorities working with children's services might be looking for you?"

"Probably not."

"What makes you think that?"

"Mainly because my foster parents likely haven't reported me missing yet. The bruises are still too fresh. If the authorities saw the bruises from the beatings they would take me away from them, and stop giving them eight hundred and fifty dollars a month to take care of me. They would then place me back into the foster care system, but I'll kill myself before I let them do that."

I looked at her, horrified. I don't know why I was so shocked. I had thought about killing myself hundreds of times during the worst of my depressions. I just couldn't believe that a nine-year-old would say such a thing.

I tried to sound calm as I said, "I would never let that happen, even if we have to move to Canada."

She smiled at me, and I asked, "Do you have a counselor, a social worker, that you can get in touch with and report what your foster parents did to you?"

"Yes. Her name is Lisa. She is very sweet, but…"

I looked at her and I could see she was getting anxious, but it was important that I got answers to these questions because the longer we went without reporting that she was living with me the worse it could get not only for her but for me.

"Are you going to turn me in?" she asked. "Because if you are, I only ask that you let me know beforehand so I can get a head start. I am not going back there."

"I'm asking because I want to become your foster parent and adopt you, and I would like to do it legally so we don't always have to be looking over our shoulders hoping that no one is following us. Isn't that what you want?"

"Yes, Joe, that is what I want."

"Bee, no one is taking you away from me and I seriously mean that. I promise!"

"Thank you, Joe."

I parked in the galleria, took Bee's hand, and we walked into a big department store.

As we made our way to the children's clothing section, I noticed that Bee was gripping my arm so tightly that it was starting to lose circulation. I could feel her little body trembling as people came and went all around us, and I suddenly questioned the wisdom of bringing her to such a busy place so soon after her escape from an abusive home. For the first time in my life, my choices and decisions were directly affecting the fragile psyche of a child, and I had to be careful.

At no time in my life could I personally relate to what Bee had already been through in her short nine years on this planet. I could sympathize with her situation, but I had no experience dealing with abusive adults, and I already felt like I was out of my depth.

Some wag — a writer — talked about being "the victim of a happy childhood," and you could almost say the same of me. While no upbringing is totally perfect all the time, mine came pretty close. My parents, aunts and uncles, and grandparents were always there for my two brothers and me. My mother came from a family of fifteen, and at one time most of her siblings and my many cousins lived within a couple of blocks of each other in the Bronx. When my beautiful mom died of cancer when I was sixteen years old, my aunt Carmela and her husband, my uncle Al, immediately filled the void left by the passing of my mom.

My aunt Carmela, who looked like Sophia Loren, and my uncle Al, who played the part of the family lawyer, became our substitute parents. This took the pressure off my father, who worked twelve-hour days as a paper handler at American Bank Note. He was able to go to work every day, knowing that we were in the supremely capable hands of my aunt Carmela, who cooked for us, cleaned, and shopped for the family. The sacrifices that she and my uncle made for us were ones that I could never repay. I only wished that my aunt Carmela had lived longer. She died at the age of sixty-six and she suffered terribly at the end. I think about her every day, and every day I regret that I didn't tell her more often how much I loved her. She was goodness personified: a kind, caring, and utterly unselfish person.

My uncle lived another twenty-five years after my aunt passed, and so I had ample opportunities to tell him how much I loved and appreciated everything he did for my family. I'm happy to say that I took every one of those opportunities. The last year of my uncle's life was spent in a nursing home in Brooklyn, near Sheepshead Bay, with a view of the water. He suffered from Alzheimer's, and occasionally he remembered me, but most often he did not.

The last time I visited him, with my two brothers, we took him outside and sat by the water and drank a few beers. My brothers went off to get pizza for us and as my uncle and I were sitting there, he stared out at the water and out of nowhere he said to me, "I miss Carmela. She was so lovely. Do you remember her?"

"Of course. She was a saint. I will never forget her."

He didn't reply, but there were tears flowing down his cheeks. He had not mentioned her in quite a few years, especially after his memory seriously started fading.

Shortly thereafter, he passed away. I missed his funeral because of an injury that I had just suffered that made any type of movement very difficult. I was gutted to miss the service, but at least with him I had no doubt that he knew how much I loved and appreciated everything he and my aunt did for us.

Once Bee started to relax, she began acting like a nine-year-old girl ... or at least my idea of how a girl her age would behave. I made it quite clear to her that I expected her to buy at least ten days' worth of clothes, plus some exercise gear for our early morning outings. She would also need pajamas, sneakers, shoes, sandals, socks, and any other miscellaneous items I might be forgetting.

She asked, "Should I buy a two-piece bathing suit or a one-piece?"

"What's the difference?" I asked.

"A two-piece is called a bikini, and it has a small top and bottom. A one-piece covers most of your body. It's looks like something a gymnast would wear."

"A one-piece," I remarked.

"Are you sure, Joe?" she asked, as she started to giggle.

"Yes, Bee, I'm quite sure."

Unbelievable, I thought to myself. She's nine years old, could pass for six, and already she's thinking about wearing bikinis. Next, she will be asking me if she should buy makeup.

Almost three hours later we walked out of the mall carrying five shopping bags filled with clothes, shoes, brushes, combs, and a pair of one-piece bathing suits. We then walked into a supermarket and bought a ton of groceries. I expected Bee to ask for a bunch of sugary snacks, but she stuck to the healthy stuff: milk, orange juice, bottled water, soda, cereal, meats, fish, vegetables, fruits, and popcorn and mixed nuts for when we looked at Yankees games and movies. Finally, we came to the beer aisle and I loaded up on my favorite beer, old reliable Budweiser.

"You know, Joe, one cannot live on beer alone," the wiseass said, and just as I was about to jokingly reply, "You're right, I need to pick up some whiskey and wine," I remembered that her parents were killed because they were drunk and drove through a red light. So, I said, "You're right. That's why I always have to remember to bring you shopping with me. You're a great reminder that I need to eat healthy food."

I reached down and kissed her on the head and remarked, "You are precious."

"Thank you, Joe."

***

Back at home, we unloaded the car and started ferrying everything into the house. Bee was small, but she was unusually strong for her size. Either that, or she had so much adrenaline running through her system that she was picking up more weight than someone her size would usually be capable of lifting. I imagined this was like Christmas for her … or more like the Christmas she never had.

I put away the groceries and Bee went into her room and started setting up her closet with all of her new clothes, shoes, sneakers, and girl stuff that I didn't ask about. I looked down at my old-fashioned landline and noticed that it showed a busy signal. The only other landline in the house was in my bedroom. I walked toward my bedroom and entered just as Bee was hanging up the phone.

"Whom were you talking to?" I asked, in what I assume was a parental tone. She looked frightened, as she looked down at the floor. "Bee, who were you just talking to?"

"Lisa," she replied. "Please, don't be mad with me."

"Lisa, the social worker?"

"Yes, she is coming over in a couple of hours. I don't like feeling like a criminal, and having you be worried that someone might notice me and report me to the police."

"Don't you think you should have told me first?"

"I couldn't help myself. I had to do it."

"I was going to hire a lawyer, and she would have handled everything legally and she would have talked to Lisa."

"It's very complicated, Joe. I read all about it on your computer."

"I also read about it, and it's not that complicated."

"I told Lisa that you were a friend of my parents. That should make it easier."

My mouth must have been hanging open while I processed the fact that she had lied. What if this statement was disproven? What if the lie became a reason to deny my application for custody? I was suddenly angry at Bee for putting us in this situation, and it must have been obvious from my tone of voice when I said, "Go take a shower, and put on your new clothes. We'll talk about this later."

She looked ashen and ran into her room. I walked into the kitchen and took out all the beer I had bought and put it back into the trunk of the car. The last thing I needed was for Lisa to think I was some kind of drunk and a possible child molester. I was still upset with Bee — something I thought was nearly impossible — but after a while I calmed down. I decided that the last thing I needed was for this Lisa person to see fear in Bee's eyes that she connected to me.

I desperately wanted a beer, but there was no way I was going to give into that temptation. The truth was that I was scared to death I might lose her. This child, who I had tried to get rid of with a two-hundred-dollar bribe, was suddenly the center of my life. I wasn't sure I could live without her, and I knew for sure that I didn't want to try.

Bee walked out of her bedroom, dressed in a lovely red blouse and dungarees that she called skinny jeans. Her new blue and red sneakers matched her outfit perfectly. There was worry in her eyes, and she looked down at the ground as she joylessly showed off her outfit.

"You look beautiful," I said, quickly adding, "Bee, I'm sorry I got mad at you. I just don't want to lose you."

She ran over and hugged me, and with tears running down her cheeks, she said, "I'm not going anywhere, Joe."

I bent down and wiped the tears away and asked, "You promise?"

"Yes, Joe, I promise."

Chapter Five

Lisa Hernandez, the social worker, showed up within the hour and knocked lightly on the door. As I let her in, she shook my hand and then looked across at Bee with a smile. Bee walked slowly from the couch to the door and slipped her hand in mine. Then she made us both smile when she introduced us formally by saying, "Lisa, this is Joe. Joe, this is Lisa."

"Thank you, Bee," Lisa said. I could tell right away that this young woman with the lovely olive skin and sparkling brown eyes was from Brooklyn. With that accent, there was no hiding her origins, any more than I could hide being from the Bronx. Everything about her immediately put me at ease.

Bee never let go of my hand the whole time we were getting Lisa settled in the living room, and I could feel her little hand tightening around mine. She was smiling stiffly at Lisa and almost crouching behind me.

Lisa saw this and reached across to gently grasp Bee's other hand. "Don't look so scared, my lovely angel, I am not taking you away or calling the police, but I need to ask you some questions. Is that okay?"

"Yes, that's okay."

Bee sat on the couch next to Lisa and I settled into a wing chair a few feet away. Bee looked a little more relaxed, but I could tell she was worried about being questioned.

"Now, why did you run away from your foster parents?"

"Because they beat me, and yelled at me for no reason," Bee replied and, just like she did with me, she suddenly pulled down her pants and showed Lisa the bruises that ran along her backside.

"Oh my God, you need to see a doctor." ·

"No, Lisa, I don't need to see a doctor. It doesn't hurt, and I don't want another person poking around on me. Joe wanted to take me to a doctor yesterday, and I wouldn't let him."

I could see anger in Lisa's eyes where I previously saw kindness. She almost seemed to be talking to herself as she said, "What type of animals would do this to a child? I warned the agency about placing her with that family, but they somehow passed the test. I will see to it, one way or the other, that they are no longer a problem." She looked up at me and asked, "Can Bee and I use one of your bedrooms? I need a private place where I can take pictures of the bruises, and I'll need to document her allegations of abuse."

"You can go into her bedroom," I replied.

"Yes, that would be a good place, Lisa, and while we're in there I can show you all the new clothes and shoes Joe bought me."

Lisa smiled and took Bee by the hand and they went to the bedroom and closed the door.

I was not a nosy person, and this was something I took a certain amount of pride in, but that was before Bee walked into my life, and I had no intention of having her walk out of it. So, like a conscientious daddy, I stood by the door and listened.

For the first few minutes, Bee talked excitedly and gave Lisa a tour of her new wardrobe, the clean sheets on her bed, and the view of the pool from her window. Then the discussion switched to the pressing subject at hand and Lisa asked, "So you really like it here?"

"Yes, Lisa, I have never been happier."

"Do you mean you're happier than when you were living with your parents before the accident?"

I heard Bee hesitate, then say, "Yes. My parents were always fighting and drinking, and they would blame me for stuff I never did."

"Did they ever hit you?" Lisa asked, and there was a long pause.

"Yes, but not like my foster parents. My real parents hit me maybe once or twice a month. My foster parents hit me once or twice a day."

Lisa was silent for a long moment, then spoke very gently to Bee. "I'm so, so, so sorry that your mom and dad hit you. No child should have to go through that. And I'm even more sorry that my agency put you in a home that was so much worse than the one you had before. That should never have happened."

I couldn't hear Bee's reply, but I heard a small sound that could have been her voice, then Lisa's again.

"You feel safe here, don't you?" she asked.

"I really do, Lisa, Joe is wonderful. I only wish my real father was like him."

"And what makes Joe so wonderful?"

"He's kind and generous and he listens to what I have to say. He makes sure I have everything I need. He doesn't yell, or threaten me, or blame me for things I have not done."

Lisa said something I couldn't hear, and then Bee kept talking while I stood on the other side of the door, listening with rapt attention.

"He took me in when nobody else would. People ran away from me, I was so dirty, but not Joe. Well, at first, he wanted to. He offered me money to go away. But then he took a chance on me and here I am. He let me take a shower and gave me dinner and a bed to sleep in and washed my clothes and took me shopping. He is so nice. I love Joe so much, and I am never going to leave him."

"I'm not here to take you away from Joe. I'm here to make sure that you're okay, and I also care very much about you too, Bee. I'm sorry it has been so difficult for you, but I'm very happy you found Joe and are now living in this lovely house."

Then I heard Lisa ask Bee to lower her skinny pants so she could take pictures of the bruises. During this, Lisa once again said that she thought Bee should go see a doctor, but Bee refused, saying, again, that nothing hurt.

I retreated to the living room and sat on the couch. Seconds later I heard Bee practically shrieking at Lisa, "No! You promised. I'm not going anywhere with you!"

"You would just be down the block from Joe. I could be fired if I left you with a man that I don't know anything about."

"I told you, he's great! Better than anyone I have ever known."

"I'm sure he is, but there's paperwork involved and a background check to make sure he doesn't have a criminal record."

"And how did the paperwork and background check turn out with my last foster parents who beat me?"

"I'm so sorry about that, but this time it's totally going to be different."

"You're right about that. I'm not going anywhere," I heard Bee scream and then slam her bedroom door. I had moved from the couch to the foyer, and could see that Lisa had suddenly found herself standing in the hallway. She looked at me and then knocked gently on the bedroom door.

"Please Bee, don't do this to me. Please."

"Go away, I never want to see you again."

I had feared this scenario, and it was the reason I wanted to get in touch with an attorney. But what happened next took me totally by surprise.

Lisa, the social worker, dropped her phone and her briefcase on the hallway carpet and started crying her eyes out, begging this nine-year-old child to let her back into the room, while the nine-year-old yelled, "Go away, and get yourself a life."

This went on for a good ten minutes. I went to get tissues for Lisa, and when I came back she was slumped against the wall opposite Bee's bedroom door, with her head in her hands.

"Lisa," I said, but she didn't even look up.

I placed the box of tissues next to her on the floor and went to the kitchen to get her a glass of water. When I came back, this supposedly professional social worker was curled up in the fetal position next to Bee's door.

"Lisa," I said.

Nothing.

I leaned over her and looked more closely and heard a little sniffling sound, like a soft snore. That's when I realized that she had fallen asleep. For a moment, I thought I had been thrown into a Charlie Chaplin movie. This employee of the state was literally out cold in my hallway. I thought about leaving her there and taking the child and running off to Canada, as per my promise to Bee, but that was almost as childish as Lisa's approach to the current situation.

I knocked on Bee's door, but she didn't answer. So I went outside and walked around to the back of the house and knocked on her window. The sound startled her and then she smiled and ran over to the window and pulled it open.

"Hi Joe. Are we going to run away?"

"No, angel, that won't do any good," I replied as I climbed through the window and into her room.

"Well, that was far too easy," I said, straightening my clothes. "I guess I'm buying window bars."

Bee smiled at that. I took her hand and we sat down on her bed beside each other and I said, "Lisa lives only two blocks away, and if anytime you feel threatened, you can run back here. I am going to give you my cell phone so you can call anytime you want to talk. I am going to fill out all the paperwork, and you and Lisa can come by later and pick it up. In the meantime, I will call a high-power lawyer friend of mine and send him copies of everything Lisa has had me fill out. He will get this resolved quickly and legally so we never have to look over our shoulders thinking someone is following us."

"But will you still love me after we have been apart for so long?" she asked.

"Good question," I said. "Hmm."

She punched me lightly on the arm and smiled.

"It won't be so long," I said. "Besides, love doesn't work like that. I will miss you so much that my love will grow to the height of the Empire State Building."

She threw her arms around me and started crying, her small body trembling. "You promise?"

"I promise."

When she let go, I went to the closet, pulled out a small suitcase with wheels, and put it at the foot of the bed for Bee to use. Then I walked over to the door, winked at Bee, and said, "Watch this." I opened the door and in tumbled Lisa, waking up as she landed on her shoulder on the carpet.

"Have a nice nap?" I asked.

"I'm sorry, I was just so tired," she said as I helped her stand up. She looked at Bee, who had started packing her clothes and accessories. "I'm sorry Bee. Please don't hate me." Bee looked at her and didn't say a word and continued stuffing her belongings into the suitcase.

While Bee was packing, I took Lisa on a tour of the house. I imagine it was part of her job to inspect the home environment that Bee was going to live in, and since the only things I collected were books, vinyl albums from my favorite musicians and bands, and a few sporting collectables from the glory days of my New York Knicks, I wasn't much concerned. But boy I was happy I hid the beer in the car, because Lisa surprised me by asking to see the inside of my fridge. She made it seem like she was just admiring an antique Frigidaire like the one her parents had back home, but I knew her real agenda. She wanted to know if I kept enough food in the house for a growing child. One day earlier she would have found a few morsels of food, some spoiled milk, a dried-up hunk of brie, and enough beer for a poker night. But thanks to my shopping trip with Bee, my refrigerator was bursting with fresh produce and meat and juice and milk. It looked like a display in a health food store.

"Nice," she said. "You don't see too many of these models anymore. It's just like the one my parents have at home."

I smiled and let her have her cover story. In truth, I was impressed that she was being so thorough.

During our tour, Lisa stopped next to a framed picture of the 1973-74 New York Knicks championship team. She scrutinized me closely, almost smiling.

"Okay, a boy from the Bronx: a Yankees fan, a Giants fan, Rangers, and of course the Knicks."

"Correct. My turn. A girl from Brooklyn: a New York Mets fan, a Jets fan, Rangers, and New York Knicks."

"Correct. And I have to admit that rooting for the Jets and Knicks is rough. But since I love my daddy and know he would never lie to his daughter, I have to believe him when he swears that at one time, before I was born, both the Knicks and Jets had good teams. I guess I was a jinx."

I laughed, and then I asked, "So Lisa, besides work, what brought you out here, and how often do your parents ask you when you are moving back home?"

"I went to UCLA and I fell in love with it out here, and yes, my parents ask me all the time when am I moving back home ... almost as much as they ask me when am I going to meet a rich movie star, fall in love, and get married. I don't have the heart to tell them that I am past the age requirement for most movie stars."

Lisa left a bunch of paperwork for me to fill out, and said that the quicker I filled it all out, the quicker Bee would be back living here. I told her I would have it all ready in a few hours, and she said she would drop by that night with Bee and pick it up. Bee walked out of her room rolling her mini suitcase behind her and remarked, "Don't believe anything she says."

Lisa looked at her and started to cry again. "Please don't say that, Bee. I love you so much."

"Of course, you do. That's why it's so easy for you to break your promises," Bee replied angrily.

I tried to correct Bee with a stern look, but she was steaming at Lisa and didn't notice. Lisa was crying steadily by that time, so I grabbed a bunch of tissues and handed them to her as we walked outside to Lisa's car. The social worker stood next to her car and wiped her eyes and blew her nose, then stuffed the tissues into her coat pocket. She opened the car door for Bee, but the little girl refused.

"I'm not getting in there. Joe and I will walk to your apartment. I don't trust where you might take me. It might not be to your apartment at all. You could be planning to take me back to that family that enjoys beating me so much."

"Bee, please, you know I would never do that."

Bee lifted her suitcase onto the front seat and shut the door and said, imperiously, "Drive slow and we will follow you."

Lisa looked at me, and I shrugged my shoulders. She sighed and shut the passenger's side door, climbed into her car, and pulled out of the driveway, then drove toward her apartment, which was only a couple of short blocks away. She kept the hazards on the whole time, and I could see her checking us in the rearview mirror every few seconds as she rolled forward at about ten miles an hour, stopping occasionally to let us catch up to her. We followed behind, and my little Bee was so furious that she didn't jump back and forth at all, but walked in a straight line for the first time since I had known her.

Lisa parked her car, and Bee grabbed her suitcase. Lisa said, "We're here. Like I said, the quicker you get the paperwork done the quicker all of this will be resolved."

"You'll have it all back tonight," I replied as Lisa motioned for Bee to follow her into the building.

Bee stood her ground. "I'm not going alone up to your apartment. Joe has to come, just in case you have something evil already planned for me. I wouldn't put anything past you."

Lisa was on the verge of crying again, and I was starting to feel sorry for the young woman.

The three of us got into her building's cramped elevator and rode in silence up to Lisa's floor. Lisa led us down a narrow, poorly lit hallway to her apartment and let us in. The apartment was very clean, but strangely barren, as though no one lived in it. There was a couch in the living room and a coffee table in front of it, but that was it. No pictures on the walls. No other furnishings.

The kitchen was immaculate, and naturally there was no table. The countertops were bare. Bee asked Lisa, "Are you sure this is your apartment?"

"Of course, it's my apartment. Why do you ask?"

"I'm not sure what to think, anymore. It doesn't look like anyone lives here. You could be kidnapping me. I don't even see a TV."

"Bee," I said sternly.

"That's okay," Lisa said. "She needs to let out her anger, and I guess I'm the punching bag." She shot a look at Bee and added, "There's a TV in my bedroom, with my computer and bed. Come see."

We walked into her bedroom, which actually looked like someone did live there ... even if it wasn't Lisa. Clothes were flung all over the place, and the bed was unmade, with sheets and blankets scattered randomly about. Bee looked at the TV, which had to be from the early 1990s. It had a curved screen, and a large back end where the picture tube was located.

Bee asked, "What is that?"

"It's a TV, silly," Lisa said. "What do you think it is?"

I looked at the TV and it brought back memories of when I was a child and had to get up and change channels, before the advent of the remote.

"Does it get the Yankees games?" Bee asked.

"No, I only have basic cable. I don't get any movie or sports channels."

"Well, I'm sorry Lisa, but I am not going to be able to stay here. I need to look at the Yankees games. Isn't that so, Joe?"

"You can watch the games on my computer," Lisa remarked.

"I didn't know the games could be seen on a computer?"

"Well, you don't actually see the games, but you get the scores in real time, and when someone gets a hit you can see a tiny figure on the bases. That's how I keep up with the Mets."

"No," Bee remarked with a nod of her head and continued, "That won't work for me. Sorry, but we are going to have to leave."

"Okay ladies, enough of this. Lisa, please call your cable provider?"

"Why?" she asked.

"Because I don't want to see a lovely and caring lady like yourself go without the basic necessaries that everybody in the world seems to have these days."

"I can't afford…"

"You don't have to," I said, taking out my wallet and holding up a credit card.

"No, no," she said. "I can't take anything from you."

"If anyone asks, tell them it was a gift from your grandfather. I have enough money to buy this building. Please, just do it."

Lisa puzzled over this for a good minute before she took out her phone and made the call. While she was on hold, I took the little wiseass, who had recently morphed into a small tyrant, into the living room.

I sat her down on the couch and said, "Please stop being so mean to Lisa. I know you're worried, but that is no reason to punish poor Lisa."

"But I love Lisa," Bee replied.

"Well, you are showing your love in a very strange way. Lisa has an important job helping stranded children find a home, and she doesn't make much money."

"I'm sorry, Joe. I just don't want to lose you."

"And you're not going to lose me. You'll be back in our house very soon. In the meantime, I expect you to be nice to Lisa. It might even help speed things up. And it's the right thing to do."

"Okay, Joe. I'm sorry."

Lisa walked into the living room and handed me the phone. I ordered the complete, platinum package for her, with every movie, sports, news, and national geography channel. I gave them my credit card and told them to bill it for a year.

I then had her go online and pick out her favorite TVs. I then called up Fry's Electronics in Burbank and instead of ordering the lesser brand, smaller TVs she picked out, I ordered and paid for two sixty-inch, flat-screen TVs that, according to the salesperson, were the best they offered. Lisa was waving at me the whole time and mouthing something about them being too expensive. I turned my back on her and finished the sale, then handed my phone to her so she could give the address for delivery. With a little extra incentive, the TVs and a cable person would magically show up within the hour. I took five hundred dollars from my wallet and placed it on her coffee table, and told Lisa to tip the person who came to set everything up for her, and to use the rest to buy food and whatever else they might need.

Lisa said, "I don't know how to thank you."

I pointed at Bee and replied, "You can thank me by taking good care of her, and getting her back to me as soon as possible. And under no circumstances does this child get placed with another family, even for an hour, because then there will be hell to pay. Are we clear?"

"Yes, as long as you fill out the paperwork…"

"The paperwork will be back to you later today."

I looked down at Bee and struggled to stop myself from tearing up. I had known the child for barely a day, and yet I felt connected to her in the way I imagined a loving father or mother would feel if they suddenly had to give up their nine-year-old child to a social worker. I hugged and kissed Bee on the head, and left the apartment with a wet mark on my shirt where she had been crying during our hug.

I rode the elevator down and left the building. I imagined the rent in this building, for a one-bedroom apartment like Lisa's, in this lovely neighborhood of Los Angeles, went for at least twenty-two hundred dollars a month … probably more than fifty percent of Lisa's monthly income. When you look at it like that, it's easy to understand why she didn't have much furniture or any modern luxuries. It felt good to buy her the TVs and one year of premium cable channels. I also imagined that her parents back home wanted her living in a safe neighborhood, especially with all the bad press the city of Los Angeles had received over the last couple of decades.

It was strange, but the amount of money I had spent in the hour since meeting Lisa was probably more than I had spent in the previous year and a half, not counting my property taxes and insurance. My monetary situation had vastly improved since I was fired from my job of twenty-five years. My lifestyle was never extravagant, and the extra money made my situation extremely comfortable, but the only thing that really changed was that I went from being a great tipper to being an extra great tipper. I still drank the same beer. I didn't run out and buy a sporty car, and I didn't for a moment consider moving into a bigger or more modern house. I even continued to buy the cheaper 'Penguin paperback editions' when I shopped for new books to read.

Yes, at sixty-one, I was living the life of an old man. Then that child walked into my life, and everything changed. Walking home, all I could think about was Bee, and when I opened the door to my house and walked in, I felt so lonely that I started to cry.

Chapter Six

I cleaned off the kitchen table and put the paperwork that Lisa had left on the table next to my laptop. They wanted my life story: Education, employment history, bank records, investments, current income, and debts. There was a section for a criminal records check, and they asked if I owned my house. Then I had to write an essay on why I felt I would make a good foster parent, and include three recommendations.

Only the recommendations worried me, because I didn't know how long that might take. I sent three emails to former customers at the restaurant that I kept in touch with, and amazingly, these three customers, who could never decide what to order at a restaurant that they ate at two hundred times a year, sent back recommendations that made me sound like the greatest human being in the world — someone who they would trust with their children and grandchildren without any concern at all. The recommendations came back less than an hour after I sent the requests. I was shocked, but extremely happy. Having recommendations from a studio head, a former mayor, and a magazine magnate looked impressive, even though I don't know if I would feel comfortable with any of them babysitting Bee.

I printed out the recommendations and attached them to the rest of the paperwork.

I then scanned everything and turned it into a single document, and made two hard copies of everything. With everything ready, I called up my lawyer. He seemed to have forgotten me until I mentioned a certain lady's name, and explained the circumstances. He promised to get on it right away, and I faxed him copies of all the paperwork and recommendations.

It was a little after six o'clock when I rang the buzzer to Lisa's apartment. Bee greeted me at the door with a big hug, grabbed the paperwork out of my hand, and handed it to Lisa who was sitting on the couch, fully engrossed in some romantic comedy. Bee said, "Lisa, get to it."

She replied, "I can't do anything with it right now. I'll look at it after the movie, and if everything looks fine, I will hand it in tomorrow at work. I promise."

I remarked, "It seems like everything turned out okay. The TV looks great. How's the one in the bedroom?"

"Great," Lisa said as she jumped over the back of the couch, never taking her eyes off the screen, and hugged me tightly. "I don't know how to thank you."

She then sat back down on the couch, oblivious to the world around her, as she looked at the movie. I asked Bee, "Have you eaten dinner?"

"No, she promised once the movie was over."

I walked over to the couch and asked Lisa if it was okay if I ordered pizza for the three of us. She said yes and told me to look for coupons in the cabinet by the refrigerator.

"That's okay, I have this wonderful pizzeria that I order from, and it's as close to real New York pizza as I have had since I have been out here."

She didn't hear a word I said, so I ordered three pizza pies and extra orders of garlic bread, just in case there was no food in the house. I didn't want Bee to go hungry while Lisa was processing my paperwork. For a second I thought, *That's if she can drag herself away from her romcoms for long enough to submit it to her bosses*, but then I reminded myself that she'd been starved for entertainment, and that a little period of over-indulging in good cable TV was to be expected.

While the soundtrack from her romantic comedy swelled in the background, I opened Lisa's refrigerator and peered in. I was surprised to see it stacked with row after row of white wine. There must have been thirty bottles in total. And this was not a fine vintage. This was the type of wine I drank when I was sixteen years old. It was the cheapest brand I could afford ... no corkscrew required, strictly twist-off tops. Not deterred one bit, I took down two regular glasses that you would usually drink milk out of — I didn't even bother looking for wine glasses — and I poured two large glasses. Then I found a lone can of soda in the fridge door and handed it to Bee. I handed Lisa a full glass of wine, and without taking her eyes off the screen she said thank you and downed half the contents in one big gulp.

I took a sip and it was as bad as I remember, but I knew that after a few glasses it wouldn't matter much. I refilled Lisa's glass as Bee and I sat down on the couch beside her and started watching the movie. Suddenly, Lisa started crying and making little mewling noises as she reached for a tissue. I turned to her and asked, "Are you okay?"

"Yes! Yes!" she exclaimed. "I just knew the son-of-a-bitch was going to leave her. It's like the story of my life."

I didn't know what to make of that, so I just nodded silently and we went back to watching the movie, with Lisa continuing to sniffle. When the pizza delivery person arrived, I paid for it at the door, then left two boxes in the kitchen and put the third box on the coffee table next to the couch with the garlic bread. We ate the pizza straight out of the box, along with the garlic bread, while we watched the end of the movie. Unlike the previous night, Bee ate only two slices of pizza, instead of seven, so at least I knew she wasn't starving. Lisa ate one slice, and before she started on her third glass of wine, I put the paperwork in front of her and said, "No more wine until you look over the paperwork."

"Mean," she replied as she smiled and put on her reading glasses. She carefully went through each page and when she got to the financial statements she exclaimed, "Holy shit, you weren't joking when you said you could buy this building. How would you like to marry me and then it would be a win/win for all of us? We would be Bee's mom and dad. How cool would that be?"

"I'm old enough to be your father," I replied as Bee gently punched me in the side.

"Nonsense, my father is much older than you. And besides, it's the 'in thing' to do in this town … a wealthy older man marrying a younger woman. What do you say?"

"Are you serious?" I asked in disbelief.

"Yes Joe, she's very serious. Just say, yes!" Bee exclaimed.

"Lisa, you're so young and beautiful, I would think you would have no problem meeting a man closer to your age."

"Is that your way of saying, 'no?' How about we just try it out and date for a while?"

Bee looked at me and said, "How about you just try it out and date for a while?" Just like a parrot.

"No, this is insane," I protested. "You're just a child."

"No, she's not," Bee interrupted and continued, "I've seen her naked and she's no child, even I could see that."

I could actually feel myself blushing at that remark. "Can we please get back to the paperwork?" I asked as I unscrewed another bottle of wine and filled Lisa's glass. She started crying, again.

"Do you see what you have done now, Joe? You've broken her heart. After our talk last night about all the beautiful girls you liked but who never liked you back. I doubt any were more beautiful than Lisa. I mean, look at her. She looks like a movie star when she's not scrunching her face up like that."

Lisa sniffled and tried to stop the flow of tears. "It's all right, sweetheart. I'm used to rejection." At that, she downed the entire glass of wine. "It's just been a terrible day. First, I take you away from Joe and that made me feel like Judas."

"Who's Judas?" Bee asked.

Lisa said, "Judas betrayed God, and then the Romans killed God. It's all very complicated."

"I didn't even know anyone could kill God, did you Joe?"

"Lisa's right, sweetheart. It's complicated. I'll explain it to you one day." I then refilled Lisa's glass and my own.

"And now another rejection from another man who thinks he's too good for me."

"I never said that, Lisa," I replied.

"You didn't have to. I could read it in your expression. I am a social worker. I'm trained to pick up on such things."

Bee was glaring at me. "I don't believe you, Joe. We would make such a perfect family, and not only do you get me, but you also get a beautiful wife. Just think of all those beautiful girls who rejected you, and who aren't so beautiful anymore. You could invite them all to your wedding and show them how much better you did than if you had married any of those losers. The least you can do is take Lisa out on a few dates. If she would just stop crying," she said, shooting a look at Lisa, "I have no doubt that the two of you would find out how much you have in common, and despite the age difference, you would fall madly in love with her. I'm sure of it."

"Thank you, my little angel," Lisa said as she kissed Bee on the cheek. She continued, "But I don't need a man so badly that I have to use the sympathy card."

"Oh yes you do, Lisa," Bee replied as I refilled my glass, this time in self-defense.

"So where would you like to go on your first date, and can I come along? I can remind you not to cry so much. Crying is the kiss of death when you're looking for a husband."

"I don't cry all the time, do I?"

"Yes, Lisa you do," the little wiseass replied.

"That's only because I'm Latin and we're very emotional."

"What's Latin?"

"People like Joe and me, who come from Spanish, Italian, or French backgrounds."

"Is that true, Joe? Are you Latin like Lisa?"

"I guess so, yeah," I replied.

"Then why don't you cry all the time?"

Lisa mockingly laughed and remarked, "Because the men are too proud and macho to ever be seen crying, unless of course they're *gay* and then they don't have any problems crying and showing their emotions."

"Maybe you should start being a little gayer, Joe. Then you and Lisa would have even more in common?"

I rolled my eyes and refilled my glass and then Lisa reached out with her glass and I simply refilled it.

"So when you two get married will I automatically become Latin, too?"

"It doesn't work that way…" I didn't get to finish because Lisa interrupted my train of thought and replied, "If you want to, my little angel," and she hugged Bee like she was a stuffed animal. "You can be anything you like, and don't you ever let anyone tell you differently … especially not a man."

"Did you hear that, Joe?" the little wiseass asked.

"I couldn't help but hear it. I'm right here," I replied.

Bee wiggled out of Lisa's hug and cuddled up to me and said, "I think I am going to go home with Joe and sleep in my own room tonight. Is that okay, Lisa?"

"No, it's not okay. What did I tell you?"

"I really don't remember, so much has happened today."

Lisa shook her head and looked back down at the paperwork and the recommendations. "My God, with these types of recommendations and all this money, you'll probably be back living with Joe by tomorrow. What is it that you did for a living again?"

Bee replied, "He was a busboy, dishwasher, cook, waiter, and a manager at a famous restaurant. Is that right, Joe?"

"Yes, very good memory Bee."

"And he knew Ernie Banks and Muhammad Ali and a whole bunch of famous movie stars, and I bet no actress was prettier than you. Isn't that right, Joe?"

"Absolutely, none at all."

"So you see, Lisa. If anyone should know it is Joe because he has seen them all."

"Oh, so why won't he marry me if am so gorgeous? Or even take me out on a date? Oh, I almost forgot. It's because he's too *old*. The lamest excuse I ever heard, especially in this town and hanging around with these types of people." She threw the recommendations at me, and Bee quickly picked them up and said, "She has a point, Joe."

"I'm so depressed," Lisa said and started crying for the hundredth time.

Bee looked at her. "Maybe if you started thinking about happy things, you wouldn't be so depressed and always crying."

"Like what, Bee? Like what? You're the only friend I have in this whole town."

"That is kind of sad, Lisa."

"And even you can't wait to get away from me."

"That's not true ... who's been trying so hard to get you and Joe married?"

"That's true, I'm sorry for saying that," Lisa replied as Bee hugged her.

"I love you, Lisa."

"And I love you, my beautiful angel."

They remained in each other's arms for an extended period of time, and then I finally realized that they were both sound asleep.

My God, I thought, miracles do happen.

I found a blanket in Lisa's bedroom and gently laid it over them. Then I stacked all of the paperwork back up, making sure the pages were in the right order, and left a note telling Lisa to take care of this first thing tomorrow. I knew there was some question now about whether she would even make it into work. I looked down at Bee and was tempted to give her a kiss on the head like I did the night before when I tucked her into bed, but then I thought that with the way things were going tonight, I shouldn't take a chance of waking her.

On my way out, I grabbed a bottle of wine out of the refrigerator. Like I said, it brought back memories, and once your body re-establishes the connection you once had with this brand, it tastes as good as ever.

I left the nut house, took the elevator down, and walked out the front door of the building. It was another lovely California night, and despite the insanity, I must admit I had had a good time. As I reversed the route I'd traveled with Bee a couple of hours earlier, I gripped my bottle of cheap wine under a twinkling sky and thought about how much easier it is to get from A to B without a little kid zig zagging all over the place, asking questions and waving at the neighbors. How much easier and how much duller, even sadder. The truth is, my life had become a lonesome journey. You would think that after working in that crazy restaurant I would welcome peace and quiet for at least the first few years after being unceremoniously fired, but it's strange how quickly loneliness can set in.

Chapter Seven

Back at home I went straight for the kitchen, where I took down a normal glass like the one I'd used at Lisa's. I filled it to the top, and just before I took my first sip my house phone rang. On the dashboard it said it was a call from me, which meant it was from the wiseass. I took a giant gulp of wine and hit the Talk button.

"Hi Joe, it's me, Bee."

"Really? I never would have guessed."

"Why did you leave without saying good-bye? Are you mad at me?"

"What? No!"

The words were barely out of my mouth when she asked, "Does this mean you don't want to adopt me anymore?" Her voice was almost strangled with worry.

"Bee…" I said, "you need to take a deep breath."

She went silent, and I heard her take one big breath.

"Are you okay now?"

I heard a sniffle on the other end of the line and a small "Yes."

"Good, because I need you to listen to me very carefully, and people can't listen as well when they're upset."

"I'm okay."

"Great. There is nothing I want more in this world than to adopt you and have you living here as soon as possible. There is nothing in this world that I want more. Got that?"

"Yes … you promise?"

"I promise. I didn't say good-bye because the two of you were sound asleep and I didn't want to disturb either of you."

"Oh," she said, and then, "I love you, Joe."

"And I love you, my little angel."

"I'll call you first thing in the morning. Is that okay?"

"It's more than okay. Good night, my beautiful child."

"Good night, Joe."

I finished the wine in my glass and hung up the phone, then sat back down at the table and re-filled my glass. I looked at the bottle closely and could barely read the ingredients list. It was almost as if the winery didn't want anyone to know what was in its product, which I could easily understand.

After I finished the bottle, I rinsed it out and dried it with a cloth. I screwed the cap back on and placed it in a cabinet above the stove where I kept other bottles that held similar memories, such as 'Boone's Farm Apple' and 'Boone's Farm Grape.' Regular price, ninety-nine cents, occasionally on sale for seventy-nine cents. Like I said, I did not have expensive tastes.

As I walked down the hall toward my room, I glanced into Bee's bedroom and turned on the light. She had only been in that room for one overnight and part of a day, yet it already seemed like it belonged to her. From the door, I could see that she left behind a T-shirt that must have fallen onto the floor while she was packing. I went into her room, picked up the shirt, folded it neatly, and left it on her bed.

I then walked into my bathroom and flossed my teeth, rinsed my mouth out with mouthwash, brushed my teeth, and then repeated the whole ritual. As much as I enjoyed my trip down memory lane, I didn't want to wake up with the taste of that wonderful vintage in my mouth. I probably should have flossed, rinsed, and brushed for a third time to really play it safe, but I was simply too exhausted and once I hit the bed, I was out cold.

I got up at my usual time, and seriously thought about going back to sleep, but then my house phone rang and it was Bee.

"Good morning, Joe."

"Good morning, angel. Did you sleep well?"

"Yes. After we talked I slept very well. You're still going to adopt me, right?"

"Yes, sweetheart, I still am, and hopefully you will be living back here very, very soon. Where did you sleep last night?"

"In Lisa's bed. She was hogging the couch and I couldn't wake her up, so I slept in her bed, even though it's big enough for both of us." She paused and then said, "I feel sorry for Lisa. She's so nice, and I know she loves me and I love her, but..."

"But what, sweetheart?"

"I just always thought that girls as beautiful as Lisa could get any guy they like. I know she cries a lot, but I also know that if she was happier, she wouldn't cry so much. If she didn't cry so much, would you marry her?"

"No, angel, and it's not because she cries a lot. It's our age difference. I could be her grandfather, and where I come from in the Bronx, guys my age don't marry girls that much younger than them. Thirty years ago, I would have jumped at the chance to go out with a girl as beautiful and sweet as Lisa, but not now. A lot of rich, older men might do it in this town, but I'm not like them. She'll find the right guy. I'm sure of it."

"I hope so."

Bee wanted to know if she could join me for my morning walk-run, but I told her it was better to play it by the rules until things were finalized. She then asked me if she could call me during the day when Lisa was at work. I said, "Of course, call all you want. Hearing your lovely voice is heavenly."

Naturally, the child took it literally and called about thirty times. Each time she asked if I still intended to adopt her. For the first dozen times or so she made no attempt to hide her concern, but by late morning she started to slip the question into conversations about other things, like what school she would attend, *if* I still planned to adopt her, or whether she would take my last name, *if* I still planned to adopt her. Finally, I said, "You can ask me a hundred times and my answer will always be the same. I am going to adopt you as soon as the agency and the courts will let me." On the thirtieth call, she never even brought it up. We just talked about whether she was going to heat up her snack of leftover pizza or eat it cold.

At about two in the afternoon, I got an email from Lisa telling me that all the paperwork had been submitted along with a glowing evaluation from her.

At about three-thirty I received another email from Lisa asking me if I had reconsidered going out on a date with her.

I felt so sorry for this girl that I did the worst possible thing I could do and replied, "Once Bee is living back at my house, I would love to take you out on a date."

A few seconds later I got another email from Lisa with a row of smiley-face emojis. Then I got a call from the wiseass, telling me that she'd heard the great news that I was going to take Lisa out on a date, and that she was "certain this would lead to us getting married." She added that she thought it would be a good idea if she went on the first couple of dates with us, to help control Lisa's crying.

I told her that would be fine, and we hung up. I believe that was call number twenty-six.

By then it was late afternoon. It was a little early for me to start drinking, but I needed to clear my head, so I took down a shot glass and a bottle of Old No. 7, Jack Daniel's, and took three quick shots. Then I walked out of the house and up to the convenience store on Moorpark Boulevard, where they have a wonderful selection of wines. I picked out two bottles of Ruffino Riserva Ducale Gold Label Chianti. I was hoping it would cancel out the damage done to my brain the night before.

Back in my house, I took out a corkscrew and uncorked a bottle of the Ruffino. I took down a nice wine glass, and like a true connoisseur, I poured a little wine into the glass, twirled it around, sniffed the incredible bouquet, and took a small sip, swirling it around my mouth and drinking it down. "Beautiful," I said to myself and then filled the glass to the top and drank it down in two gulps like I was drinking an ice-cold beer. I refilled the glass and put on a collection of Frank Sinatra's greatest hits, starting with "Moonlight Serenade."

I sat down on the couch and was just starting to let the music and the wine take me to a nice, peaceful place when I was interrupted by a call from my lawyer. He had looked over all the paperwork, submitted it to the courts, and didn't see any problems with me getting custody of the child. Just when I thought we were done, he asked, "Why?"

I replied, "Because I see potential in the child, and could one day see her playing for my beloved New York Knicks."

He paused as though I might have gone soft in the head, and then said, "Great! I'll be in touch. Have a wonderful day." He hung up and I went back to the music and wine, only to be interrupted by another call from the wiseass, who said, "I have some bad news Joe. You were too slow. Lisa was just asked out by this super-hot guy, and since she's not the type to date two men at a time, she felt it was her duty to tell you."

"But you're telling me," I replied.

"I know, but that's only because she was too embarrassed and felt terrible about breaking your heart. She did say that if things don't work out with the super-hot guy, she would still love to date you."

"How very nice. So what you are telling me is that I am her second choice?"

"Exactly, Joe. I knew you would understand. She also wanted to know if this meant you were going to take away her TVs and cable subscription."

"No, they were gifts and I would never take them back."

"That's what I told her, Joe. I love you so much, and once I'm back home you and I will get to spend even more quality time together."

"That's true, my little angel."

"What are you doing now?"

"I am listening to Frank Sinatra…"

"Who's that?" she asked.

"The Justin Bieber of my time."

"Can I come over?"

"No, I do not want to take any chances."

There was a pause on the other end of the line.

"You're still going to adopt me, right? You promised."

"Yes angel, you do not have to worry about that."

"If it makes you feel any better, if I was older, I would immediately marry you."

"Thank you, but I really love the idea of being your dad."

I hung up the phone, got up off the couch, took down the bottle of Old No. 7 and poured two shots down my throat. I wanted to make sure that I wasn't imagining this whole scenario, and I knew Jack Daniel's would set me straight.

Chapter Eight

In less than a week I got the little wiseass back for what was referred to as a *probation period*. Lisa dropped her off at the house in the morning, and before I had a chance to say a word, Bee reached up and hugged me so tightly that I thought I might suffocate. She was tiny, but there was a lot of strength in that little frame. Lisa, who was late for work, took off immediately.

Bee and I spent the rest of the morning getting her set up in her room. I pulled a reading lamp and a clock radio out of storage and set them up on a little night table next to her bed. She squealed and reached for a book that happened to be sitting on the bottom shelf of her night table. She plopped herself onto the bed and cracked the hardcover tome open to a middle page.

"Principles of Restaurant Management?" I asked.

She inspected the cover and frowned. "Not too exciting, huh?"

"I seem to remember buying that about fifteen years ago and never reading it. I guess I was too busy reading novels."

"And managing the restaurant."

"That, too."

That got us thinking about food, so we ordered pizza for lunch, even though it was only 11:00 a.m.

"We should always have pizza for Elevensies," she said, and I had to agree that this sounded like a great plan.

She had been gone a little less than a week, but it didn't feel like she had been gone at all. That might be because we'd talked a few hundred times over the phone.

We sat at the kitchen table and Bee insisted that I tell her a "true story," so I told her about my uncle Tony who passed away like fifty years ago on Valentine's Day. She listened with an intensity that was quite amazing, and it wasn't like I was some great storyteller. In fact, she kept having to ask questions because I would forget she didn't know him and say things out of order.

"What do you mean he walked with a limp?"

"Ahh," I said, clarifying. "Uncle Tony had polio as a child."

"Oh. Is that bad?"

"Polio? Yes, polio was very bad. A lot of people got it before there was a vaccine, and some of them could never walk again. My uncle Tony could walk, but it was hard for him to get around, and he could never play sports."

"Did he get to go to school?"

"He did, yes, but not for very long. Because of the illness he would have to stay home a lot or be at the hospital. But he loved to read, and he was very knowledgeable."

"Did he get to have a job?"

"Oh yes," I said. "He worked as a doorman in a rich part of Manhattan called Sutton Place."

"Did he like it?"

"He did. He liked it a lot. He met a lot of famous people, including some big Broadway stars and a few well-known directors. But he didn't talk much about them. He was more interested in American history, and he loved to talk about courageous historical figures who made a difference, like President Theodore Roosevelt, General Ulysses S. Grant, George Washington, and General George S. Patton. Have you heard all of those names before?"

"I think so, but I don't know that much about them. George Washington, but not the others."

"Okay, we'll work on that."

Then I guess I wandered onto some tangent about a story that my uncle used to tell about Teddy Roosevelt, because Bee broke in and said, "But what was he like?"

"Teddy Roosevelt?"

"No," she laughed, "your uncle Tony."

I smiled and said, "Well, he was just about the kindest and most generous and loving person that anyone could ever hope to meet."

"Wow," she said simply, almost like she was a bit envious, or impressed. I couldn't tell.

"Are you sure you want to hear about my happy family? I mean, does it make you sad that you didn't get that?"

"It does make me a little sad, but I want to hear," she said, with a maturity that I couldn't even fathom. "It'll be almost like I was there and he was my uncle too."

I must have been wearing a stupid grin on my face because she poked me on the arm and said, "What was so great about him?"

That's when I told her all about how he lived with my grandmother and grandfather and my aunt Rena, and how he didn't make much money but he still gave my two brothers and me an allowance each week."

Bee's eyes went wide, and I added, "It wasn't about the money. He gave us a quarter each. But he made us feel like we were the three most important kids in his life."

She nodded like she knew exactly what I was talking about, and with that encouragement, I kept going.

"I couldn't wait to see him at night," I recalled. "I would take a bath and put on my pajamas and then I would run downstairs and sit with him while he ate dinner. He would get home at about eight o'clock at night from work, after everyone had already eaten. My grandmother would keep his dinner warm and he would sit down at the kitchen table, with the night owl edition of *The New York Daily News* and a quart of Rheingold beer, and I would sit across from him and listen to his great stories. I was about eight or nine years old at the time."

"That was so nice of his mom to keep his supper warm. He must have loved her a lot."

"Oh, yes. He was always telling me that my grandmother was the greatest person in the world, and his favorite thing was to say it in front of her. Then he would tell me to go give her a kiss from him, and me, and I would run off and kiss her twice."

Bee laughed at that, but when I added, "He used to say that his only wish was to die before her," she suddenly frowned.

"Why?"

"I guess he couldn't imagine life without his mom. He never forgot all the things she did for him when he got sick with polio, taking him to doctor after doctor, and rushing him to the hospital in the middle of the night. She never left his side the whole time he was being treated, even though she had other children to care for."

Bee was quiet for a few moments, and then said, "What else do you remember?"

"So many things. He was old school. He taught me that only cowards hit women, and that any man who ran away from a fight where he could have helped a friend was not worth having as a friend."

"What did he look like? Can you show me a picture?"

I left the room and came back with a single framed photo of my uncle standing next to my aunt Rena and their mom and dad. "That's him there."

"He looks a little like what's-his-name … Rocky."

"Sylvester Stallone?"

"Yes. He looks kind of like Sylvester Stallone."

"It's funny you should say that because he had huge hands, like a boxer, and everyone used to say he looked like a movie star. But the Rocky movies weren't made until later, so he would have been more like Kirk Douglas in *The Champion*."

Bee shrugged as if to say "Before my time," and asked, "Did he have any kids?"

"No, he never got married, and he never left my grandmother. I guess that was kind of sad for him in a way, but it meant that he belonged to all of us. He was everyone's favorite uncle. He was a mythical figure and there was something so very special about him."

"How did he die?"

I let out a sigh and told her the whole story. "On a Tuesday morning while he was getting ready for work, he had a stroke and was rushed to the hospital."

Bee gasped and I nodded as if to say, "It gets worse," and continued. "They told me he was getting better and would be coming home from the hospital very soon, and they said he would be mad if I took off from school or didn't do my homework just so I could go see him in the hospital."

Bee was holding her face in her hands as if she knew what was coming.

"Three days later when I came home from school, I walked into the house and found my mother and my aunt Carmela crying. I never even thought anything had happened to my uncle Tony. After all, he was invincible … he was the man who took the devil by the throat and flushed him down the toilet when he tried to tempt him into doing bad things. When I asked my mother what was wrong, she tried to speak but nothing came out. My aunt Carmela finally said that my uncle Tony is now in Heaven with God."

Bee shook her head in dismay.

"I asked, 'When is he coming back? I have so much to tell him,' and my aunt said, 'He's not coming back.' But she told me to say my prayers and ask God to tell him what I wanted to tell my uncle, and that she was sure he would get the message."

Bee stayed silent for a long time. She finally said, "That must have been hard on you and your brothers and the whole family."

"It was. I remember I dropped my schoolbooks and ran into the bathroom and for the first time in my life I cried for a person who had passed away. It was Valentine's Day, and my uncle got his wish. He died before his mother. It wasn't long after that that she died, too. Whenever I visit their gravesite I look down at grandmother's name engraved on the tombstone and directly below her name is my uncle Tony's. I always think of that saying from the Bible: 'In death they were not parted.'"

After a few quiet moments I said, "I have never celebrated a Valentine's Day since."

"That is not what your uncle Tony would want," Bee remarked. Her eyes were nearly brimming with tears.

"Maybe not," I said, but I didn't sound sure.

"You said he loved to have people around him, and that he was everyone's favorite uncle. And in the end, he got his wish to die before his mommy. I think he would hate the idea that you are still mourning him after all these years."

Bee got up from her chair and walked over to me and hugged me around my neck and kissed me on the cheek and said, "I think it is wonderful how you remember your uncle, and I think you honor him every day. You have never hit a woman or a child, right, Joe?"

"No, no, gosh no," I said as I kept my head lowered.

"And you would never desert a friend who was in a fight, right? You're kind and generous, and I love you so much."

I looked up at her and asked, "Has anyone ever told you that you are awfully smart and perceptive for your age?"

"Before meeting you and Lisa, no one ever cared what I had to say, or asked for my opinion."

"Well, that was their loss," I said. Then I became self-conscious and said, "Here I am going on and on about losing my uncle, and you have been through something a thousand times worse."

"I have," she said. "But I meant it when I said I want to know about your family so they can feel like my family."

"I get that, but I want you to know that if you ever feel ready to talk about your parents, I'm right here and will listen to every word you have to say."

"Thank you, Joe. Not right now," she said, and I nodded my understanding.

"How about a walk?" she said. I laughed and said yes, as long as she didn't force me to run.

"After all, we're all clean and you look so lovely in your new clothes."

As we headed outside, I realized that we had talked so long that the sun was now heading toward the horizon and a soft breeze was rifling through the trees. It was one of my favorite times of the day. The diffused afternoon light was like a tranquilizer that eased the day's worries and filled me with a sense of peace.

I held Bee's hand, and kept her away from the street, and for the first time in my life I felt the joy of being a parent.

Chapter Nine

After a light dinner and some TV, I tucked Bee into bed and gave her a peck on the forehead, then went to my own room and climbed under the covers. As I stared at the ceiling, I thought about how quickly my life was changing. Not since working at the restaurant had things seemed to move so fast.

I fell asleep quickly, and before I knew it I was sitting at the dining room table back in our apartment in Parkchester, watching my aunt Carmela. She was standing in the kitchen, dressed in a simple red housedress, marinating chicken breasts for one of my favorite dishes. She looked as lovely as I always remember — prettier than any movie actresses I met during my twenty-five years of service at the restaurant. I stood up just as she was about to place the big pan of chicken breasts into the oven. I took the pan from her and placed it in the oven.

She smiled and said, "Thank you, Joseph."

I looked at her, and tears were suddenly pouring down my face. She looked surprised and right away asked me if I'd hurt myself.

"No, No," I said, "I just love you so much."

"Oh, Joseph, that's so sweet. I love you just as much."

"I'm so sorry for not telling you enough times how much I appreciate all that you and uncle Al did for us."

"Don't be foolish," she said, touching my cheek. "You have told me plenty of times how much you appreciate what we have done. You're my sister's son. How could I do anything less?"

"But you and Uncle Al had your whole lives before you. You had no responsibilities. You could have traveled the world drinking gin martinis all day long and no one could have said anything."

Aunt Carmela laughed and said, "It's not like we didn't drink gin martinis all day. Surely you didn't think there was water in those glasses."

"No, but you loved being in the sun and laying by a pool and going to the beach."

"We still did those things. Maybe not as much, but the joy of helping raise you and your two brothers outweighed any suntan. Who knows? Maybe you saved me from getting skin cancer!"

I chuckled at this but got serious again quickly and said, "I wasn't there for you at the end."

She stopped and stared at me, uncomprehending. "But you were living in California! I didn't expect you to spend your whole life right next to me. You had your own life to live. Besides, I remember all the phone calls and the kisses you sent to me over the phone. That meant as much to me as if you had been there."

"But I should have been there! I could have easily got off from work. I should have been by your side like you were by my side all those years after my mom died. How could you forgive me so easily?"

"Because it was so easy to love you, and I never doubted that you loved and appreciated everything your uncle Al and I did for you." She opened the oven to check the chicken and I could smell the rich aroma of lemon, white wine and thyme.

"Dinner should be ready in about an hour," she said. "Why don't you go relax for a little while? I'll call you when it's time to eat."

I kissed her on the cheek and said, "Okay," then walked into my parents' bedroom, where I found my father sitting in a plush, red chair, next to the window that overlooked the basketball court. He was young and handsome, the way I remembered him before he was forced to go on dialysis three times a week after his kidneys stopped functioning. He lasted fourteen years on dialysis, which was like a miracle because most kidney patients are lucky to last four or five years. As I looked at him, I suddenly remembered the time we were driving back from Stony Brook University and he said to me, "The only reason I continue on dialysis is because I love my family so much. Otherwise, I think it would be easier to just die."

"What are you doing sitting in here by yourself?" I asked.

He looked up at me and smiled. "Just thinking, Joseph. It's so good to have you back home."

"I'm happy to be back home. No matter how long I live in Los Angeles this will always be my home."

"That's what I used to tell my parents when I moved from Lawrence to the Bronx to marry your mom. You remember your grandparents from Massachusetts?"

"Of course, I do. I remember going to visit them at Salisbury Beach. We would stay for two weeks every summer. The beach was right across from their house, and if you walked out the front yard and turned left there was that amusement park. I remember walking to the hotdog stand with you and buying footlong hotdogs."

"That's right. You always did have a great memory. Your mother used to worry because you were such a picky eater, but God, did you love those hot dogs."

I sat down on the bed, across from my father, and asked, "After mom had the surgery and they told you that the cancer was too far along to do anything, you chose not to tell my brothers and me. That had to be a really difficult time for you."

"The doctors told me that your mom would have about three or four good months before it got really bad. I discussed the situation with your aunt Carmela and your uncle Al and we decided that the best thing was not to tell you boys. Your mom never knew, and if you remember, she wanted to go back to work. Besides the three of us, no one in the family knew. We wanted the next three or four months to be as normal as possible, and with Christmas coming we wanted it to be as special as ever. Being Catholic, we also never gave up on the possibility of a miracle happening."

"That was one of the happiest Christmases I can remember. She was still so vibrant. I remember her cleaning and decorating and baking cookies. I had no doubt that she was perfectly fine. What a difference it all would have made if we knew."

"Yes, it worked out perfect, and if you remember, your mom lasted a whole eight months after the surgery. The doctors had told me it would be at most six months, but your mom was a very strong person."

"Yes, she was," I said as I stood up and looked out the window where the basketball court had been, but was no more. I looked at my dad and asked, "When did they take down the court?"

"Oh, it's been years now. Things have really changed, Joseph."

"I remember Mom calling for me through this window. I'd be in the middle of a game, and she'd be yelling 'Joseph! Dinner!' I would finish the game, run into the house, inhale my dinner and be back out on the court in five minutes so I wouldn't miss the next game. She used to get so mad."

"But she always let you go. She knew how much basketball meant to you."

As I continued to look out the window, I thought about the night before my mom passed away. By then everyone knew she was dying and she was resting comfortably, heavily sedated, and sitting up in her bed at Montefiore Hospital, on Gun Hill Road. There was a line outside her door to see her — so many aunts and uncles, cousins, friends. I stopped off at a newsstand and bought her the Sunday edition of the *New York Daily News*. She loved to read the comics, especially in the Sunday edition. I laid the newspaper on her lap and she smiled as she gently touched my face. She was dressed in a blue nightgown and to me she did not look like she was dying. Even at that point, it was inconceivable to me that she could die. I was the last one to leave, with my cousin Grace, who was a nun, and my father. Just as the elevator arrived, I said, "Wait for me, I'll be right back." I ran back into my mother's room and found her looking down at the comics. I reached over and kissed her one last time and she said, "Please take care of them." I knew she was referring to the family, and I promised I would. The following morning, at exactly 10:15, the phone rang, and the doctor told me my mom had passed away comfortably just a short time earlier.

I heard my aunt Carmela yelling that dinner was ready, and I turned from the window and walked toward the kitchen, alone.

In the dream logic that combines past and future and sense and nonsense, I jumped ahead to the present and realized that the promise I had made to my mother was one that I never kept. It was just one more thing I would carry to my grave.

Chapter Ten

When I woke up, the sun was just beginning to peek over the horizon. I propped myself up on a pillow and looked out the window at a little shed where I kept my lawn mower and an old bicycle. The shed, which I knew to be grey, was tinged with early morning pink.

My dream from the night before came back to me with such intensity that I lay there mulling it over for twenty minutes, then went down memory lane, pulling up other family stories that I hadn't thought of in years.

Something about leaving the restaurant, having more time, and now having Bee in the house, had opened the floodgates, and I could not seem to move from my bed until I had devoted some time to reflecting on these long-ago events.

A lot of my memories focused on my aunt Jeannette. When I was very young, we lived with my family in the top apartment of my grandmother's home, and I used to go downstairs all the time to sit with my grandmother and my aunt Jeannette.

My grandma was barely five feet tall, and suffered terribly from arthritis. My aunt Jeannette was mentally challenged and had difficulty walking. She would sit in a special chair in the kitchen and she and my grandma would entertain visitors throughout the day. Despite their illnesses, they were both very sociable and their personalities were definitely on the sunny side, except on a few days during the year when they both seemed very quiet and reflective.

When that happened, I would ask my mom what was wrong with Grandma and Aunt Jeannette, and the reason would almost always be that so-or-so had died on this day. The so-or-so was usually my aunt Angie, who died when she was thirteen years old from a ruptured appendix, or my aunt Philomena, who died of cancer.

My aunt Angie I never knew, and by this time in my life she had already been dead for over thirty years. My aunt Philomena, who I barely remembered, had been dead eight years. I found it unusual that both my grandma and my aunt Jeannette remembered the exact day my aunt Angie died, and suffered every year as though it had just happened yesterday. It was like it was programed in their minds.

Today, the dates that my uncle Tony, mom and dad, grandma, and aunt Carmela died are seared into my mind, like they were in both my aunt Jeannette and grandma's minds. Valentine's Day, March 8, Dec. 2, June 5, and Feb. 16. Each one of my departed family members had been gone for more than twenty years. My uncle Tony died forty-eight years earlier, and my mom had been gone for forty-four years. I lay there listing the dates of their deaths until I was certain that they were lodged in my memory, never to be forgotten as long as I could remember how to brush my teeth or pick up a fork.

When I finally got up, I walked into the kitchen and Bee was sitting down eating a bowl of cereal with cut up strawberries.

"That looks healthy," I said.

"Would you like me to fix you a bowl?"

"No sweetheart, I never eat breakfast."

"You did the first morning I was here."

"That's because you went to the trouble of cooking, and there was no way I could say no to that."

"How about I fix you a bowl and instead of milk, I use beer?"

"How about I spank your little butt?"

"You said you would never hit a girl."

"There's always an exception."

She made a funny face, finished her cereal, got up, and cleaned and dried her bowl. She turned to me and smiled, and for a moment the dreams that I had woken up to dissipated and I was just looking forward to another day with my little girl who looked like an angel, and who had a bit of a wiseass in her.

＊

We stepped out of the house and started our walk, and just as she had a week earlier before the separation, she jumped back and forth, every which way but straight, like a bumblebee.

After about a mile, she decided it was time for a short run. I followed her lead, and my hip felt great as we came to stop after a block and a half. Bee was totally out of breath, and when I suggested that we stick to one block for a while, she said, "But then I won't improve. If I do a little more each day, I'll get better quicker."

I couldn't argue with that logic. She was determined, and I could respect that. I was also pretty sure she knew that if *I* did a little more each day, I would build up enough confidence to start running the whole six miles again, like I did for over thirty years.

As we were walking, Bee said, "I have an idea. Since Lisa is going to come by and drop off the adoption papers, why don't we invite her to stay for dinner? I know she loves Chinese food."

I looked at her and wondered what kind of scheme she was cooking up to marry me off to Lisa, but I said, "That's fine with me, as long as you make the phone call. I don't want her to get the wrong idea about my intentions."

"And why would she do that?" Bee said. "She wants to continue going out with the super-hot guy she has been seeing, and according to you, you're not super-hot."

"That's for sure…"

Pivoting, she asked, "Did you like the movie stars you met at the restaurant?"

"Sure. Yes. Most of them."

"And was there something special about them? Did they glow like stars in the sky?"

I shook my head slightly as I remembered a line from the Beatles' manager, the great George Martin. An interviewer had asked him about fans and the way they adore actors, musicians, and other artists. Mr. Martin's advice was, "If you have heroes, try never to meet them because you will always be disappointed."

Yes, I met many movie stars at the restaurant and had long conversations with a number of them. They were almost all very nice and polite. I actually cried when a few passed away, like Sam Shepard and Don Rickles, whom I got to know on a friendly basis. Whenever either of them came into the restaurant, we would have a big old chat about whatever was happening in our lives, from everyday events to worries, concerns, and happy moments with family and friends.

"As for movie stars glowing like stars in the sky, no, I never saw that," I told Bee. Then I turned and put the brakes on the bumblebee by placing my hands on her shoulders and said, "But you, my child, glow like a magical orb of miraculous light."

She looked up at me with a quizzical look that turned to a smile, and said, "Thank you, Joe." I let go of her shoulders and in a flash, she was back to jumping every which way but straight like a bumblebee.

"So, will it be Chinese food for dinner with Lisa tonight?" she asked.

"Sure."

"Great. I'll call her once we get back home, and then you can teach me how to play basketball, and then can I go for a swim in my new two-piece bathing suit?"

"What two-piece bathing suit?"

She giggled and said, "I'm only joking, Joe. In my lovely new one-piece suit."

We ran another block and a half five different times during our six-mile walk, and arrived home sweaty.

The second we got into the house Bee called Lisa, who said she would love to have dinner with us. How could she possibly turn down Chinese food? She asked what she should bring, and Bee asked, "Joe, Lisa wants to know what could she bring?"

"Just herself," I replied and Bee repeated to Lisa, "Just yourself." There was a long pause and then Bee repeated, "Just yourself."

I took the phone as I sensed the conversation going off into a different dimension … the Bee dimension, where time and space were strangely out of sync. I told Lisa that there was no need to bring anything. She would be over at six o'clock. I hung up and looked at the child.

"Time to play some basketball," I said.

We walked outside by the pool and toward the basketball hoop that I put up at the end of the backyard. The area was about the size of a half court one might see in a park — roughly forty feet long and about thirty feet wide. I used the official NBA measurements, with the foul line fifteen feet from the basket and the three-point line twenty-two feet around.

Back when I first put the court up twenty-five years ago a group of my friends from the restaurant would come over and we would play three-on-three games for hours at a time, and afterward sit around the pool and drink beer. That lasted for a few years, until like everything else, it simply stopped. I was left playing by myself and pretending, at forty years old, to be Walt Clyde Frazier, the famous New York Knicks guard, who back in the early '70s lead the Knicks to two championships, including their last one in 1974.

The bumblebee kept jumping around while I used a foot pump to fill the ball with air. It had been a while since I played, and basketballs have a way of going flat over time. I tossed the newly full ball to Bee, and she started bouncing it with two hands like she was beating down on a beach ball. I walked over to her and said, "What you are doing in the world of basketball is called a double dribble. It's a violation."

"What's a double dribble?" she asked innocently.

"It's when you bounce the ball with both hands." I took the ball and showed her how to bounce it correctly, with one hand and a light touch. I handed the ball back to her, and for about fifteen seconds she bounced the ball a little more softly and with just her right hand. Then she went back to using two hands. I grabbed the ball and simply looked at her.

"Double dribble," she said guiltily.

"Yes, double dribble. Just concentrate."

"Yes, Joe, okay, just concentrate," she said, half to me and half to herself. I handed the ball back to her and, once again, after fifteen seconds she was back to double dribbling and, once again, I grabbed the ball.

"You know, there's a simple cure for this?"

"And what's that?"

"I simply cut off your left arm and just like that the problem is solved."

"Very funny. Maybe I should try shooting?"

"Not until you are able to bounce the ball with one hand for a least a minute." I took hold of her left hand and handed her back the ball. "Let's try it this way."

She started bouncing the ball with her right hand, pulling me this way and that way like when we were out walking. For a tiny creature, she was quite strong. After about fifteen seconds, she asked, "Has it been a minute?"

"I don't know, but I'm so dizzy I have to stop." I let go of her hand and sat down on one of the deck chairs I kept next to the court. After a moment she sat down beside me, holding the basketball in her lap.

"Are you okay, Joe?"

She sounded a little anxious. I looked at her and smiled. "Oh, I'm fine. It's just that you jump around like a bumblebee. I'm surprised you don't make yourself dizzy."

"Maybe that's the problem ... like a bumblebee, I'm just too small to play basketball."

"Nonsense! When I was your height, I was playing basketball ten hours a day."

She stood up and bounced the ball a few times with only her right hand. She then held the ball with both hands and threw it at the basket underhanded. It sailed over the backboard and into the neighbor's yard. "Oh, no," she said as I shook my head and wondered if maybe she just didn't have it in her to play basketball.

I retrieved the ball from the neighbor's yard and laid it off to the side and said, "Enough basketball for today."

"I'm not having such a good day, am I Joe?"

"It's early and I'm sure it will get a lot better."

She looked so nervous that I took her by the hand and sat her back down. "You know what it is to have a bad day, Bee? Getting beat up by your foster parents, or seeing your parents killed in a car accident. That's a bad day. Not throwing a basketball over the backboard. That's funny."

"Thank you, Joe."

I turned her face toward me and said, "I am going to see to it that there are no more bad days like that. I will do everything in my power to protect you." She smiled and hugged me tightly. I could feel her tiny body trembling against mine, and it didn't take a psychologist to know that a child her age should not be so frightened about missing a basketball shot, even if it did go over the backboard.

"You know what? I think it's time for you to try out the pool," I said, and that perked her up right away. She ran to her bedroom, and came out minutes later dressed in her blue Speedo. She twirled around and asked, "What do you think?"

"Looks great," I replied.

"Thank you, Joe. I'm curious. Is it just me you don't want to see in a bikini, or is it all girls you don't want to see in a two-piece?"

"It's nine-year-old girls that I don't want to see in bikinis."

"You know, that's kind of sexist on your part."

"Is that so. I guess you're part of the 'me too' movement?"

"Of course, I am. Every girl should be. I don't want any old men groping me, or young ones, for that matter, and I want equal pay and equal rights. But who are we kidding? You don't want me wearing a bikini because you want to protect me, and I love you for that."

"I love you too. And just for the record, I am all for equal rights, and equal pay, and any guy harassing a woman should get his ass kicked."

"Good," she said. She walked toward the sliding glass door that opens out onto the pool and asked, "Okay if I go swimming now?"

"Of course, but what's the rule about swimming?"

"I always have to tell you before I go into the pool."

"And the first time you don't, the pool will be drained. It's not like I go swimming."

"Why not? It would be great for your hip," she said.

"Hmm," I said. "I'll think about it."

I followed her out to the pool and watched her walk into the shallow end. The sun was reflecting off the rippled surface in little circles, like a bed of dimes. Bee smiled at me just before she pointed her hands in front of her and disappeared into the water. Then she surfaced and swam effortlessly from one end of the pool to the next, cutting through the water like a baby dolphin that had never been out of the water.

When she surfaced and leaned against the edge of the pool, I said, "How did you get to be such a great swimmer?"

"Our apartment building had a pool. It was usually full of leaves and junk and my parents never took me, but there was a woman one floor up who liked to swim and pretended I was her daughter so I could be in there with her."

"That was nice of her. And now look at you. You're like a fish."

She smiled and swam a little more, and when she came back, I ventured another question.

"What were your parents doing while you were swimming that they couldn't go with you?"

"Fighting. Drinking. Blaming me for everything that went wrong."

Then Bee started floating on her back as she continued.

"When I was six or seven, my mother used to tell me how much better her life would be if she had aborted me. I didn't know what it meant, until a girl I met at the pool told me. My mom was saying her life would have been better if she had just killed me in the womb. It's legal, and I don't know why she just didn't do it. I guessed the world would be better off if I wasn't born."

She flipped and was about to start swimming again when I called out, "Hey, come back here!" She stopped and swam back to the edge of the pool while I leaned down painfully on my knees until I was able to reach out and place one hand on her forearm.

Now I was the one shaking as I said, "I don't know what the hell was wrong with your parents, but don't ever let me hear you say that the world would be better off if you weren't born. Don't you ever say such a thing. Never! Do you understand?"

She looked shocked and a little scared at my reaction, and asked quietly, "Is this another rule?"

"Yes, it's another rule, and you had better not break it. Understand? The world is a *much* better place with you in it, and don't you ever forget it."

"I won't, Joe," she said, and then sank under the water, reappeared, and swam off.

I watched her as she glided back and forth, back and forth, from one end of the pool to another, with an effortlessness that I assumed only occurred in children who were destined to become swimming stars.

The idea that a parent could say that to a child was frightening, yet it was not surprising. I knew from experience that this kind of behavior wasn't restricted to families like Bee's, who were having financial struggles and other problems. I had seen families from the extreme other end of the socioeconomic spectrum behaving the same way. Almost every day at the restaurant, successful parents came in with their young children and didn't say a word to them throughout dinner unless it was to scold them. The nanny ordered for the children, helped feed them, and cleaned their smudged faces. Privilege had its shortcomings, and never was that more on display than when you looked into the faces of these children.

I grabbed a towel and wrapped it around Bee when she finally got out of the pool. She lay down in a chair and I sat down beside her. "Remind me to buy sunscreen. I have a feeling you are going to be spending a lot of time out here."

"I do love the water. Maybe one day we can go to the beach and I can swim in the ocean? I bet that would be a lot of fun."

"Yes, that would be fun," I said, as I looked at her unblemished face, pure and luminous, like the face of a celestial being leading one safely through a dark forest and up and through the gates of heaven. She smiled as though acknowledging my thoughts, as I lay back in my chair and felt the sun on my face and wondered if this was all a dream.

Chapter Eleven

The doorbell rang, and I let Wang Wei into the house. He was carrying a large bag filled with all kinds of wonderful Chinese food. Wang worked at Rice Wok, which was located on Moorpark and Laurel Canyon, and I had been ordering from there for more than ten years.

Wang was always the delivery person. He was very friendly, and we had been on a first-name basis for years, although I called him Wang, which was actually his family name. The food was wonderful — as close to New York Chinese food as I had found in all my years living in Los Angeles — but I had grown to like Wang so much that I would probably have ordered from almost any Chinese restaurant that employed him. It was just my luck that he still worked for the best place in town.

"Ah, Joe, big order tonight."

"Yes, I have guests." I took the bag from him and placed it on the kitchen table. "Can I get you something to drink?"

"Not tonight Joe, very busy." Over the years Wang and I had shared beers together about a dozen times. He could be very chatty, and I was often very lonely, so we complemented each other well.

Bee walked out of her bedroom and I introduced them.

"Wang, this is my adopted daughter, Bee. Bee, this is Mr. Wang Wei."

"My God, so beautiful! Your daughter? Why have I never met her before?"

"Because I just adopted her."

"Congratulations, Joe. You chose very well."

"Thank you, Wang. She actually chose me. Isn't that so Bee?"

"Yes, Mr. Wang, I could not have chosen better."

"Joe is a great guy. We have known each other for many years."

"Yes, we have, and thank you for that endorsement, my friend."
I paid Wang in cash and gave him a generous tip, like always. Bee
shook his hand and said, "Very nice to meet you, Mr. Wang."

"Very nice to meet you, Miss Bee." Then he ran back to the car
and got something out of the front seat and came back and held out
his hand to Bee.

"Extra fortune cookies for good luck," Wang said.

As soon as we had closed the door behind him, Bee said, "What
a nice man."

"Yes, he is, and believe me, you will be seeing quite a bit of
him. I order from there at least once a week and sometimes two or
three times."

Bee started setting the dinner table and thankfully I had three
cloth napkins, and enough silverware, plates, and bowls for the three
of us. I usually used the plastic utensils that came with the order,
and ate straight out of the boxes, but tonight I wanted things to be a
little more formal. I unpacked the bag and put the food on top of the
stove: two wonton soups, two orders of chicken fried rice, shrimp
with lobster sauce, fried dumplings, and an order of chicken chow
mein, which I personally didn't like but every other New Yorker I
knew simply loved.

I called Bee over and raised a dumpling to her mouth with a pair
of chopsticks that came with the order. She bit into it and her face lit
up with delight, and then she asked if she could have another. With
a face like hers it was impossible to say no, so I placed another in her
mouth. I suddenly knew what it was like for birds to feed their
young, and I told her that, and we had a good laugh.

Before ordering the Chinese food, I had taken a trip to the
convenience store on the corner and bought five bottles of the

Ruffino Gold Chianti I had a few days earlier. I figured five bottles should hold the Latin beauty in good stead, and if not, I could always get more.

Lisa arrived about ten minutes after Wang left. Despite being told to bring only herself, she arrived with a box full of Italian cannoli from the Monte Carlo Deli and restaurant in Burbank. Bee moved about the house as though she had been living there her whole life, and Lisa watched her with a big smile on her face.

Before anyone sat down, Bee handed Lisa a plate with three dumplings and said, "You have to try these." After one taste, Lisa said, "Rice Wok on Laurel Canyon?"

"Exactly," I replied.

"I love that place. It's by far the closest thing to New York Chinese food I have found outside of New York. I have food delivered from there at least once a week."

"Do you know Mr. Wang?" Bee eagerly asked.

"Yes, I know Mr. Wang. Outside of the people from work, I have probably talked to him more than any other person since I have been living out here."

"Isn't he so nice?"

"He's the best."

During dinner, Bee recapped our day together, and each time the child smiled it was like a bolt of pure joy jumped from her brow and encircled the kitchen. She told a funny story about her performance on the basketball court, complete with a slapstick demonstration of her illegal double bounce. I talked up her swimming career like she was the next Amanda Beard, or a female Michael Phelps. Lisa laughed and exclaimed happily in all the right places until Bee finally came over and sat down next to her and rested her head against Lisa's shoulder. Lisa looked like she was about to cry, but she managed to blink the tears away and said, "Now that you've tried Rice Wok, what are your favorites?"

Bee said she loved the dumplings and the noodles in the wonton soup. Then she explained that she would think of me every time she ate a dumpling, because I fed her dumpling and we'd had a big laugh about her being a baby bird.

After we capped off our meal with delicious cannoli, Bee excused herself and ran off to the bathroom but promised to be back in just a few minutes.

Lisa turned to me and said, "Never in my life did I think I would see that child so happy."

"I imagine the happiness gene has always been in her, but she's never had an opportunity to express herself."

She smiled and patted my hand and said, "And I'm eternally grateful to you for making that possible. I should *never* have sent her to live with that family…"

"And if you hadn't, she never would have run away, and I never would have met her."

"That's true," she said. "Thank you for saying so. I have been flogging myself for days over what happened to her."

"Stop! None of that was your fault, and she's here now. Everything will be fine."

"Thank God," she said.

Then she turned to me and put on her business face and said, "I've been meaning to speak to you about your compensation. Once everything is approved and Bee is living here, you will get a monthly check, possibly as much as eight hundred and fifty dollars, for being a foster parent."

"I don't want their money."

"Oh, yes you do. I know you live a comfortable life, but in a very short time Bee is going to be a teenager, and that will add a whole new set of expenses to your monthly bills … expenses you've never once thought about. Take the money, and if nothing else, put it toward her college fund."

"I tell you what, I'll take the money if I can write out a check to you every month for the same amount. Would you agree to that?"

"Seriously, Joe, you've already given me two expensive TVs and a complete cable package for a year. I can't accept another thing from you!"

"I'm sorry to play hardball, but these are my terms. You take the money or I will walk down to your building tomorrow, with the child, track down your landlord, and pre-pay your rent for a year. The choice is yours."

"But…"

"But, nothing. You have been through my finances, and you know I don't need eight hundred dollars from foster care, and that I can easily afford to pay your rent for the next ten years. Come to think of it, I will make the choice for you. Case closed."

"If this is how you treat a lady who cancels a date with you, I can only imagine how great a boyfriend or husband you would be to some lucky woman."

"You know as well as I do, Lisa, that a thirty-five-year difference in our ages just wasn't going to work."

"I guess…"

I snuck in a question while the wiseass was still out of the room. "About schools, which ones do you recommend around here?"

"Well, there are public schools, private schools, and Catholic schools. They're all rated fairly well, but their safety records vary a lot. I've actually had something different in mind for you and Bee."

"Such as?"

"Well, you're quite a well-educated guy … NYU, John Jay College of Criminal Justice, Stony Brook University, graduate school at Loyola Marymount University, and a few courses shy of a master's degree in education. I know this is a lot, but would you consider homeschooling Bee for the next year or two, or beyond that if you like?"

"Am I even qualified?"

"You're over-qualified. All you need is the equivalent of a high school diploma. You have to follow a regimen, teach to the curriculum, and keep careful attendance records, but it can be a great option. I usually don't recommend homeschooling to foster parents, but I think you'd be great, and Bee will thrive."

Lisa looked anxiously toward Bee's bedroom and whispered, "Honestly, I'm not sure Bee is ready to be around other children every day. She has been through a lot, and not just with her foster parents. Her biological parents treated her terribly. The first time I visited her after her parents were killed, she showed absolutely no emotion. I told her that if she felt like crying it would be perfectly normal, and that it's terrible to lose one's parents, but she just said, 'I don't feel like crying. They always told me how much better everything would be if they never had me.'"

I nodded and said, "She told me that today, and I haven't been able to get it out of my mind. I can't help thinking that the world, and Bee, are better off without them."

Lisa looked at me as if she'd had the same thought, and said, "Believe me, Joe, I am no stranger to such stories and I have heard a lot worse. Sometimes the kids turn out like the parents. But Bee is different. There is something about her that just pulls you in. How any parent could look into that child's face and say, 'It would have been better if I just aborted you' baffles the mind. She's an angel ..."

Lisa stopped talking as Bee emerged from her bedroom and sat back down. Bee smiled, showing off her gleaming white teeth and her adorable dimples and said, "I like to floss and brush my teeth right after I eat. I don't want any nasty cavities."

Lisa laughed as she ran her hand through Bee's hair and said, "You see, Joe? You are not only adopting an absolutely beautiful child, but a possible future hygienist. How lucky are you?"

"I feel like I have won the lottery ten times over."

Lisa left shortly after nine o'clock, and Bee and I raced through the dishes so we could watch the Yankees game. She ran off to her bedroom to put on her clean pajamas as I sat down on the couch in the living room and turned on the game.

The Yankees were playing the Orioles and were comfortably ahead 8 to 1. The Yankees had a really good team, and in the off-season they had signed a couple of star starting pitchers, and were expected to seriously compete for a World Series title. Considering that I had already given up on my New York Knicks before the basketball season was about to start in a couple of months, I could at least take comfort in the fact that the Yankees might win it all.

Bee, dressed in her pajamas, sat next to me on the couch. After a minute or two of watching the game, she asked which ones were the Yankees, and I said, "They're the ones wearing the pinstripes. They're ahead 8 to 1." She smiled and said, "Great! That's the team you root for, and from now on I will be rooting for them, too."

"You mean, you didn't look at the Yankees games while at Lisa's?" I asked.

"I would have watched them on the TV in the bedroom but I didn't have the heart to leave her alone in the living room, watching sad love stories and crying her eyes out."

"Such a thoughtful young lady you are. Did you have a good time tonight?"

"Yes, I had a wonderful time. Lisa is so nice, and so is Mr. Wang, and the food was delicious. I love the cannoli."

"While you were out of the room, Lisa and I talked about what might be a good school for you to attend."

"Oh," she said. "I figured that would eventually come up."

"Not looking forward to going to school?"

"No, but it's not like I have a choice."

"Well, Lisa and I agree that for the next year or two, or possibly longer, I could homeschool you. Do you know what that is?"

She looked puzzled, so I explained that instead of going to a regular school, she would stay home and I would be her teacher. "We would have to keep strict attendance records and cover all of the same material they teach in school, but you would be at home the whole time. Do you like that idea?"

Her eyes widened and she said, "I love that idea!" She reached over and hugged me tightly.

"I don't want you to think that it is going to be easier than if you were attending a normal school. I am a firm believer in education and one day I hope to see you graduating college and doing something important with your life. You understand?"

"Yes, yes, I understand. I love it here so much and I love you so much that I never want to leave."

"That's what you say now, but in a few years, you'll be thinking differently."

"No! I never want to leave."

"Okay, you never have to leave. There's nothing that would make me happier than you never leaving. That's how much I love you. But if you change your mind later, that's okay too."

"I won't."

"We'll see."

"I won't."

She rested her head against my shoulder as we watched the game. For the first time in my life I was totally responsible for another human being: for feeding, clothing, sheltering, educating, and providing unconditional love and support.

In a sense, I had trained for this job since I was a kid. I never knew anything but unconditional love and support from my parents and my large extended family. But like so much in my life, the training I received went unrealized and was never put into practice. Lisa reminded me of that when she listed off my academic degrees, alongside the fact that I spent my working life in the same restaurant for over twenty-five years as a busboy, waiter, part-time bartender, and manager. The only time my education was put to use was when I was called on to serve as an occasional orator and speechwriter at memorial services for family and the occasional friend. And when I sat down with a very special customer at the restaurant. He was a friend, much more than a customer — a person whose intellect, creativity, knowledge, kindness, and generosity were unmatched by any other individual I met in the more than thirty years I have lived in Los Angeles. Our conversations will remain with me until the day I die.

My father, aunt Carmela, and uncle Al would never say anything, but I knew they had to be disappointed that I failed to use my education for a higher purpose. Yes, I made good money at the restaurant and I got to know fascinating and creative people, but I never could honestly look into the mirror and say that I was proud of my achievements and profession.

My uncle Al had certainly tried to set me on the right path. When I was eight years old, he and I used to sit down at my parents' kitchen table and he would take out mimeographed copies of words from the dictionary, and each night we would go over ten new words. Some of them were derived from Latin, while others were Greek, Germanic, Gothic, English, and Dutch. It was my task to learn and memorize the origins and the meanings of the words, and my uncle Al would test me on them the next night, and randomly throughout the next seven years. Needless to say, I had a big vocabulary by the age of nine, and an even bigger one at fifteen, when his tutoring sessions ended. I didn't always love these lessons, but I knew my uncle Al wanted the best for me. He firmly believed that with the right education, I could escape the family pattern of working in a factory and someday do meaningful and important work that would enhance the lives of many unfortunate people.

I doubt he was happy with my choices. After I graduated from college and pursued master's degrees in a number of different areas of study, I could have gone on to do almost anything, but I stayed at the restaurant for the money. I'm sure that wasn't my uncle Al's idea of meaningful work that would enhance lives. At least, now, I would be able to put my education to use, helping a girl who had all the potential in the world, but until now, none of the advantages.

The game ended with a final score of 11 to 3. The Yankees hit a couple of meaningless homeruns in the bottom of the eighth, which made their victory a little more impressive. The child with her head on my shoulder was out cold, and I tried not to disturb her too much as I picked her up and carried her into her bedroom. I swear, she was no heavier than a case of beer. I tucked her into bed and kissed her on the forehead.

I started walking out of the room and heard Bee's sleepy voice say, "I muv you, Joe."

I laughed and said, "I *muv* you too, Bee," and she laughed a groggy little laugh before falling back to sleep.

Chapter Twelve

As I stepped into the soft light of the hallway, leaving Bee's door slightly open, I reached into my pocket and pulled out a key to the third bedroom in the house. It was actually the master bedroom and the only room that I kept locked. I hadn't always done that. Until a month ago, this was the part of the house where I spent most of my time.

I padded down the hall in my socks, unlocked the door, and walked into the room. As I looked around, I immediately felt a sense of calm excitement. The walls were lined with mahogany bookcases that reached from floor to ceiling. Wedged between them, in front of the only window, was my desk. Inside the bookcases were my best friends, and at the same time my deadliest enemies. Thousands of books, arranged alphabetically by author, filled the cases. I had read nearly all of them, some multiple times. On my desk, between two plaster lion bookends, were nine books: Joseph Conrad's *Heart of Darkness* and *Under Western Eyes*, James Joyce's *A Portrait of the Artist as a Young Man*, Hemingway's *The Sun Also Rises*, Dostoevsky's *Crime and Punishment*, Dante's *Divine Comedy*, Byron's *Don Juan*, *The Federalist Papers*, by Madison, Hamilton, and Jay, and finally, in honor of my uncle Al, a dog-eared copy of the *Oxford Dictionary of English Etymology*. These nine books were my favorites and had had the greatest influence on me. They had occupied that spot for thirty years, and had been taken down and re-read, in part or in full, more times than I could count.

Next to the books was a bright, colorful framed illustration of Dante's final sphere — the Ninth Sphere — from the final book of the *Divine Comedy, Paradiso.* This is where Beatrice explains to the poet the creation of the universe and the role of the angels, and where Dante sees the blinding light of God. To me, it has always symbolized, apart from the religious aspect, the worldly possibility of a Paradise on Earth, if we work diligently and never abandon our moral obligations toward our fellow human beings.

The illustration was given to me by an elderly owner of a used bookstore in Burbank after we had been discussing Dante's work and how it is still as powerful and relevant today as it was when he first wrote *The Divine Comedy* nearly five hundred years ago.

I had started locking this room a month earlier because, rightly or wrongly, I started viewing all of these books, and the time I had spent reading them, as the reason why I hadn't achieved my potential in life, despite having had so many advantages.

I moved to Los Angeles at the age of twenty-three, determined to chase my dream of working in the film industry. Specifically, I hoped to write award-winning screenplays about important subjects, like the wars in Central America and Angola and the scourge of Apartheid in South Africa. But this dream required grit and a willingness to be constantly on the move. After making a few visits to a couple of these countries, never putting myself in any real physical danger, except for the possibility of drinking to excess and dying of alcohol poisoning, I lost interest in travelling, apart from occasional visits to the Bronx to visit family and friends.

From there I drifted into my first job at the restaurant, and quickly rose through the ranks. When I wasn't washing dishes, waiting tables or managing the staff, I could often be found reading. I became caught up in the world of books, devouring novels, short stories, poetry, biographies, and history, and even picking my way through textbooks on medicine and science. Instead of visiting places that I wanted to write about, I read about them. Instead of writing, I read and read and read, convinced that I was doing research for my own stories. Then, after spending a year or so drilling down into a topic, such as dark money in politics, I got bored and moved on to different subjects and authors. My own stories remained unwritten.

As I sat there in my study, I thought about my obsessive tendencies, going back to when I was a teenager in the Bronx. Back then, my entire life revolved around the game of basketball, beer and cheap wine, drugs, movies and *The New York Times*. Later, I would add books to that list. When I first started John Jay College at seventeen, I wanted to work for the FBI. I had graduated high school in three years, not because I was some type of genius but because I hated the institution so much that I doubled the number of credits I needed to take each semester and after my third year I was off to college.

While at John Jay, I took an introductory course in psychology and suddenly became hooked on Sigmund Freud and psychoanalysis. In one year, I became so well-versed in Freudian theory that I could easily hold my own with my teachers, who were all licensed psychologists. I used to go down to the famous New York City Public Library on 41st Street and read esoteric and archived material written by Freud, before the advent of psychoanalysis, that few people had ever heard or read about.

Then one day, while in the library at John Jay, I picked up a book called *Crime and Punishment*, by some guy named Dostoevsky. I thought the book had to do with the criminal justice system in New York, but when I started reading it, I realized it was about a Russian student who commits a dastardly murder. I got so caught up in the story that I read the six-hundred-page novel in a couple of days. That was the beginning of my long-lasting love affair with literature, and an end to my fascination with the man who believed that women and girls suffer from penis envy.

Literature and books, basketball, and family have been the three consistent supports and pillars in my life. When I've been short on money, or going through severe bouts of depression or other health issues, they have always been there for me. Yes, most of my relatives are gone now, buried in Saint Raymond's Cemetery in the Bronx, but the memories remind me of how blessed I was to have them in my life.

Playing basketball, especially shooting by myself and pretending to be my favorite basketball heroes, is probably the only time in my life that I felt a sense of invincibility, a sense of freedom that I have never been able to recapture playing any other sport. Running up and down an empty court, pretending to be a player I idolized, was always a magical experience. No one was judging me, and it allowed me to feel perfect in an otherwise ugly body and a troubled mind.

Books provided me with other freedoms and forms of escape. They alleviated my sense of failure every time I walked through the doors of the restaurant, allowing me to forget that I was destined for more meaningful work. They softened the sense of rejection I felt every time a screenplay I had worked hard on was rejected by agents and producers who had promised to help me. And books whisked away the pain I felt when girls whom I really liked, and whom I would have treated like gold, showed no interest in me, remaining indifferent to my very being.

I sat in the chair in front of my desk and looked around at all the books. Each author represented a different time in my life, and reminded me of the ups and downs, and the times when I felt complete uncertainty about everything and everyone. I was leaning back in my desk chair, surveying the room and thinking about the different phases of my life that coincided with the discovery of each author's work, when my eye happened to catch the dust jacket of Nelson Mandela's autobiography, *Long Walk to Freedom*.

At that moment, Bee walked into the room and stood next to the door with her mouth open. "Oh—," she said, unable to speak as she looked all around at the thousands of volumes on display in this makeshift in-home library. I looked at her, in her pajamas, her face aglow like a child let loose in a candy factory.

"What are you doing up?" I asked. "It wasn't that long ago that I tucked you in and you looked like you were out for the night."

"The light woke me up. Have you read all these books?"

"All but a very few. Some of them I've read many times," I said. She walked up to me and I reached down and picked her up and sat her on top of the desk. She saw a typewriter that lived on the desk just below the window and asked, "What's that?"

I laughed and said, "It's a typewriter, sweetheart. It's what us old folks used to write on before computers came along."

"Why do you keep it, if you don't use it anymore?"

"Because my mother bought it for me, and it cost quite a bit of money, and it wasn't like my family was rich. But, she knew I would need it in college. It was the type of sacrifice she made for her children, even if it deprived her of things she needed."

Bee ran her fingers across the typewriter, and then looked wide-eyed around the room and asked, "Am I allowed in this room, or is there a rule against that?" She giggled as I helped her down off the desk.

"Yes, you're allowed in this room as long as you always put the books back in their proper place. I was actually thinking of making this your classroom when we start your homeschooling. Would you like that?"

"Yes," she replied as she walked around the room, running her fingers gently across rows of books.

"When I'm gone this will be all yours," I remarked.

She turned and looked at me and with a worried expression she asked, "Where are you going?"

"You know, when I'm gone, I'll be leaving all this to you."

"No!" she exclaimed. "No! No! No!" she screamed as she put her hands over her ears, and ran out of the room and into her bedroom and slammed the door behind her.

All of this happened before I could say another word. I sat, dumbfounded at her behavior. It was as though some sort of extreme bodily pain had suddenly attacked her. Surely, she understood that one day I would no longer be here … that I would die, like everyone else. I mean, it wasn't that long ago that she sat in her parents' car and experienced the trauma of seeing both of them killed. She had also heard her parents talk about having her aborted, and had listened to my stories about my dead relatives. Surely, she didn't expect me to live forever?

I got up from my chair, walked out of the room, and knocked on her bedroom door. She didn't answer, but from inside her room I could hear heaving and crying so loud that I decided I had to go in. I opened the door and found her there, bundled up like a ball, crying hysterically as her tiny body trembled like she was having an epileptic seizure. I walked over to her and asked, "Did you hurt yourself? Are you in pain?" When she shook her head, I reached down and picked her up. She grasped me so tightly that for a second I lost my breath. I gently rubbed her back as she continued to heave and cry, and after a few minutes my entire back was bathed in her tears.

"Did I upset you by talking about … going away?" I felt her head nod up and down as more tears splashed onto my shoulder.

"Well, I'm not going anywhere," I said. "I promise. I would never leave you." It was like the words came out of my mouth without thinking, like someone had programmed me to say them.

Her grip loosened slightly, yet she continued to heave and cry and after about fifteen minutes her body went totally limp. She had fallen asleep in my arms. I laid her down on the bed, arranged the covers over her, and watched over her for a long time, until I was satisfied that she was okay. Her breathing was normal and the color had returned to her lovely face. I walked out of the room, but left the door wide open. I turned off the light in my library and locked the door.

***

After changing my tear-stained shirt, I walked into my bedroom and lay down on my bed, exhausted. I closed my eyes and suddenly I was in front of Rizzo's Funeral Home on Westchester Avenue in the

Bronx, dressed like I was fifty years ago. I entered the building and there in the lobby was a placard that read, "Anthony Caggiano, Room # 2." I remembered that the first time my parents allowed me to go into a funeral home was when my uncle Tony died. Back then, it was customary for a family to lay out a deceased relative between three and five days before the funeral mass and burial. It was quite morbid, and my parents felt I was too young to experience such a ritual, even though relatives and friends of the family were constantly dying because my mother's side of the family was very large. I insisted on going to see my uncle Tony, especially since my parents didn't allow me to go visit him in the hospital and I loved him so much.

Suddenly my uncle Nick was there, taking me by the arm and leading me to Room #2. The room was packed with friends and family. The lights in the room were dim and the cries and sobs of the bereaved were piercing, like the sound effects one might hear in a horror movie. I had heard that guests often went to these events inebriated, with a flask of whiskey in their pockets, and that there was usually a barroom within a half a block of any given funeral home, and I thought: *It's no wonder.*

My uncle Nick stood beside me at the open casket as I looked down at my uncle Tony lying there with his hands crossed, holding a pair of rosary beads. It looked just like him, but he didn't move or speak or laugh like he always did. Then the lights dimmed and the cries dissipated, and in a flash, I was there alone with my uncle Tony, who suddenly got up from the casket as though he was getting up from his bed after eight hours of sleep. He laughed as he looked at me and asked, "What, you never seen a dead person come back to life?"

"You're not really dead? This is some type of joke you are playing on all us, isn't it?" I said, hoping more than anything that it was true.

"You would think that after all these years, you, of all people, would know that I was dead. As for resting in peace, now that's a totally different thing, especially with you bombarding me constantly with your guilt-ridden thoughts and prayers and the countless stories you tell about me. You're worse than my sisters, your aunts and mother, constantly hitting me up with requests and scolding me for drinking too much, but with them I have no choice. I'm stuck with them for eternity."

"It's because I miss you so much," I said, starting to cry.

"Now, now, stop that. I thought if I taught you anything it was to behave like a man."

"And that only cowards hit women," I continued like he used to tell me all the time.

"Exactly!" he exclaimed as we sat down in front of the casket. "You wouldn't remember which of your aunts decided to bury me in this God-awful suit?" He stretched his arms and legs out and it was quite apparent that the suit was tight on him. He was quite a muscular guy.

"I think it was my mother and Aunt Carmela," I replied.

"The rooster and the movie star. That's what I figured, but every time I ask them they just run off, giggling." He used to call my mother the rooster because she had red hair, and my aunt Carmela was the movie star because she looked like Sophia Loren. "So what is it now that's bothering you? Is it that pitiful, dirty little girl you picked up off the street?"

"Yeah, sort of ... she's been through so much. Her parents..."

"I know, you have retold the story to me at least a thousand times in the last three days."

"I didn't know you were listening," I remarked.

He laughed and reached over and planted a kiss on my cheek. "Of course I have been listening. Don't you think I love and miss you as much as you do me?"

"So you saw what happened in my study?"

"Yes! You remember what I always told you my one wish in life was?"

"To die before your mom," I replied.

"That's right. And do you know why? Because she is the one person who always looked out for me and took care of me and prayed for me when I was stricken with polio. Her caring never stopped, and the idea that one day I would not have her there was too much for me to handle." He waited to see if I was making the connection, then drove home his point. "You're the first person Bee has ever known that has loved her unconditionally and cared for her like your grandmother cared for me. That's why she behaved like she did when you mentioned being *gone*, twice if I remember correctly." He looked at me like I was a bit of a dolt for not knowing that she would react that way, and I had to agree, but his kind eyes told me that it was all going to be okay.

"I am so proud of you," he said. "So very proud. But hopefully your beautiful little girl grows up to be like your mother and aunt Carmela … strong and independent, yet loving and caring, and also realistic. Just give it time." He reached into his pockets and shook his head and said, "And not only do they put me into this suit but they bury me with no money."

"I have money," I said.

"Great! Now why don't you run over to the grocery store across the street and buy me an ice-cold quart of Rheingold beer and a night owl edition of the *Daily News*? They have everything up there but my favorite beer," he said, pointing skyward.

"I'll be right back and I will also get myself a quart. I'm old enough to drink now."

"I'm quite aware."

I ran out of the funeral home and across the street to the grocery store. I picked out the two coldest quarts of Rheingold beer and a night owl edition of the *News*. I walked back into the funeral home and into Room #2. I walked toward the casket but he was no longer sitting in front of it. I looked down into the casket and he was lying down, with his hands crossed, holding the rosary beads, and he didn't move, or talk, or laugh. I placed the two quarts on both sides of him, and the newspaper above his hands. I then reached into my pocket and took out all the money I had on me. I put it into his side coat pocket and then reached over and kissed him on his forehead and said, "Thank you."

I tried not to cry, but I couldn't help myself. Was it my fault that he loved and cared for me so much, that I would never stop loving and missing him or telling stories about him?

I woke up, and now it was my tears that showered down upon my shirt.

***

I walked into the bathroom, peeled off my soggy shirt, and splashed cold water on my face. As I examined my craggy features under the harsh light, I thought about my Freud phase from forty years earlier. Back then, I would have analyzed that dream for weeks and come up with some tortured explanation about hidden sexual fantasies or aggressive desires toward my father that I had repressed since the age of five.

Fortunately, those days were over, and I was free to enjoy the dream about my uncle as though it were a visit from him. I took it for what it was: a message, a nugget of sound advice, and a confirmation of how very much I missed and loved him.

I put on a clean shirt and the rest of my exercise gear and left the bedroom, expecting to find Bee in the kitchen eating breakfast, ready for our next run/walk. Instead, I looked straight ahead through her bedroom door, which was still wide open, and saw a child sleeping so soundly that I didn't dare wake her. I looked at her face and could have sworn I was witnessing some sort of deep healing in action. She was so perfectly still that I imagined her young brain stitching itself together and recovering from those first nine years of chaos. I stood in the doorway, transfixed, blew her a kiss, and padded quietly down the hall.

I decided to take a day off from running, and walked into the kitchen and opened the refrigerator. Despite the early hour, I could have gone for an ice-cold beer, and I probably would have had one, but I still had not taken the beer out of the car, and I certainly wasn't going to have a warm beer. I took out an otherwise foreign object from my refrigerator, a bottle of orange juice, and poured myself a glass.

I sat down at the kitchen table, turned on my computer, and read an email from Lisa thanking Bee and me for a wonderful night. As promised, she attached links to all the information and forms I needed to apply for a license to homeschool Bee. Lisa was right; I was fully qualified to educate Bee from home. There weren't many requirements, and one did not need a college degree. The curriculum was fairly straightforward, with an emphasis on math, history, and English at each grade level. The record-keeping requirements were strict, especially when it came to attendance. I had to wait until I was officially Bee's foster parent to submit the required paperwork. Fortunately, the deadline was not for another three months.

I switched over to *The New York Times* website, a newspaper I have read religiously since I was a delinquent teenager sitting on the roof of one of the many tall buildings that made up the projects called Parkchester, drinking beer at eight in the morning, with my basketball beside me, catching up on news and sports. Back in the day, I thought the Watergate scandal was the most serious case of political corruption I was likely to see in my lifetime. Boy, was I mistaken.

After reading half a dozen articles about the unfolding circus in Washington and across the country, I turned off the computer. The early morning sun was already passing through the kitchen window and bathing the room in a soothing yellow light. I turned around and saw Bee walking toward me, still in her pajamas, rubbing cobwebs from her eyes.

"Did you already go for our walk?"

"No, I thought today we would give our bodies a rest."

"I'm sorry I slept so long," she said as she plopped down in the chair beside me.

I got up and fixed her a bowl of cereal and put it in front of her. She played with the spoon as she looked at me and asked, "What have you been doing this morning?"

"Reading the newspaper, and going over the application to apply for a homeschool license."

"Have you talked to Lisa?" she hesitantly asked.

"No, why would I be talking to Lisa at this time in the morning?"

She looked down into her bowl and replied, "Because of the way I acted last night."

"The way you acted? I thought you were the perfect host."

"The way I went crazy in your study and started crying and slamming the door."

"And why would I tell her about that? It was my mistake for bringing up a topic that I should have known would be very sensitive for you, given everything you have been through, in the past few months especially."

Bee was continuing to look down at her bowl.

"Bee," I said, touching one of her hands lightly. "Listen to me. It was my fault. You did nothing wrong. I'm not used to being a father yet, and I forgot that I need to be sensitive. You've been through a lot."

When she still couldn't look at me, I said, "To think that I have a daughter who loves me so much that even mentioning going away makes her cry makes me feel like the luckiest parent in the world. Do you know how great it feels to know that I have someone in my life that loves me so much?"

At this she finally looked up and met my eyes. I was worried about making her cry, but I had to say it: "You know, don't you, that having you in my life is the best thing that has ever happened to me?"

She dropped her spoon into the bowl, stood up, and threw her arms around my neck and buried her head in my shoulder. The arms on that kid! She was a swimmer all right, with all that upper body strength.

Then the dream became a kind of vision, playing out before me, as I suddenly felt like my uncle Tony was nearby, watching with approval, or maybe orchestrating events. For all I knew, he had sensed my loneliness and had led Bee to my door. It wouldn't be the first favor he had done for me.

I held on to that little girl for dear life, and as her latest round of tears splashed down my back and onto my new clean shirt — tears of joy, this time — I whispered, "Thank you, Uncle Tony."

Chapter Thirteen

Bee took a quick shower, changed into clean clothes, brushed her teeth, and jumped into the passenger's seat of my car. She didn't know it yet, but we would be going on a shopping spree, after first making a stop at the CVS Pharmacy not far from my house. I bought four bottles of sunscreen and handed the bag to Bee. "You are not to go into the pool without putting that lotion all over your body."

"Does that include the parts of my body covered by my one-piece bathing suit?" she asked.

"Keep being a little wiseass, and I'll have you wearing 50 SPF to bed."

"So, this is another rule?"

"Yes. An important one. If you don't put it on, your swimming privileges will be revoked for a week. It's to protect you from the sun."

"Thank you, Joe."

"And now we are going to buy you your own computer and cell phone."

She looked surprised by this and said, "Can't I just use yours?"

"I want you to have your own. You'll need a computer to do your homework and I'm going to be using my own computer a lot more over the next couple of months, getting ready to homeschool you. And knowing you have a phone on you all the time will give me peace of mind. I need to know that we can always get in touch with each other if we are separated."

"Okay, but we should compare prices and not get the most expensive thing."

"I agree with you in principle, but let's see how it goes."

We turned into the parking lot at Fry's Electronics in Burbank and parked.

"They have everything here," I said.

"I don't want you spending so much money on me," she complained.

I put my hand to my ear and made a fake radio static sound. "Sorry, can't hear you. Going — krrrkkkchhhkkk — through a tunnel." This was only faintly amusing. "I'm right here, silly," she said. "Oh, that's right, you are." I held her hand as we walked into the store and made our way to the computer and cellular departments, where a knowledgeable salesperson helped us pick out a powerful laptop computer for the wiseass. Bee's eyes kept darting across at the computer games on display next to the laptops. I asked, "Which two games would you most want, Bee?"

"I don't need any games."

"Okay, I'll just pick out any two, then."

"No," she suddenly replied, "I'll pick them out, if you insist on buying them." She picked out a game called "Tomb Raider," about a teenage girl stranded on an island who beats up bad guys, and one named "Horizon Zero Dawn," starring another ass-kicking female heroine who beats up monsters or some sort of alien creatures.

Next we went to pick out a phone. We got a basic camera phone, with room for a few apps and games, but not so many that she would spend her whole life on her phone. At least I hoped she wouldn't.

Then I asked her if she wanted a TV for her room and she said, "No, that's okay. I like watching TV with you."

"Okay," I said, not-so-secretly pleased.

***

Back at home, Bee jumped out of the car with her shopping bag filled with electronic gifts. Naturally, she forgot the bag with the sunscreen and I grabbed it as we walked into the house.

She immediately called Lisa on the house phone, and told her all about her gifts as she walked randomly around the house. As I listened to her account of our day and watched the light bouncing off her dimples, she smiled up at me, and I felt my heart do a little flip. I was quite sure that Bee was the kindest, smartest, funniest, and most beautiful creature in the world. If other fathers could marvel at their daughters, I felt I had every right to do the same.

She started to run into her bedroom with her shopping bag, and I stopped her and handed her the bag with the sunscreen. "Forget something?"

"Oops!" she said, and took it from me with a bashful smile. "Don't worry. I won't forget the pool rule."

"Good. Are you going to set up your computer?"

"I'm going to see how far I can get without help from you or Lisa. But first I'm going to take it out of the box and stare at it for a while because it's so pretty."

I laughed and promised to check on her in a little while, and she left for her bedroom, laden down with bags. "Good luck," I called out, struggling with the temptation to follow her, but deciding to leave her to work it out on her own. It was entirely possible that someone of Bee's generation would have an easier time setting up a computer than I would. And if she did ask for help, we would tackle it together.

Suddenly alone, I did what I always seem to do, at least since leaving the restaurant: I wandered around the house, thinking. *Musing*. In the months since I was laid off, it was almost like I'd been inhabited by the ghost of Marcel Proust. At some point every day, I found myself staring out a window, searching for lost time by running through all of the stories that have made me who I am.

On this occasion I ended up in the kitchen, gazing through the window at my quiet street. For five minutes, no one walked by, and no cars drove past. This fact alone underscored how different this area of Los Angeles was from my native Bronx.

As I took in the quiet, I remembered the night before I left to go live in Los Angeles, back in 1982. My brothers, Paul and Sal, Sal's girlfriend, Donna, and my friend Howie, had ended up at a bar. We stayed well past midnight and drank our weight in beer while swapping stories. Halfway through the evening, Donna pulled out a little box and put it in front of me on our table, which was littered with glasses. From the look on Sal's face, he obviously had no idea what Donna was up to. I opened the box and inside was a gold chain with a carved head of Christ. "For good luck and safe travels," she said. Nearly forty years later I still keep the chain and the box in my desk drawer, next to a stack of letters from my father, brothers, and uncle Al.

After we left the bar, we drove back to our house on Sacket Avenue and sat outside talking until after two in the morning. My flight was leaving from Kennedy Airport at 8:00 a.m. The price of the one-way ticket was $350, which was a lot of money at the time, so there was no way I could afford to miss that flight.

We all hugged and said our good-byes and then I went upstairs with my brothers to get a little sleep before we had to leave for the airport. I had shipped all of my stuff to Los Angeles a few days earlier, and my friend Anthony, who was a godsend to me during those first few months in Los Angeles, had all the boxes put into my studio apartment in the complex where we would live for the next three years.

Just before going to sleep that night, I looked out the kitchen window and down at the street, which was oddly well-lit for the hour. In the distance, I could hear delivery trucks unloading supplies for the market not far from the house. Occasionally, a car would pass under the street lamps. I remember thinking about how the time had flown in the four months since I had decided to move to Los Angeles. At the time it had seemed as if the moment might never arrive, and there I was, hours away from boarding a flight to my new life on the other coast.

I remember being scared, excited, and full of hope. When I had told people that I was moving to Los Angeles and that I planned to work in the movie business and write screenplays, they were surprised and impressed by my ambition and drive. Not many people who grew up in my part of the Bronx ever left, and if they did it was to move to Long Island or upstate New York. It was a different time, years before everyone would be walking around with cell phones that were also cameras and everyone was an amateur filmmaker.

Later that morning, after what felt like about two minutes of sleep, my father and brothers drove me to the airport. Sal was still feeling the effects from the night before and stayed in the car while my father and Paul walked me into the American Airlines terminal. When it was time to board, I kissed my brother and father and surprisingly did not cry. I looked back one last time before boarding and waved to my dad, who was standing alone, silhouetted against a background of travelers coming and going. It was then that I broke down and wept.

I must have had an inkling, at least, of what I was leaving behind. How stupidly lucky I had been. My whole life, up to that moment, I'd had nothing but unconditional love and support from my family, my aunt Carmela, my uncle Al, and all of my other relatives. I wasn't born with a silver spoon in my mouth, but I won the lottery when it came to knowing that I had the love of my whole family. As I got in line to board the airplane, I remember thinking, *I could die right now and have no complaints.*

It was my first time flying, and if I was nervous, I really don't remember. I do remember being homesick before we even took off from Kennedy Airport, and turning to books for comfort. I reread all of Steinbeck's *Grapes of Wrath* and was on the last chapter of Joseph Conrad's *Heart of Darkness* by the time we touched down at Los Angeles International Airport.

My friend Anthony met me at the terminal, and I could tell at a glance that he had acclimated to southern California like a pro. He showed up at LAX in shorts and a tank top, looking more like a surfer than a kid from the Bronx. I wondered out loud if I would look the same way within a couple of months, but I knew that was wishful thinking. Anthony's golden skin and chiseled features had given him a big head start.

He was bubbling over with optimism as he drove us back to the apartment complex. He spent the whole ride talking about how we were going to make it big in this town and turn the movie industry on its head. We were part of a new generation of filmmakers and would reshape the industry. He was sure of it. And he was half right; he made it big as an editor, while I got sucked into the restaurant business and stayed there for thirty years, spending my off-hours reading instead of writing.

In a sense, my story was no different than that of a million other wide-eyed newbies who came to Los Angeles to work in the movie business, only to end up with their dreams derailed. Unlike in the Bronx, nobody in LA was impressed when you told them that you were an aspiring screenwriter ... so were a couple of million other hopefuls. The only thing that got a less enthusiastic response was telling them you were an aspiring actor.

As I thought about all of this ancient history, I moved around the kitchen like a zombie, distractedly pulling together some leftovers from the night before for a quick lunch. I served myself an egg roll and some fried rice and piled the rest of the dumplings onto a plate for Bee. Then I set aside the last three cannoli.

I called out to her, and when I didn't get a response, I walked down the hall to her bedroom, balancing both plates on one arm and holding a glass of milk in my other hand, waiter-style. At first when I looked into her room all I could see were opened boxes and discarded plastic bags and big chunks of molded Styrofoam strewn all over the floor, but no Bee. Then I glimpsed a little form under the desk.

"I find it usually works better when you sit in the chair," I called out.

"Ha-ha," she said, crawling out from under the desk with a big smile on her face. "I was plugging it in."

"See, I knew you were a genius." I walked over and put her plate down on the desk.

"Ooh, thank you," she said, and sat down at the desk chair. I sat on the edge of her bed and started in on my egg roll and fried rice.

She turned to me and asked, "Do you know your Wi-Fi password?"

"Yes."

"Really."

"Yes, and why do you look so surprised?"

"Because I…"

"Because you were quite certain I didn't," I replied as she giggled. "Why don't you eat a little of your lunch, and then I just might give it to you?"

She looked like that might be considered bribery, but she picked up a dumpling and started eating it while I wrote my password down on a scrap of paper and handed it to her.

She looked at it and said, "I should have known: nyknicks70/74. What does the 70/74 stand for, the only two years they won the World Series?"

"The World Series is baseball. In basketball they called it the Championship."

"Oh, still, a really long time ago," she replied with a giggle as she typed in the password and finally said, "I'm in."

"You seem pretty good at this. Did you have a computer at home?"

"No, this is my first one. I was allowed to use the computers at school, but only to look up information for school projects. Now I can have my own email account. What email address do you think I should use?"

"Wiseass@mail.com," I replied. She shot me a stern look and said, "Hmm," and then, "Oh, I have the perfect one." She started typing and happily added, "And it's available."

"What is it?"

"You'll see. I am going to send you my first email from my lovely new computer."

"Okay, while you're working on that I will call up the phone company and have them put you on my cell phone plan." I kissed her on the head, took her phone off the desk, and walked into the kitchen, where I called my provider and had Bee's phone added to my account.

Half an hour later, I brought the device back to her. She now had her own phone and her own number and the ability to text, send emails, and connect to the internet. I only hoped I wouldn't come to regret all of the extra features.

My laptop dinged from the kitchen, so I went back to the kitchen and checked my email. In there was a new message from daddysgirl70/74@mail.com. It read, "Dear Joe, I love you, I love you, I love you, with all my heart and soul. Thank you for my new computer and phone and thank you for loving me." I stared at this until my eyes were swimming with tears. After a few minutes I wrote back, "Dear Bee, You're welcome, sweetie. Love, Dad (Joe)."

Then my cell phone dinged and it was a text from Bee. "Can I go for a swim?" it said, followed by about twenty emojis, including two rows of multicolored hearts and little people doing cartwheels and pictures of sushi and fortune cookies and a cupcake and zebras and horses and horseshoes.

"Sure," I wrote back, adding a few emojis of my own, although it was obvious from my paltry selections that I had work to do to become more fluent in emoji.

She sent back four big smiley faces and another row of hearts, and for some reason that got the waterworks going again. I was having trouble keeping up with all the times I had cried big fat man tears since Bee came into my life. I couldn't remember crying more than a dozen times in all the years since I'd left the Bronx to live in LA. Now here I was having one or two big happy cries a day.

I was relieved to have a few more minutes to compose myself while Bee changed into her suit. "No more crying for today," I told myself, but in truth, I had no idea what else the day would bring.

Chapter Fourteen

Bee stepped out of her bedroom dressed in her bathing suit and holding up a bottle of sunscreen. "Would you like to inspect?" she asked, and as she turned around, I could see that she had not missed a spot. Her entire body was aglow with newly applied lotion.

"Very nice job," I said.

"So, you approve?"

"If I could give you an A-plus for sunscreen application, I would."

"Great! Now it's your turn," she said as she opened the bottle and started applying sunscreen to my face and arms. I squirmed a little when the cold lotion hit my skin, but I couldn't very well object.

"You protect me, I protect you," she said.

When she was finished slathering goop on my arms and face, I followed her out to the pool and watched her swim back and forth. It was another beautiful, sunny, southern California day — the kind that makes you wonder why anyone lives anywhere else. Bee crisscrossed the pool in alternating lengths of crawl, breaststroke, and backstroke, looking like she'd been taught by a pro. Then she practiced treading water and did some porpoise dives. Half an hour later, she climbed out of the pool, wrapped herself in a huge beach towel, and sat down beside me.

"Nice swim?" I asked.

She was a little out of breath and looked like she couldn't even sum up her feelings. "It was so perfect. I feel so free when I'm swimming, like no one can catch me or harm me."

I looked at her and said, "No one is ever going to harm you, again." She looked at me like she couldn't be sure that was possible, but then she smiled and lay back in the chair with her eyes closed.

"We need to get you a nice pair of sunglasses," I suggested.

"Then I'll look like a movie star," she giggled.

"I have known movie stars and none were as pretty as you … not even close."

She opened one eye and looked at me like that was the most ridiculous thing she'd ever heard. Then she shut both eyes and asked, "Did you swim much in the Bronx?"

"Not so much. Private pools were pretty rare."

"But they had a lot of basketball courts, so that made you happy, right?"

"Yes. Like you, I felt free and safe on a basketball court, and no one could harm me."

"Who would harm you?"

"No one, angel," I replied. Physically, no one would hurt me, but words and taunts from schoolmates hurt very deeply … so deeply that fifty years later I still remember them.

Once she was mostly dried off and had caught her breath, Bee insisted on playing basketball, but instead of trying to play a game, she focused on bouncing the ball with just one hand. She managed quite well. Twice in a row, she used only her right hand to bounce the ball for five minutes. I asked her if she wanted to take a shot, and she said, "No, I just want to concentrate on one thing at a time and when I get good enough at bouncing the ball then I'll move on." Suddenly, I saw before my eyes a student whom I could teach how to play the game I loved so much, *correctly*.

It was that attitude of mastering one aspect of the game at a time that eventually produced a complete ballplayer who could advance right through high school, college, and possibly into the pros. I could visualize my little Bee playing one day for my Knicks. Actually, that was seriously underestimating my girl. As much as it hurt, I started visualizing my girl playing for the Lakers. At least they won championships.

She handed me the ball to put away, but instead I handed the ball back to her, picked her up, and placed her on my shoulders. I moved as close to the hoop as possible and told her to gently toss the ball through the basket. She did exactly like I said, and the ball swished through the net. Yes, she definitely had potential.

We walked back into the house and she quickly ran off to her room to take a shower. I turned on the stereo, and put on the Beach Boys' *Endless Summer* album. Bee walked out of her bedroom all clean and sparkling and squealed, "I love this music!" She started to bounce back and forth to the beat. I took her by the hand and twirled her around, and with her hair tied back and her angelic face, she looked like the most beautiful ballerina in the world ... even if she wasn't the most graceful.

I took her by both hands and started to teach her the simple box step waltz ... right, left, back, right, left, one, two, three. She quickly picked it up, which was quite amazing because I still had not perfected this supposedly simple dance move after sixty years. Then again, mine was a low bar. I had been kicked out of the only dance class I ever took, back in college. The teacher took me aside and said, "You know, dance isn't for everyone." I replied, "You're right," and never came back.

As I taught Bee the waltz, I couldn't help feeling that this might have been the first time in history that the waltz had been performed to the sound of the Beach Boys. Bee didn't seem to mind. She laughed and laughed, occasionally stumbling, and as for me, the music of the Beach Boys was more to my taste than traditional waltzing music, and I didn't care if I was making a fool of myself.

As we glided around the living room, I remembered how upset Bee had been the night before, and I gave silent thanks for how well she seemed to have bounced back. I just had to remember not to mention anything about *leaving* or *not being around.*

Except for the previous night and a few earlier episodes of anxiety concerning her place in my life, she seemed to be a remarkably secure and happy child. This in itself was astonishing. In all my years of being obsessed with Freudian psychoanalysis, I couldn't point to anything that would explain how a girl who had experienced so much trauma and abuse could still seem like such a stable, secure, and happy kid. A piece of me worried about repressed trauma and crises yet to come, but I felt sure we would be able to face those troubles together when and if they showed up.

One thing was certain: Bee made me feel younger and better than I had in years. In a sense, she gave my life new meaning. But kids had a way of doing that for older folks.

I remembered how happy my grandmother and my aunt Jeannette had always been when I was around as a little kid. Whenever I did something wrong, like stuffing my face with a bag of chocolate chip cookies before dinner, which always got my lovely mother upset, I would run downstairs and sit with my grandmother and aunt, and it was like entering a protective bubble. My mother would follow me downstairs, swearing and yelling, and suddenly when confronted with my grandmother on one side and my aunt on the other side of me, she would become as meek as a mouse. She would calmly explain the situation and how worried she was about my poor eating habits, and my grandmother would remind her that she was no different as a child and that she still occasionally caught her with her hand in the cookie jar.

My mother would eventually give up and shake her head and ask me, "Are you at least going to come upstairs and try to eat a little bit of the dinner I have been preparing for the last two hours?" My grandmother would nod for me to go, but first I would kiss her and my aunt and tell them that I would be back downstairs to watch TV with them after my bath. My mom would take me by the hand and lead me back upstairs, never failing to ask, "Do you know how hard I work to prepare a proper dinner for all of you?"

"Yes mom, I'm sorry. I just couldn't help myself."

I would sit down at the dinner table and my mother would put my dinner in front of me and beg, "Please, try to eat a little bit."

I would try my best but there was never anything on my plate that tasted nearly as good as the cookies.

***

I asked Bee to show me her cell phone, and of course she already had two phone numbers programmed into the contact list: mine and Lisa's. I gave her a piece of paper with her own phone number printed on it, and asked her to keep it in a safe place, along with a record of her password. I stressed the importance of carrying the phone with her whenever we went out … if we ever got separated, we could easily reconnect by sending a text. It quickly became apparent to me that Bee knew more about cell phones and computers than I did, even though I had been using them for twenty years before she was born. It was like the children of today came out of their mothers' wombs instinctively knowing how to use such devices.

The first call she made was to my cell phone and when I answered she said, "I love you, I love you, I love you, with all my heart and soul." I called her back, from one couch cushion over, and repeated the same sentiment, which sent her into a fit of giggling. She then called Lisa and gave her a recap of the day, and explained at length how much she loved her new phone, computer, and especially me.

We then drove back to the CVS Pharmacy, and I had her pick out a couple of pairs of sunglasses. She asked me what I thought of them, and I said whatever she liked was good with me. I thought it was important to protect her eyes when she was out in the sun, and besides, it seemed like all girls and boys her age were wearing sunglasses, and I wanted her to fit in.

I paid for the glasses and we drove back home. It suddenly occurred to me that the beer was still in the trunk of the car, but I was just too lazy to carry it all in.

We ordered pizza and bread sticks for dinner, and I made sure to order enough so that she could have cold pizza for breakfast in the morning, which she greatly enjoyed.

I was fairly certain that after dinner I would lose Bee to her computer games and the internet, but instead of disappearing into her lair she came out dressed in her pajamas and plopped down on the couch with me to watch the Yankees game. We shared a bowl of popcorn as I answered her questions about the rules of the game and the history of the team. I could tell she was eager to learn more about sports because it was something that I cared about.

By the sixth inning, with the Yankees comfortably ahead, she fell asleep with her face up against my shoulder. Her breathing was so soft that unless you looked down at her you would never know she was asleep … that, and the fact that she stopped asking questions and clapping every time a Yankee hit the ball.

I carried her into her bedroom and tucked her into bed, kissed her on the forehead, and whispered, "I love you."

Chapter Fifteen

With Bee asleep in bed, I went back into the living room to finish watching the game. They won comfortably again. The Yankees lineup was one of the best in recent years, and they were expected to go far. That was great, because my NY Knicks were having another terrible year. It was getting so bad that at times I really thought they could be beaten by a really good college team.

I shut the TV off and walked over to the sliding glass door that opened onto the pool area. I looked out at the pool and the swaying branches of the surrounding trees reflecting off the surface of the water. I was wishing for an ice-cold beer, but all the beer I had was sitting in the car and it would take at least an hour and a half in the freezer to get just a few beers as cold as I like them, so I didn't even bother going out to get them because I would most likely be asleep in the next hour.

As I stared at the rippling surface of the pool, I realized that it had been a full week since I had that old familiar feeling that my life was basically over, and that I was just running out the clock. Many of my friends from the restaurant had either died or moved away, and the rest didn't bother returning my phone calls and messages. I was financially in a good place; my house was all paid for and was probably worth close to a million dollars.

Unlike many of my friends, I had put money away every week, and over thirty years it had piled up nicely. I also owned stocks and had a 401k plan. But the thing that really put me over was an unexpected inheritance from a really good customer, my friend, Simon, whom I had known for years and whom I had always taken care of when he came in to eat. He was a famous movie producer, and he used to love talking to me about literature, artists, history, sports and politics. We exchanged books all the time. Actually, we would buy books for each other and then discuss them.

We never talked about movies. He said he "had enough of that shit every day," and that it was "our conversations about everything *but* movies" that he cherished. He always came in by himself, early in the evening or late at night, and so I always had plenty of time to talk to him. He made me feel like my education was precious and that my love of books was a gift. The level of ignorance in this town was, in his words, "astonishing."

One night I sat down with him while he was eating, and he said, "You probably won't be seeing me for a while. I just got back the results from a biopsy, and it looks like I have pancreatic cancer."

I didn't say anything right away. I knew the prognosis for this type of cancer was very poor and to give him false hope would be to insult his intelligence. I simply asked, "When do you start treatment?"

"Tomorrow. I will probably be living at Cedar Sinai for the next three weeks or more. You guys don't deliver, do you?"

"No, but it's no trouble for me to bring you food. I'll just call you up in the morning and you can tell me what you're wishing for, and I will bring it over."

"No, I would never put you through that, and besides, I probably won't have any appetite."

"One way or the other I will be coming to see you all the time, so why not take advantage? You must have spent a couple of hundred thousand dollars in this restaurant over the past two decades, and besides, you're the only one who keeps me sane in this place. Our conversations throughout the years have in many ways been the highlights of my career in this restaurant."

"We'll see. Please, if anybody asks about me, just tell them that I went on vacation."

After he finished dinner, I walked him out to his car, and just before pulling out of the parking lot he lowered the driver's side window and shook my hand for the second time in less than thirty seconds. "It's been a pleasure, Joe."

I watched as his car drove down Santa Monica and into Beverly Hills. Richie, the head parking lot attendant, walked over to me and said, "Such a nice guy."

"Yes, a lovely gentleman."

I walked back into the restaurant, looked at our hostess at the front desk, and turned and walked into the empty coatroom and started to cry.

The following day I called up Simon's cell phone at about five o'clock and asked him what he wanted for dinner. He laughed and replied, "How about a piece of prime rib, some creamed spinach, and a piece of cheesecake for dessert?" He gave me his room number, and I told him I would be seeing him around nine o'clock.

I left the restaurant at about eight thirty and drove to the hospital, which was only about ten minutes away but I knew that finding the room would take some time and at exactly nine o'clock I walked into his private room and he said, "Wow! As punctual as if I was eating at the restaurant."

I laughed as I took the food out of the shopping bag that I was holding and set a plate from the restaurant on his food tray, along with a steak knife, a fork, and a cloth napkin. I placed the food on the plate and took out a bottle of red wine, with two wine glasses, and poured a glass for each of us. He sat up, and immediately started eating. I asked, "So how did the first day of treatment go?"

"Not bad at all. Actually, a lot better than I had anticipated."

I looked around the fairly large, private room and was kind of surprised that there were no get-well cards or flowers from relatives and business associates. I had visited other customers who were in the hospital and at times there were so many floral arrangements that you were barely able to fit into the room.

We talked for over two hours and finished the bottle of wine and he ate every last bit of food I brought him. He didn't show any side effects from the treatment, and I was so encouraged by his demeanor that while driving home I actually thought that there might be a glimmer of light at the end of what is usually a very dark tunnel.

The following ten days were no different. His appetite did not seem to diminish one bit, and instead of bringing one bottle of wine I started bringing two bottles because our conversations about literature, history, sports, and politics went on for three to four hours. In an odd way, in a hospital room with a friend suffering from pancreatic cancer, I was having the time of my life. The conversations were some of the most stimulating that I had ever had, and Simon seemed energized. I remarked, "The treatments don't seem to have had that bad of an effect on you."

"No," he replied as he touched the abundant crop of wavy grey hair on his head. "I haven't even lost any of my hair. I thought that would be long gone by now."

"Well, you do have a forest growing up there," I joked.

"I have a jungle of baobab trees growing up there. They are the most fire-resistant species of tree, and apparently not even chemo and radiation can take them down." We both laughed as we continued our conversation on Lord Byron's four-part narrative poem, "Childe Harold's Pilgrimage."

It wasn't until the end of the second week that Simon took an abrupt turn for the worse. I walked into his room, holding the shopping bag filled with food and two bottles of wine, and he was sitting up in bed with a morphine drip, hanging from an IV poll, inserted into his veins. He was undeniably woozy from the morphine and I asked, "Tough day with the treatments?"

"Yeah, it was eventually going to happen. I've been lucky so far."

"Well, hopefully that luck returns tomorrow. How about we try eating something?"

"I'll try as long as you're willing to risk getting barfed on."

"It wouldn't be the first time," I replied.

He had difficulty holding the knife and fork, and so I cut up the New York steak into tiny pieces, but he only managed to eat a couple of pieces of the steak and a droplet of creamed spinach. I waited a few minutes and took out our famous New York cheesecake that the restaurant shipped in from the Bronx. We had better luck with the cheesecake and he ate about half of it, as I lifted his glass of wine to his mouth and he took a few sips. A nurse stopped by the room to check the morphine drip and looked suspiciously down at the two glasses of wine. I asked, "Would you like a glass? It's a really good wine, a Brunello."

"I would love to, but I can't while on duty and I still have eight more hours to go."

"How about some food?"

"I really can't, but it looks delicious."

"It's from the best steakhouse in town, and I'm fairly certain that I am not contagious," Simon remarked.

The nurse laughed and picked up a piece of steak and ate it. "You weren't joking," she said. "That's delicious." She quickly picked up another piece and ate it and then turned to Simon and said, "If you need anything, please don't hesitate to press the buzzer."

"Thank you," Simon replied as we watched her leave the room. "They work their butts off and probably don't make in a year what a useless movie executive makes in a week."

"But at least they have the satisfaction of knowing they helped, and made a difference, in a meaningful and productive way. I imagine that is a greater sense of accomplishment than the useless executive will ever feel."

"Yes, Joseph, you're..." Simon fell in and out of consciousness for the remainder of the time I was there. Just before leaving, I squeezed his hand and leaned in and kissed him on the forehead and said, "You're a great man, Simon. I'll see you tomorrow." A flicker of a smile crossed his face. I was wiping away tears from under my eyes as I walked out of the room and accidently bumped into the nurse. After apologizing, I said, "He seemed to be doing so well these last couple of weeks, but…"

"It's a dastardly disease," she remarked.

"Yes, it is. Like millions of other people, I have seen it take too many family members and friends."

"You're the only person he allows to visit him. The two of you must be really close."

"We share a love of literature, poetry, history, politics and sports."

"Do you work with him in the movie business?"

"No, I actually know very little about his movie career. I can't name a single movie he has produced. I know him from the restaurant I work at. He has been a regular customer of mine for many years, and we have never talked about movies."

"Well, a couple of the nurses who are also aspiring actresses say that he is very big, and that he could easily make any of them a star in no time if he chose to."

"I don't doubt it, but for the two of us it has been a love of other things, not the movies, that has forged our friendship."

"You coming here every night to see him and feed him is really very nice."

"It's what friends do, and besides, he is the only person I know who can discuss the works of Dante, Byron, and Yeats, World War II, The Civil War, the Revolutionary War, and the Crimean War." I laughed as I remembered our many discussions. I said good night and walked out of the hospital, crying.

I didn't need to ask the nurse about his prognosis; that was answered the second I walked into his room that night. He hadn't come to the hospital to receive treatments, but to die. It was no miracle that he kept all of his hair and maintained a relatively healthy appetite until the day he didn't. He had refused to receive any chemo or radiation.

I knew he had only a couple of days left, at best. The morphine, and whatever other pain medicine they were giving him, would greatly reduce his suffering. I was all too familiar with the routine. Cancer struck my mother's side of the family like an atomic bomb, but that was mainly because they all started smoking cigarettes at fourteen. There were no warnings on the packages back then, and at times I wonder if that would have even stopped them.

I got into my car and drove down Beverly Boulevard, past The Hard Rock Café, and turned onto La Cienega Boulevard. At this late hour of the night, the streets were fairly empty, and the traffic was nonexistent. The silence was deafening, especially in an area that is usually bustling with traffic and people, and the despair I felt was like a separate entity, outside my body, attacking me from all sides.

I drove across Sunset Boulevard and onto Laurel Canyon, and into Studio City. I turned onto Ventura Boulevard, past Du-par's diner and CBS Studios, then turned left onto Colfax and parked in my driveway. I got out of my car and sat on the trunk and looked up at the blanket of stars shining down upon me. The universe was infinite and immense, and I felt lonelier at that moment than I thought possible.

I continued to go to the hospital, but instead of bringing Simon food I brought along the complete poems of Byron, Keats, and Yeats and read his favorite poems out loud to him. He was barely conscious, but when I squeezed his hand, he gently squeezed back. He had once asked, "If you were on your death bed and James Earl Jones agreed to recite you one last poem, what would it be?" I had chosen Poe's "Annabel Lee" because it was the poem that made me fall in love with poetry.

Simon had said he would choose Yeats's "Sailing to Byzantium," so I brought it and read it to him numerous times each of the next few nights.

That is no country for old men. The young
In one another's arms, birds in the trees,
—Those dying generations—at their song,

The salmon-falls, the mackerel-crowded seas,
Fish, flesh, or fowl, commend all summer long
Whatever is begotten, born, and dies.
Caught in that sensual music all neglect
Monuments of unageing intellect.

An aged man is but a paltry thing,
A tattered coat upon a stick, unless
Soul clap its hands and sing, and louder sing
For every tatter in its mortal dress,
Nor is there singing school but studying
Monuments of its own magnificence;
And therefore I have sailed the seas and come
To the holy city of Byzantium.

O sages standing in God's holy fire
As in the gold mosaic of a wall,
Come from the holy fire, perne in a gyre,
And be the singing-masters of my soul.
Consume my heart away; sick with desire
And fastened to a dying animal
It knows not what it is; and gather me
Into the artifice of eternity.

Once out of nature I shall never take
My bodily form from any natural thing,
But such a form as Grecian goldsmiths make
Of hammered gold and gold enamelling
To keep a drowsy Emperor awake;
Or set upon a golden bough to sing
To lords and ladies of Byzantium
Of what is past, or passing, or to come.

The heart and oxygen machines attached to Simon's body started to sing an all too familiar tune aptly named, *The Death Code*. In the moment before the doctors and nurses rushed into the room, I looked one last time at my friend, and recited,

Whatever is begotten, born, and dies.
Caught in that sensual music all neglect
Monuments of unageing intellect.

I picked up my books and walked out of the room as the nurses and doctors rushed in. I sat in a chair in the hallway and tried to block out all the noise coming from Simon's room. A few minutes later the nurse who had been taking care of Simon sat down in a chair beside me and asked, "Would you like to see your friend one last time before they remove the body?"

I shook my head and replied, "No thank you. I have already said my good-byes." She placed her hand on my shoulder and asked, "Is there anything I can do?"

"No. Simon did leave next of kin to get in touch with?"

"Yes, his assistant, Annie. She is on her way down. She asked if you would wait until she arrived?"

"Of course," I replied as I stood up. "Can you please let her know that I'll be in the waiting room?" She nodded as I shook her hand and said, "Thank you for being so kind."

I walked down the hallway and took a seat in the empty waiting room. I started reading Byron's "Don Juan," and after a short while a lady walked into the room. It was apparent she had been crying. She asked, "Joseph?"

I stood up and replied, "Annie."

"Yes," she said as she took a seat beside me and took my hand and continued, "So we finally get to meet. In all the years I worked with Simon, he never spoke more highly of a person than you."

"We loved many of the same things, and no customer made my job more enjoyable than Simon." Annie was most likely in her late fifties. She was quite attractive and she had an eloquence and grace about her that seemed to belong to a different age. She spoke with a British accent that had become somewhat Americanized over the years.

"I have one request to make of you. Actually, it was Simon's request. At his burial tomorrow, at Forest Lawn, he asked that you choose a poem to recite as his casket is being lowered into the ground. Would you be able to do that?"

"Of course. When should I be at the cemetery?"

"The burial is at two, but I can have a limousine pick you up at your home."

"No, that will not be necessary. I don't live far from Forest Lawn."

"It will be a private burial. Just his two daughters, you, and me."

We exchanged all relevant information, including phone numbers and emails. I stayed with Annie as she filled out all the hospital information and made final arrangements with the funeral home. I then walked her to her car and before getting in she hugged me tightly and said, "Thank you for loving my friend so much." I watched as she drove off and then I got into my car and drove home.

***

After my run the next morning, I returned home to find an email from Annie. It included a reminder about the service, a map to the section of the cemetery where the burial would be taking place, and an invitation to go to the Smoke House restaurant afterward for a little get together.

I arrived at the cemetery early and waited for the funeral procession. I had decided to read Yeats's "Sailing to Byzantium," even though it wasn't the type of poem one would usually recite at a burial with a rabbi standing nearby.

Simon was not very fond of religion, especially organized religions like the Catholic Church, Judaism, Islam, Hinduism, or the many different institutions under the heading of Christianity. In fact, he thought the world would be a safer and much more peaceful place if religion did not exist at all. "Sailing to Byzantium" immortalized *art*, not human beings in general. According to Mr. Yeats, the only thing that would exist forever was art ... *Monuments of unageing intellect.*

My gut told me that I should read the poem rather quickly, but that also felt like it would be a disservice to the man and his memory. Instead, I would read it slowly and with as much power as I could muster.

The hearse and one limousine arrived and passed through the gates. I followed the limousine and parked about thirty feet behind it. The family and the rabbi exited the limo, and the back of the hearse was opened. Four pallbearers, who I gathered worked for the funeral home, lifted the casket onto a gurney and rolled it to the gravesite. Annie and the rabbi followed the pallbearers, along with two women in their early- to mid-thirties who turned out to be Simon's daughters. I caught up to Annie, and she grabbed my arm as though she was holding onto a life preserver. She was having a very difficult time and couldn't even manage to introduce me to Simon's daughters, who didn't show any obvious signs of grief, or any interest in my sudden arrival.

I knew from Simon that his daughters were married and that he had a number of grandchildren. *Why aren't they here*, I wondered. I knew it was a private ceremony, but even at the most private burials there were usually ten to fifteen members of the family and close friends in attendance.

The rabbi said prayers beside the wooden casket. It was a Jewish tradition that the dead be buried in a wooden casket, and that the bodies not be embalmed. In Jewish tradition, the dead should not be distinguished from each other. Unlike in life, where people are distinguished by professions, or by the amount of education they receive, or by the amount of wealth they accumulate, the dead are considered indivisible. A wooden box will decompose like human remains over time and all will turn to ashes. Very few Jews are cremated, and that is largely because of the Holocaust and the indiscriminate way that merry gang of fun-loving Nazis gassed and burned six million Jews.

The rabbi introduced me, and told the small group of mourners that it was Simon's wish that I choose a poem to recite over his gravesite. I felt I needed to say a few words about my friend before reading the poem, and so I remarked, "Simon was a dear friend. We shared a love of literature, art, history, sports, and even politics. He was undeniably one of the most intelligent and knowledgeable individuals I have ever known, and our conversations over many years provided me with countless hours of enjoyment. Even at the very end, while he was in the hospital, our discussions continued. He will be greatly missed, and I doubt I will ever be able to read another word by Byron, Keats, Shelley, Yeats, or Eliot without thinking of Simon and his deep affection for their works, or his many interpretations of their poems. I have chosen to recite Yeats's "Sailing to Byzantium." It honors the timeless nature of art, and I have no doubt that it represents Simon's feeling that art is the one thing that will survive and outlast all other worldly endeavors."

As I started to recite the poem, almost from memory, I looked past the faces and out over the rolling vista of bright green grass and weathered headstones. By the second stanza, I had all but forgotten that I was reading for this small group of mourners, most of whose names I didn't know. Instead I felt like I was alone with Simon, soaking up the words of a beloved artist and getting ready to talk for hours. I didn't know if the people standing around his gravesite loved Simon. Perhaps they did, or perhaps they were only there out of duty, or expectation, or the hope of an inheritance. I had no way of knowing. I only knew that the words I had chosen to read in Simon's honor carried me up and beyond the world of things and people into communion with a friend the likes of whom I would never see again.

Chapter Sixteen

I pulled into the driveway of the Smoke House Restaurant, parked, and went inside. A hostess escorted me to the back, where Annie sat at a round table with Simon's two daughters. I was finally introduced to the daughters, Emily and Rachel, and then sat down next to Annie. Both daughters were stylishly dressed — more in accord with a party than a funeral — and spoke with distinctly southern California accents. If either shed a tear at the burial, it did not show. They looked like they had just emerged from the makeup chair on *The Young and the Restless*.

In contrast, Annie was a mess. Her eyes were bloodshot from crying and her cheeks were speckled with mascara that had run down her face and been imperfectly blotted away. She gently patted my hand and said, "The little speech you gave before reciting the poem was beautiful, and the poem you chose was perfect."

The daughters nodded and smiled, but with a robotic blandness and sameness that I suddenly found chilling. I wondered whether they had understood a word of the poem or bothered listening to my preamble.

Annie ordered a bottle of chardonnay and made a short, heartfelt toast to Simon, and we all drank to his memory. She said a few words about his film work, and I had the feeling that she cut her speech short because she was about to cry, but she wrapped it up so smoothly that I couldn't be sure. I turned to Rachel, who was sitting next to me, and spoke to her for barely a minute, and by the time I turned back to Annie, she had finished her glass of wine and was ordering another bottle.

We ordered a late lunch, and throughout the meal, Emily and Rachel talked about their children and husbands. They couldn't understand why Daddy did not want their families to attend the service. They were his blood, after all, but then, that was Daddy. "Unpredictable if nothing else," Emily said as she played with the diamond-studded Rolex on her tanned wrist. The daughters didn't down their glasses of wine, but they kept up with Annie by taking sips every ten seconds. I switched to beer after my first glass of wine, and by the time lunch was over, Annie and the daughters had gone through four bottles of wine.

During dessert, Emily dragged a finger along Annie's sleeve and slurred, "Annie, Annie, you simply *must* come out to the house to see the children. You know how they *adore* you."

"They do," Rachel echoed loudly. "They *adore* you."

Emily raised her glass and winked luridly at Annie. "Any friend of Daddy's…"

"That's right," Rachel parroted.

"Thank you, girls," Annie said. "That's kind of you."

Over the next hour, as Emily and Rachel became visibly drunk, their voices began to drown out all of the other noise in the restaurant. Annie, meanwhile, stayed as sober as a judge. I felt sure that Simon's daughters must be getting on her nerves, but she never betrayed a moment's irritation.

We ordered a few desserts to share, and with them coffee and after-dinner drinks. At about five o'clock, Emily and Rachel decided that it was time for them to get home to their families; even though both daughters had wonderful and caring nannies who loved the children, they still wanted to spend a little time with them before the nannies put them to bed. I could only hope that they didn't breathe on the children. Annie had the company limousine drive Rachel and Emily home, and after the driver dropped them off, he came back to the restaurant, where he ordered dinner for himself and ate at a separate table.

Annie turned to me and asked, "Are you sure, Joseph, that you don't have to be at work or somewhere else?"

"Absolutely sure."

When she heard that, she ordered another round of after-dinner drinks for the two of us. Then she looked at me and said, "Those two girls are going to have a surprise coming their way in a very short time."

I raised my eyebrows and nodded but decided not to pry. If Annie wanted to tell me the surprise she would.

She smiled at my restraint and said, "I really do appreciate you staying and talking to me. My husband is on location in Angola shooting a documentary, and I didn't want him to fly back here for such a simple and short ceremony."

"You don't have any children?" I asked.

"No," she said, and I thought I detected a note of sadness.

"I'm sorry. I shouldn't have asked that—"

"No, no, it's all right. I tell people we weren't able to conceive, but in the back of my mind I have always suspected he had a vasectomy before we got married, and just never got around to telling me. Children would only have cramped his style."

"Not the fatherly type?"

"Ha ha, no … especially since he has never taken our wedding vows very seriously. He's probably been with more women than Warren Beatty, and that's only counting his conquests since our wedding day."

"Wow!" I exclaimed as I shook my head.

"Oh gosh, listen to me…"

"No, no. This is LA, right? We talk about everything," I said. "I appreciate your trust."

"I suppose you must hear stories like this from other women at the restaurant."

"Occasionally, but not usually from women as beautiful as you."

"Thank you," she said, blushing a little. "Besides Simon complimenting me, I think that might be the kindest thing I've heard from a gentleman in decades."

"I'm surprised by that," I said. "But not surprised that Simon had a crush on you. Did the two of you ever date? I think you would have made a perfect couple."

"I have no doubt that Simon has always been in love with me, and I have always been in love with him, but circumstances got in the way."

"You're referring to your respective marriages, I take it?"

"Yes and no. I mean, our course was set long before either of us got married. A little before the start of World War II, in fact," she said.

I cocked my head in surprise and took a sip of my drink as she continued.

"My parents were British diplomats, living in Berlin, and they had many friends who were Jewish. They were quite aware of the persecution of the Jews by the Nazis, even if the rest of the world looked the other way in the hope of appeasing Hitler.

"Just before hostilities broke out between Britain and Germany, my parents were recalled back to Britain. Before they left, a Jewish couple that they were especially close with asked them to take their one-year-old son with them. They were able to smuggle the little boy out with them, and for the next sixteen years the child lived with them."

"Simon?" I asked, and she nodded.

"In every sense of the word, he became their son. The original plan was to send Simon to America to live with an uncle once they got him safely out of Germany, but that wasn't such an easy task. The Americans, like most of the world, were not too keen on accepting Jews ... despite Eleanor Roosevelt's protests to her husband and to members of his administration about the slaughter of the Jews by the Nazis.

"So, Simon lived with my parents. In 1949, I was born, and even though I don't remember very much of Simon, he remembered me quite well, and would often joke about rocking me to sleep in my crib. In 1954, his uncle insisted that he finally travel to America to live with him. My parents were heartbroken, as was Simon, but the uncle insisted, and that was what his biological parents had always hoped for, so they had to let him go. Simon was almost seventeen by then, and when it looked like he would be going to live with his uncle for at least a couple of years, he applied to USC and was accepted. His uncle only lived for another three years, but it did honor his biological parents' wish and the promise his uncle had made to them."

"I gather his biological parents never made it out of Germany alive?"

"No, Simon found out later that they died in Auschwitz-Birkenau."

We both fell silent until I said, "Imagine how proud they would have been of him."

"Yes, I think about that a lot."

"Your parents must have missed him terribly."

"They did. But he never forgot them, not for a single day, and he and my parents kept in constant contact with each other over the next ten years. We flew to California twice to visit him. I was still a young girl at the time, but I remember thinking what a handsome and charming young man he was, and he called my parents Mom and Dad. They were the only parents he ever really remembered."

"And then you followed him out here?"

"Sort of. When it was time for me to decide on a college, I chose USC, which was bittersweet for my parents. They were sad to lose another child to America, but they were happy that Simon was living in LA and had promised to take care of me."

"Was he already established in the film industry by then?"

"It was still the early days, but he had produced and written the top-grossing movie that year, which had also picked up several Academy Award nominations, so yes, he was well on his way to making a name for himself. And he generously took me under his wing, of course. He picked me up at the airport in a limousine, and as he often described it, he 'opened the door to the limousine, and in climbed the most beautiful, intelligent, and caring young lady I have ever seen.'"

"That sounds like Simon, and I have no doubt that you were a vision."

"I was a trembling teenager! But I did my best to hide that fact, and he made it all feel so natural," she said. "He took me in hand. I was supposed to live in a dorm on campus, but Simon wouldn't hear of that. I would be living in his house — 'our house,' as he put it — in Malibu. I was told all this within my first ten minutes in the limo, while sipping Dom Perignon. My ears were still popping from the flight!

"By the time we got to his house, he had convinced me to drop out of USC and come and work for him. As he put it, what he could teach me about film and many other subjects, I 'couldn't learn in USC in twenty years,' and of course he was right. I was so overwhelmed, a little dizzy from the champagne and the long flight, that I forgot about the tall task of telling my parents about my change of plans. Not to worry, he had already talked to our parents while I was en route, and they had agreed, as long as I was happy to go along with Simon's grand plans."

"And were you?"

"Happy? It was a dream. I would be living in a palatial estate with this handsome, single, dynamic man. The only problem was that from the start he was calling me 'Sis,' and when speaking about my mom and dad, calling them 'our parents.' I know the British have a long history of cousins marrying, and at some earlier point, even brothers and sisters married, but my parents weren't members of the royal family, and I was brought up properly, and both my parents looked down on such behavior.

"I figured that this couldn't last too long, that a man as brilliant as Simon had to realize that the taboo against incest did not apply to us ... that, despite the fact that the same man and woman helped raise us, we were not biologically related, and therefore exempt. In fact, I hardly knew Simon. I had few recollections of the first four to five years of my life, when Simon was still living with us, and even though he and my parents were in constant contact, I wasn't privy to their conversations. Once he got a job in America, he would always send me beautiful gifts for my birthday and Christmas, and I would always send him beautiful thank you notes.

"And being a naive little girl, I was certain that from the moment I stepped into the limousine at the airport, and sat beside him, sipping champagne, that he was definitely attracted to me. The Malibu house was breathtaking, and naturally Simon helped design it. He considered the architecture in Los Angeles to be childish, and he was particularly appalled by the mansions in Beverly Hills, which were hideous hybrids of different European styles, featuring Italian, Spanish, and French elements thrown together with no vision or coherence.

"Before I even had a chance to take in the amazing ocean view, Simon took me by the hand and showed me his library. It was the biggest room in the house, with books lining every wall from the floor all the way to the vaulted ceiling. In the middle of the room sat two large, mahogany desks. One was his, and the other he had hired a carpenter to build for me. It even had my name engraved in it. He told me that he'd sent pictures of the room to our parents and that this was what had eventually convinced them that he could tutor me better than any university. I was a good student back in London, but I doubt I had read more than thirty books in my entire life. Suddenly, my prince charming was expecting me to read thousands.

"I asked him, 'Have you read all these books?' and he said, 'About eighty percent.' I knew I would be lucky to make a small dent in that total during my lifetime, but when I told him that, he just said, 'Oh, you are going to make more than a small dent. Remember, I promised our parents that I would give you a proper education. Being a great filmmaker requires great and diverse knowledge.'

"I looked down at my desk, and he had written out a list of about fifty books that he considered *required* reading. The idea of dorm life and going to classes five days a week suddenly seemed very appealing. But then, he picked up my luggage and led me up to my room. Naturally, my name was engraved on the door. He opened it and I walked into the most beautiful room I have ever seen, with a breathtaking view of the ocean. I remember being so astonished. I said, 'My God, Simon, you did not have to go to all this trouble and expense for me. This is a room for a princess.' But he said, 'That is exactly what you are — a princess — and Mom is a queen and Dad is a king.' When I tried to call him a prince, he said he was just 'the lucky recipient of a lot of love from a brave man and woman who took in a one-year-old child who would have otherwise never known life.'

"That night we ate at a quaint seafood restaurant. I asked Simon what he remembered of the war years in London. He said, 'For the longest time, it seemed like every night the sirens went off and you could hear the harrowing whistle of bombs falling. I just remember Mom throwing her body over mine like a protective shield, and then the explosions. Afterward, the sound of fire engines everywhere, and then the darkness of night was replaced by blazing sunlight. In the morning, I would go with Mom and stand on long lines in hope of buying some food; and where just the day before there had been buildings and churches, now there was just rubble and medical personnel carrying out bodies on stretchers. Mom tried to cover my eyes, but I saw it all — bodies in the street, destruction, mayhem. The indiscriminate murder and butchery of innocent people. But then the Americans joined the fight, and a semblance of normalcy returned to the city. And after it was all over, the most beautiful gift in the world arrived, and her name was Annie, and I'm looking at her right now, and she is lovelier than one could ever imagine.'"

I realized that I'd been holding my face in my hands. "He loved you for everything you represented, including his own survival," I said. She nodded with her eyes closed.

Annie ordered two more after-dinner drinks and said, "If we stay much longer, we can order dinner. I love their filet mignon. Have you ever had it?"

"Yes, it is quite good."

"But not as good as at your restaurant?"

"I try not to judge. I've ordered the filet here and have never been disappointed."

"Not that it's any of my business, but you are so smart, Joseph, and forgive me for saying so, but it seems surprising that you would choose to spend your career in the restaurant business. Not that restaurant employees aren't smart, but someone who shared so many of the same interests as Simon wouldn't typically be found working in a restaurant. You usually find them teaching at places like Harvard or Yale."

"Harvard or Yale sounds like a tall order," I said with a laugh. When she kept smiling at me expectantly, I realized that I would have to try to explain a career path that had often been as mysterious to me as it obviously was to her.

"Before moving out here for graduate school, I had never even thought of working in a restaurant," I began. "I doubt if I ate at a restaurant, apart from pizzerias and Chinese take-out, more than twice a year. My family wasn't poor and my two brothers and I were never denied anything essential, but eating in restaurants once or twice a year was still stretching the budget. Like millions of other youngsters, I came out here with the hope of working in the movie business. I wanted to write screenplays for documentaries about war and other important subjects."

She raised her eyebrows in obvious interest. "So serious," she said, and I agreed with a laugh.

"After about six months of not being able to find any work at all, never mind work in the movie business, my friend talked me into doing a few shifts at the restaurant where he was working as a busboy. We had come out here together and were good friends back in college, and he promised me that it would be temporary, and that in the meantime we would be making good money and forging connections with powerful people in the business. He was right about two things: Yes, I was making over five hundred dollars a week, and that was great money back then. And I had no problem making connections. In fact, in no time I was one of the most popular employees at the restaurant. Heads of studios, executives, agents, actors and politicians would call me over to their tables to settle questions about historical events, literary works, silent movies, and political figures. A few of the customers started calling me 'the professor.' At first, their level of ignorance startled me. After all, how could someone not know who wrote the United States Constitution? You might not know that Governor Morris of Pennsylvania wrote the final draft, but how could you not know that James Madison was the Father of the Constitution?"

"I didn't know that," Annie remarked, looking embarrassed.

"Okay, but you're British," I said.

"True, but I became a US citizen over twenty years ago. I'm fairly certain I knew that Madison and Alexander Hamilton had a lot to do with the Constitution, but I didn't know that Governor Morris wrote the final draft."

"Most people don't know about Governor Morris, so I forgive you on that point, but at least you knew about Madison's contribution and, more impressive, Hamilton's contributions. Most of them didn't know who Madison was, never mind Hamilton."

Annie smiled to herself and said, "Simon was fond of saying, that 'the level of ignorance in this town was *astonishing*.'"

"Yes, I remember hearing him saying that," I said. "He felt that people had a responsibility to be informed." I took a sip and looked at Annie, and before I knew it, I was saying out loud what I had repressed for years. "My friend was also right about the temporary job at the restaurant, at least when it came to him. He was just as outgoing as me. Maybe not quite as knowledgeable, but very smart and driven. He wanted to work in the film industry and would not be denied. He approached the same people I knew, but he took the next step, which I was always too shy to do. He made them know that he wanted to get into the business and was willing to start at the very bottom. Eventually, Larry Brezner gave him that chance and he made the most of it, and my friend has gone on to become a very successful filmmaker.

"Ironically, I knew Larry as well as anyone in the place. We came from the same part of the Bronx and we were both huge Yankees fans. He actually taught in a public school in the Bronx, a few blocks from where I lived, before marrying and managing Melissa Manchester and moving to Hollywood and becoming a very successful manager and producer.

"A few months before he died, I talked to him on the phone and he asked me about any regrets. I told him one of my biggest regrets was never working in the film business, which was the main reason I moved out here. He said, 'I was always under the impression you wanted to be a novelist. You should have let me know. I would have gladly helped you before anyone.' I said, 'Yeah, I always knew that but I was just too shy to ask.'

"I always had a problem talking about myself. I could talk to people about a lot of different subjects, and I was always a great listener, but when it came to talking about myself or even writing down my qualifications on a job application, I found it very hard. Part of it had to do with my dislike of bragging, but more importantly it had to do with being so shy. It's a curse that kept me from realizing many of my dreams. The story about Larry was just one example. Believe me, there were so many similar stories that I could tell you from the restaurant, but it just doesn't matter anymore. By the time I overcame my shyness, I had lost all interest in the film business. I had become very comfortable working in the restaurant, making good money, being able to buy a home, and living a fairly relaxing life."

"That last part doesn't sound so bad," Annie said.

"No, but I have regrets. The major one that I'll carry to my grave is how much I feel I let down my parents and a special aunt and uncle. They put a lot of faith in me, and, given the support I received, I could not have disappointed them more. They would never admit it, because they loved me unconditionally. But I can't help feeling that they would have been prouder if I'd made minimum wage and worked for the International Red Cross. At least then I would have made a difference."

Annie had been listening intently and finally broke in. "But you have made a difference! Just look at Simon. He wouldn't let me visit him, nor would he tell his own daughters or any of his colleagues that he was sick. You were the only one he allowed in during those three weeks in the hospital. And I'm sure he was happy to know that it was you at the grave today, reciting one of his favorite poems."

I picked up my glass and took a long sip and wondered if Annie knew that Simon refused to receive treatment for the cancer. If she did not know, that was the way Simon wanted it, and I wasn't about to break his confidence. I remarked, "I think it might be time to order the filets we talked about, and maybe a nice bottle of red. How would you like to try a bottle of Brunello?"

"I think that sounds wonderful," Annie replied as a busboy came over and cleared away the desserts from lunch and the empty glasses. We then ordered dinner and the waiter opened the bottle of Brunello, and Annie took a taste and said, "That is divine, thank you." The waiter filled her glass and then my glass and we sipped and clinked our glasses together and sipped again.

As the house lights came down and a waiter lit a single candle in the center of our table, Annie looked even more radiant than she had looked all day, which was saying something. I guessed that she was around my age, in her late fifties, and the more time I spent with her, the more charmed I was. She had a laugh that, when fused with her British accent, was irresistible. Like Simon, there was nothing pretentious about her, despite her refined elegance and her refined speech. As I looked across at her, I found myself thinking, quite randomly, that she would have made a great mother. Why her husband felt compelled to cheat on her was a mystery. But the same could be said about countless other husbands in this town.

Los Angeles was a different type of beast when it came to marriage. A pervasive rot seemed to affect at least half of the unions, at least among the Hollywood elite. Annie was right to assume that I must have heard it all. But I was used to hearing about women responding to their husbands' habitual philandering in one of three ways. Some stayed with the man, took their own lover, and spent their husband's money freely while living in luxury. Others stayed for the children, sacrificing their own happiness in the process. And a third subset divorced their husbands and took them to the cleaners, then moved onto another man as easily as their ex-husbands had jumped from one mistress to another.

Annie's story was different. For one thing, she was richer and more successful than her cheating spouse. She could have left him at any time. But for whom? The man she loved considered her his sister. It had to be hard, working with Simon, and for a time living in the same house with him, yet never being able to express her feelings until it was too late. Being rich, living in luxury, and achieving success would all have been wonderful, but having no one to share those accomplishments with could make a person feel bereft, especially if there were no children involved.

To get myself off of this train of thought, I asked her what it was like to work for Simon. She seemed eager to take the opportunity to speak about him some more.

"It was not at all what I expected," she said. "Back then, Simon had his offices on the back lot of the Warner Studios. After seeing Simon's library at the beach house and how he had organized everything, I naturally expected a work atmosphere that was more like the army. Instead, it was like a dorm atmosphere, with a lax dress code and back and forth banter that you would expect to hear at a restaurant or bar."

"Sounds like fun."

"It was! Simon had eight people working for him. Two of them were beautiful young ladies who wore summer dresses that barely covered their behinds, and that left little to the imagination. My first thought was, no wonder Simon wanted to keep our relationship as brother and sister. I couldn't compete with them on my best day.

"Simon introduced me as his sister, and jokingly said that if anyone treated me harshly, they would have to 'pay with their lives,' and on the flip side, that if anyone treated me preferentially, they would also pay with their lives. I was there to learn and do my share of the work, and would start off making the same salary as any new employee.

"And he wasn't joking. I started at the bottom and stayed there for over a year. If not for the fact that I was living at the beach house for free, never had to pay for a meal, and was given a generous clothing allowance, I might have been considered a 'starving student.' I was barely making minimum wage, poor me." She laughed as she took a drink from her glass, and then stared down into the remaining wine in the glass and gently swirled it around.

"And how many books did he have you reading a week?" I asked.

"He went easy on me. I was only required to read one a week, but some of the books he chose for me, like *Anna Karenina*, were eight hundred pages long. Every Sunday evening we would discuss the book over dinner and drinks. As you well know, Simon loved intelligent and insightful conversation."

She took another sip of wine, as her mind seemed to wander. As I watched her lovely eyes drift, I was reminded of my uncle Tony's saying, that "the past can be either your tutor or your poison."

I asked, "Did you and Simon ever admit your feelings to each other?"

"Yes, but not until it was far too late. I spent more time with Simon over the past thirty years than any other person. In a sense, I guess you can say we were married, just never intimate … never sleeping in the same bed. By the time we admitted our mutual passion for each other, the idea of actually having an intimate relationship felt both dirty and faintly ridiculous, and we both laughed at the idea. It was like the idea of being *brother and sister* had fully implanted itself in both of our brains. And it was about this time that Simon started feeling sick. He had a canny sense for when things were going wrong, and he was usually able to correct whatever it was before it was too late. But this was a disease, a problem that didn't play by the usual rules, and there was no antidote to the venom that was invading his body.

"Simon didn't like people to feel sorry for him. He believed he was the luckiest person in the world, and that every day was a blessing bestowed upon him by our mother and father. It's the reason he wanted no one to know that he was sick or in the hospital. He refused to let me visit him, and he only allowed me to call him once a day. The very idea that he let you visit him in the hospital just goes to show how much he thought of you, and how comfortable you made him feel. He talked about you often, you know. He used to say that the only antidote to a dull week surrounded by movie people was 'dinner and a conversation with Joe.'"

"What an incredible honor," I said. "But you know we spent so much time talking about big ideas that we almost never discussed family. If he was bored by movie people, was he at least stimulated at home?"

"Not so much," Annie confessed. "Simon would say he wished that his daughters would show one-tenth of the interest that you showed in the really important things: art, literature, and politics, to begin with. He felt responsible for their deficits and would say it was his fault they turned out the way they did. I'm really dishing on the gossip here, but I feel I can speak to you candidly."

"You can," I said.

"After the divorce, Simon's wife kept their daughters as far away from their father as possible. It was pure spite. They split up when the girls were still very young, and her influence over them was great. They were raised in luxury, and Simon's ex-wife encouraged them to think that they were entitled to all of it and more. She had them believing that the only thing they had to do to maintain that way of life was to look beautiful and marry rich, which is exactly what they did.

"At one point, after they had both graduated from high school, they told Simon that they had decided to become actresses, and asked if he could help them out. At first, they would accept small roles in his movies, but in time they hoped to be the stars of his films. Simon gave them screen tests, and they were so terrible that it is impossible to describe. He took them into his office and told them that while he saw potential, he seriously recommended that they take acting lessons. He knew a number of great acting coaches and he would get in touch with them and, under their tutelage, he had no doubt they would become wonderful actresses if they worked really hard at it. They literally sat up, and walked out of his office as though he had insulted them. They couldn't believe they were being asked to mingle with the common folk who were struggling and working their butts off to become better at their chosen craft and hopefully one day make a living as actors."

As I took in this story, the waiter arrived with two gorgeous servings of filet mignon, each with a side of creamed spinach. We ordered another bottle of Brunello and sliced into our filets. They had been cooked perfectly, and after we had each taken a taste, we said at the same time, "Delicious." Annie laughed and took a sip of wine. I was starting to feel the effects of drinking for five straight hours, whereas Annie seemed to be rebounding from earlier on when she almost got a little sloppy. I had read somewhere that a person's size had nothing to do with how well they could hold their alcohol. Annie, an elegant featherweight, was proving the point.

After finishing dinner and the second bottle of wine, we ordered after-dinner drinks and a couple of double espressos. Annie insisted that her limo driver drop me off at my house and since there was no way I was getting into my car and driving I took her up on the offer. We slid into the back seat of the limo and I gave the driver my address. As he drove out of the parking lot, Annie turned to me and put her hand on my coat sleeve and said, "Considering the circumstances, I had a wonderful time with you today. You made it much easier on me, and now I can easily understand why Simon liked you so much."

I looked at her and before I could speak, she had her lips pressed up against mine. I recovered from the surprise quickly and we kissed for what felt like a long time, though I could not say how much time actually passed. When we had come up for air, she leaned in and said, "The night doesn't have to end in a few minutes. I would love for it to continue, if you'd like that?" Before I could answer her lips were once again pressed up against mine and it wasn't like I was showing any resistance. She asked, "Is that a yes?"

"Any other day, it would have been a definite 'yes,' but not today. You are so unbelievably attractive, and any other day…"

"It's Simon?" she asked.

"Yes," I said, looking around the inside of the limo as though I would suddenly find him there. "It just doesn't feel right." I reached over and kissed her for another long time, then surfaced and said, "I'm sorry."

"It's not like I am not used to it. The difference is that the excuse usually comes from my husband. At least this time it came from a gentleman."

The driver parked in front of my house, and before getting out I reached over and kissed the beautiful lady one last time and said, "Please give me a call tomorrow."

"I will. Thank you, Joe."

"Thank you," I said as the limo disappeared down the street.

Chapter Seventeen

Inside my brightly lit kitchen, the second thoughts were coming at me so furiously that I almost picked up my phone and called Annie to come back.

It wasn't easy having a beautiful woman ask me to spend the night with her and feeling honor-bound to say no. It's not like I had had women throwing themselves at me all my life, but deep down I knew I did the right thing, and after the impulse to reverse my decision finally passed, that made me proud. It's never right to take advantage of a person when they're vulnerable and grieving, even if they're taking the initiative. Grief makes a person do strange things, and I didn't want Annie to wake up two weeks or two months later and regret her decision.

I slept soundly that night and woke up at my usual time, and to my surprise, after drinking so much, I felt pretty good. I went for my run, and when I arrived back home my phone rang, and it was Annie. She apologized for calling so early, but said she could not wait any longer, after the way things had ended the night before.

Suddenly I had a terrible feeling that she remembered things differently than they actually happened, but then she went on to say that she meant everything she'd said the night before, and that she would have had no regrets if I came over this morning. In fact, she was certain it would have been great, and it would have been the first time in decades that a man had made love to her because he was attracted to her, and not because it was his responsibility.

She wanted to know if I was interested in having a relationship with her, and I replied, "Absolutely, I can't think of anything I want more, but what about your husband?"

"You mean my soon-to-be ex-husband. I've already made an appointment with my lawyer later this morning and will be filing for divorce. It's something I should have done years ago, Joe, and maybe if I had gone to a few of those dinners with you and Simon, I would have found the courage before now. I have no doubt that I would have fallen in love with you then, as easily as I did last night."

The words slipped into my ear and rendered me speechless. When I finally recovered, I said, "And I have no doubt that I would have fallen in love with you."

"Joe," she said.

"Annie. *Annie.* Have I told you how much I love that name?"

"You haven't, but I love hearing you say it."

We hung on the line like a couple of teenagers, until I asked, "How do you want to handle this?"

"Very carefully. I hate to sound tactical, but I am going to have to play it very low for now. I don't want to give my husband any ammunition in our divorce settlement. He might have cheated on me a thousand times, but it's not like I have any record of his conquests and he's the type that would use our relationship to show proof of my infidelity, even though I have always been faithful."

"I understand."

"Can you wait for me?"

"I can wait."

"It may be a while before we can spend any amount of time together. Please remember that I meant every word of what I just said."

"I will."

"Just the idea of waking up next to a man who loves me for who I am and who is a total gentleman is so exciting that I'm shaking right now. It's as though Simon had a hand in all this, like he's watching out for me."

"Yes, it definitely feels that way."

"Oh, before I forget, Simon's lawyer will be getting in touch with you in the next couple of days."

"Should I be worried?" I jokingly asked and she laughed.

"Just the opposite. It's about his will."

"Oh," I said, genuinely surprised. "Am I reading another poem?"

"Very funny. No, I can almost guarantee you that that's not why you've been asked to attend."

"Okay," I said, still confused. "Is there anything I should know?"

"No, I don't even know what's in it," she replied. "Just take the call. Whatever happens, it will be another chance for us to see each other."

"Well, I guess we'll find out together."

"I guess we will."

***

Before I had time to even process my conversation with Annie, Simon's lawyer called. He was reaching out to inform me that the reading of Simon's last will and testament would be held in one week at his Century City office at 10:00 a.m. He gave me the address, said a few kind words about Simon, and with a crackle in his voice he said, "I'll see you next week. Have a wonderful day."

I sat down at the kitchen table, and for a short moment it seemed like my life was suddenly in a state of blissful turmoil: A woman, who for all practical purposes, was totally out of my league — a beautiful, intelligent, and amazingly successful woman — was talking about the two of us having a serious, romantic relationship. For most of my life, I couldn't manage to have a relationship with a woman who was *in* my league. And now I was one of four people mentioned in the will of one of the most successful movie producers of the last thirty years. Strange times, indeed.

Chapter Eighteen

I sat next to Annie as we gathered in the lawyer's room. It was the first time I had seen her since we'd spoken on the phone the morning after Simon's funeral. She was dressed simply but elegantly in a knit dress and low black heels. She looked beautiful, and I couldn't help feeling that she would come to her senses one day soon and realize how ridiculous it was to think that she and I could make a go of things. In the meantime, I wasn't about to give up on the dream of having her all to myself. I thought of that Ernie Banks quote again: "Once you stop dreaming, you stop living."

The lawyer, John Ratner, entered the room and shook each person's hand and then sat down in the chair behind his desk. He was a distinguished-looking man, in his mid-fifties, who wore an expensive suit and spoke with a Boston accent softened by years of living in LA. Directly behind his desk was an amazing view of Century City, a prominent business and real estate district with skyscrapers that form a distinctive skyline on the Westside of Los Angeles. On either side of the big picture window were framed posters from silent films starring Tom Mix, whom I knew as the cowboy actor who owned the land that Century City now sits on, back when it was still ranch land, before it became the back lot for 20th Century-Fox.

Mr. Ratner flipped through the pages of a thin document and then laid it down in front of him on his desk. Looking at the four of us, he said, "I had the honor of knowing Simon for over thirty years and I considered him a close friend. Yet, I was as surprised by his death as anyone could possibly be, and it is still very difficult for me to process. Simon and I had many wonderful discussions over the years, and as long as we stayed off the subject of the movie business, our conversations were always very civil and insightful." He laughed and then cleared his throat.

"I had absolutely no idea that Simon was sick, and I was just recently informed by Annie that the only person who knew the extent of his illness was Joe, the gentleman sitting next to Annie."

I nodded to each of the people in the room as Mr. Ratner continued his preamble.

"Simon's will has more or less stayed the same over the last ten years, except for a change he made about five months ago that was witnessed by my secretary, Martha, and another attorney, Ronald Smith. They both can attest to Simon's healthy and clear state of mind when he made the change." Mr. Ratner opened the will and said, "First, let me quickly go over the charities that Simon left significant amounts of money and assets to: the Holocaust Foundation, the United Nations Refugee Rescue Agency, the Red Cross, and Saint Jude Children's Research Hospital.

"To my daughter Emily, I leave one million dollars, and to her two children, Michael and Benjamin, my grandchildren, I leave two hundred and fifty thousand dollars each, to be held in trust until they reach the age of eighteen. At that time, they can do as they please with the money, but I sincerely hope that they use it to further their education.

"To my daughter Rachel, I leave one million dollars. To her two children, Robin and Peter, my grandchildren, I leave two hundred and fifty thousand dollars each, to be held in trust until they reach the age of eighteen. At that time, they can do as they please with the money, but I sincerely hope that they use it to further their education."

I looked at Simon's daughters, who did not look at all pleased. They shook their heads and crossed their arms and sighed in unison.

The lawyer then looked at me and smiled before he continued. "To my great friend Joe, who provided me with countless blessed hours of insightful and educated conversation, I leave not my books ... which I imagine you might have thought I would be leaving to you, but they are going to Annie, who still has not read half the books in my library, but who has promised me that someday in the future she will finish them all..."

Annie laughed at that, as did the lawyer before he continued reading. "To you, my wonderful friend, I leave half a million dollars and fifteen percent of my company, and the hope that Annie will allow you free access to my library." Annie grasped my hand and held onto it tightly as Emily and Rachel let fly another round of audible sighs.

"And finally, to my Annie, the loveliest and most caring and gifted lady I have ever known, whose parents gave me the gift of life, I leave the above-mentioned books and the remaining forty percent share of the company. In so doing, I give you controlling interest, with eighty-five percent ownership of the company. I also leave you the house in Malibu and the one in Bel Air, along with all of their contents, and all other assets and bank accounts as will be explained to you by Mr. Ratner.

"You, my precious Annie, 'Walk in beauty, like the night of cloudless climes and starry skies, and all that's best of dark and bright, meet in your aspect and your eyes' (with thanks and apologies to Lord Byron)."

And with those concluding lines from the reading of Simon's last will and testament, Annie's grip on my hand loosened, the color drained from her face, and she fainted. Just as she was about to hit the floor, I caught her, and for the next half hour, Mr. Ratner and I took turns supporting her and helping her sip water until she was well enough to sit without slumping. Rachel and Emily stayed in their chairs, looking aghast, and made their excuses before their aunt-by-adoption had fully recovered.

"You'll be hearing from us," Rachel said, and Emily lifted her chin in defiant agreement as they left the room.

***

The full extent of Simon's gift to me did not become apparent for several more weeks. I didn't tell anyone at work because that would have unleashed a flood of requests for help. I would suddenly have had a dozen new best friends, all of them addicted to drugs, booze, or gambling, or just incapable of managing their own finances. I had already loaned money to quite a few people at work over the years, and I was almost never paid back, so I stopped asking, because it was pointless.

Keeping the news to myself turned out to be one of the best decisions I ever made because less than a month after the reading of the will, I was fired from the job I had held for twenty-five years. After a few too many drinks one night, I got into an argument with the general manager, and I unloaded about a bunch of things all at once, complaining about how shabbily I felt the restaurant was being run, and telling him that employee morale, the quality of the food, and customer satisfaction had all taken a nose dive. And yes, I threw a couple of punches at the GM, but they barely grazed him. And that was the end of my career in the restaurant business — a career that I never foresaw when I got off the plane at LAX, nearly twenty-six years earlier, hoping to work in the film business.

When I got home that night after being fired, I sat at my kitchen table and actually thought about calling the owner of the restaurant, who lived in New York and whom I was fairly close with, to ask him if there was anything I could do to get my job back. I decided to have a beer before making the call, and as I drank, I started opening up mail that had accumulated over the previous five days. When I came across a letter from Simon's company, which was now Annie's company, I half-expected to find out that the inheritance was being rescinded because someone — likely Rachel and Emily — had successfully challenged my right to any of Simon's estate, or that it had all been a joke or a mistake. *Wouldn't that be the topping on the cake*, I thought. I slowly opened the letter and looked down at a bunch of figures. I couldn't make out what I was looking at until I realized that it was a bank statement telling me how much my fifteen percent share of the company was worth ... a mere thirty-seven million dollars. I sat there staring at the page until zeroes were swimming before my eyes and my hands were starting to shake. Needless to say, all thoughts of calling the restaurant owner to beg for my job back flew out the window.

It was late, but I still had to call Annie and verify this game-changing amount of money. She answered after the fourth ring, and I could immediately tell that she had been asleep.

"Joseph," she said, "is everything okay?" I was struck by the raw huskiness of her voice in her half-awake state. I hadn't realized how much I missed her.

"Yes, Annie. I am so sorry for waking you, but I have to be sure of something and it can't wait. I just got a letter from Simon's — I'm sorry, your — company and it seems to be saying that my fifteen percent share is worth thirty-seven million dollars. Could that be correct?"

"First off, it is still, and always will be, Simon's company. And yes, the amount is correct." There was a long pause on Annie's side and then she asked, "Does this mean you are no longer interested in seeing me, now that you have all the money you could possibly want and can trade me for two twenty-year-olds?"

"What? Are you crazy? I'll marry you tomorrow if you're free." She laughed and said, "Nothing would make me happier, but there is still that small problem of me being legally married to my current husband."

"Oh, yeah."

"But I would greatly appreciate it if you would wait for the divorce to be finalized, and then I will marry you the very next day."

"Of course, I'll wait. I said I would, and I will. I want to. I only wish I could see you occasionally."

"Nothing would make me happier than to be in your arms right this minute, but Simon's legacy is at stake, along with the company that he built from nothing. Believe me, my husband would have no qualms trying to get a stake in it, and I have to do everything in my power to stop that. We can't give him any ammunition."

"I understand."

"I would be remiss if I didn't tell you that you can sell your share of the company at market price anytime you might need the money."

"And why would I do that? There is no part of that company that I helped build. If you are serious about being with me, I'll give you the shares back for nothing the day we marry. Then you'll have complete control over the company, as you should. I might have to borrow money from you for groceries and clothes, but that's it."

She laughed and said, "Simon was a great judge of character, and never was his judgment more on the mark than when talking about you. I love you, Joseph."

"And I love you, Annie."

After we hung up, I sat at the kitchen table and continued to drink one beer after another as I stared at the bank statement and mulled over my past and my future.

It was all so funny. I spend years writing screenplays, some of which I thought were quite good, and knowing full well that if I was a son, or a nephew, of a movie executive I would probably have sold all of them. Studios were quick and willing to buy screenplays. The cost to them was relatively cheap: thirty-five thousand if you had a lousy agent, fifty thousand if you had a good agent, and maybe a hundred thousand if you had a great agent or were the son or nephew of an executive.

But if you had no agent or no relative in the business, you could write the next *Casablanca* or *Gone with the Wind*, and it would still end up in the round file. At best, you might get a short letter telling you that they loved the story, and the characters, but that it's not something they're interested in pursuing at this time. They're really interested in doing just comedies, not realizing that was exactly what you sent them. They took fools like me for exactly what I was … a fool.

Yes, they were superb liars. Once a producer told me that he really liked my script, and he would have loved to do something with it, but it just wasn't in the budget. I asked, "How would you know?"

And he replied, "Because I read it."

"That's not what I heard, and I heard it from a very reliable source. The source told me that you gave it to a reader, and said if you have the time can you please take a look at this script. That kid from the restaurant gave it to me. The reader ripped off the summary page and flipped the script into the trash. That's what I heard."

The producer just looked at me, dumbfounded, that an irrelevant punk like me would have the audacity to question him. I got that bit of information about my script from a former secretary of his who had just relocated back east to study medicine and become a doctor.

As I was remembering this encounter, I thought about Annie's comment that I could easily afford to exchange her for two twenty-year-olds. That made me laugh. If the twenty-year-olds weren't interested in me when I wasn't rich, I surely wasn't interested in them now that I was nearing sixty and set for life. But I knew that this put me in the minority. Love was for sale in this town, just like anything else. Integrity, honor and morals might get you a few compliments, but money and power got you the twenty-two-year-old beauties.

When I first started working at the restaurant, a really great, successful customer in the movie industry started dating one of the most gorgeous women I had ever seen. I had seen plenty of pretty women at the restaurant, but she was something else. After about a year, they got married, and had one child. He continued to come to the restaurant, but I never saw her on his arm anymore. I finally asked him if his wife was okay. He said, "Oh, she's great. Better and richer than ever. We recently got divorced, and now she has moved on to another sucker."

Surprisingly, from that day on I saw this customer walk into the restaurant with more beautiful, stunning women than any one guy deserved to have. He seemed to have a gorgeous new dinner date every other night. I asked him, "Any chance any of these beautiful women might be in the running to become your next wife?"

He laughed and laughed and said, "Joe, don't you know a high-class call girl when you see one? Two thousand a night, dinner, and whatever I want afterward. No strings attached, no pretending, no taking me to the cleaners after a few years. And every one of them is better looking at this moment than my first wife, who isn't looking so drop-dead gorgeous anymore. I learned my lesson once, and don't ever intend on repeating it. What it cost me in girls a year is one hundredth what my ex-wife cost me a year and is still costing me to this day."

No, I wasn't turning anyone in, especially Annie, for two twenty-year-olds. And if my fifteen percent of the company was worth thirty-seven million, Annie's eighty-five percent was worth hundreds of millions, and that wasn't including the homes, other accounts, and the library. Yes, Annie had hundreds of millions of reasons to be concerned about her husband.

I would be less than honest if I said I didn't have my doubts about Annie and myself. Her first and one true love was obviously Simon, and I imagined that would be as true in twenty years as it was then. I was no substitute for Simon, despite all we had in common. We both loved books, literature, and history, but beyond that, the gap between us was as wide as the Pacific Ocean. Simon came to America with very little and built a company that garnered more film awards and box office receipts than any of the major studios or independent production companies. He was a creative genius. I was born in this country, and although my parents were far from wealthy, my brothers and I never lacked for the necessities of life. I went to Los Angeles, and despite all the excuses I might want to use, none were truly justified. I amounted to nothing. While Simon was building his empire from the ground up, I was coasting through life as a busboy, waiter, part-time bartender, and part-time manager.

By some miracle, I was able to preserve my moral compass and avoid harming other people. I was never a back stabber, I never stole credit for things I didn't do, and I tried my hardest to be fair to everyone, even when turning my back could have helped me financially or professionally. Those traits were instilled in me by my parents, by my extended family, and by my religion.

I had known Annie for a very short time. As impossible as it sounds, we fell in love over an extended lunch that stretched into dinner and included a few dozen drinks, and we nearly ended up in Annie's bed. I learned quite a bit about her and Simon during that dining experience at the Smoke House, but in fact I still knew almost nothing about her, and she knew almost nothing about me. You might think you have learned a lot about a person in a short time, and occasionally that might be true, but it's usually not the case.

***

Over the next year, I talked on the phone with Annie about twice a month, but never once did we get together for a drink or dinner. The lovey-dovey talk died down and all mention of romance and marriage dropped out of our conversations ... and so, when I turned away from the sliding glass door in my living room and unexpectedly saw Bee standing there in her pajamas, all thoughts of Annie and marriage had more or less floated away.

I asked, "What are you doing up?"

"I've been up for quite a while, just watching you standing by the door, looking out at the pool. What were you thinking about?" she asked.

"About an old friend."

"A dead friend?"

"Yes, a dead friend."

"You have a lot of dead friends," she said.

"Yes, I do, but I have more friends who are alive."

I sat down on the couch and patted the cushion next to me and she came over and sat down next to me and wrapped her arms around one of mine. I looked at her angelic face and asked, "Where did you get that face from?" A rhetorical question if ever there was one.

"I don't know," she answered.

"No idea at all?"

She shook her head and shrugged her shoulders. "Nope."

"Curious."

"Did the Yankees win?" she asked.

"Yes, but I think they missed your clapping and cheering those last few innings you fell asleep."

"I try to stay up, but I get so tired."

"That's okay. You do enough clapping and cheering while you're up to carry them to the end, and another win." I gently ran my hand through her hair and asked, "Have you always kept your hair pulled back in a ponytail?"

"Yes, my mother said it was cheaper that way, and by always keeping it in a ponytail she could easily cut my hair instead of taking me to a hairdresser." She hesitated for moment as she bit her lip and asked, "You don't like it combed like this?"

"Sweetheart, your face is so perfect that it would be a crime to cover up any part of it with, I don't know, bangs or, what do you call them, layers. But if you ever want to try a different style just let me know and I will take you to a really good hairdresser."

"You already spend too much money on me."

"That's because I have the money, and I can't think of anyone more deserving to spend it on than you."

"Thank you, Joe. I love you so much," she said as she rested her face against my shoulder. "I have never been happier than I am now."

"And I plan on keeping it that way," I said. I looked down at her face, and in a matter of a few seconds she was sound asleep again. For the second time that night, I picked her up and carried her to her room and tucked her into her bed.

Then I walked into my bedroom and got into my own bed and stared at the ceiling, absorbed in thought again.

It was amazing how much things had changed for me in just a couple of years. I had inherited a share of a movie company worth many millions of dollars, and an extra half million dollars that was sitting in my bank account. I had been fired from my job after twenty-five years, and whereas I had never planned on working in the restaurant business, I had the restaurant to thank for introducing me to Simon. Meeting him had been one of the highlights of my life. He became a treasured friend, and our conversations kept my mind active and stimulated when it could have withered away from lack of use. Our conversations were the highlights of my day, and because of Simon, I was now financially set for life. And then, literally out of the blue, when I was feeling especially lonely and depressed, Bee entered my life, and my existence took on a new meaning and purpose that I had not felt since I was a kid in the Bronx, surrounded by a loving family and many friends.

I lay there, mulling over this strange series of events, and just as sleep was about to carry me off, I looked up, or dreamed that I looked up, and saw a woman's face floating high above my own, near the ceiling. She seemed to be smiling down at me, though I couldn't tell what was happening because her features were obscured by what looked like gauze or heavy fog. Then the ceiling became a night sky, and the woman was no longer tethered to my world but moving steadily away, her bright eyes and smiling mouth receding until they became tiny dots in a sea of stars.

Chapter Nineteen

The next morning, Bee and I went on our six-mile walk-run. She already had me running five straight blocks, four times, during our near-daily sojourns through Studio City. My hip was holding up great, and we must have made a striking pair, because the same neighbors who never noticed me in all my years of running started to wave at us every time we passed.

Back at the house, Bee continued to practice dribbling the basketball and she was definitely getting better. After she finished, I picked her up and raised her up to the hoop so she could drop the ball in easily. It was better that we try to master one part of the game at a time. After basketball practice, she would always go for a long swim.

Later that morning, I decided to go visit Simon's grave. Since losing my job, it had become my ritual to go there at least twice a month. I would set up a beach chair and talk to Simon a little bit and read some of his favorite poems out loud. The grave always sported a fresh bouquet of flowers, and it was easy enough to assume that Annie must have been responsible for that lovely gesture. I had little reason to think that either of Simon's daughters had anything to do with it.

I stopped by Bee's room and told her I would be gone for a couple of hours and that if she needed to get in touch with me to call me on my cell phone. She was playing on the computer and as I told her this, her face turned a ghastly white as though I had told her the worst news ever.

"Can't I go?" she asked. I looked at her, perplexed. 'Death' had become a tricky subject with her, especially after her meltdown in my study when I told her that one day all of my books would belong to her when I was gone. On the other hand, talking about other people dying or about people close to me who had died did not seem to have the same effect on her. I decided to risk telling her the truth.

"I'm going to Forest Lawn Cemetery to visit the grave of a friend of mine."

"Oh, I love Forest Lawn. We took a class trip there last year and visited the museum and looked at all the murals from all the wars the United States has fought in, and all the statues of the famous soldiers. Can I please go with you?"

"Of course, you can," I replied.

We picked up a few beach chairs, put them into the car, and drove off to Forest Lawn. We parked beside the section that held Simon's burial plot, took out our chairs, and walked over to the grave. I did what I always did and kissed Simon's name engraved on the tombstone. This was an old habit of mine from back in the Bronx. Usually, it was the engraved picture of a Saint or Jesus on the stone that I kissed, but since Simon was Jewish, I just kissed his name.

As usual, the tombstone was topped with a beautiful bouquet of fresh flowers. Bee went straight for them, living up to her name, and inhaled their scent. Who knew if she grabbed a little pollen while she was in there? I teased her about that, and she rolled her eyes, and for the first time in my life I knew what it was like to be a dad making a moderately funny dad joke that landed a little flat. We had a laugh about that, and while I set up the chairs, Bee looked at the inscription below Simon's name.

"And therefore I have sailed the seas and come to the holy city of Byzantium," she read out loud. "What does that mean?"

I thought about it for a moment and then tried to explain it in the simplest language possible without upsetting her. "Byzantium is a metaphor for Heaven, and it is the place all great artists and their works go to after they have passed away."

"Was Simon a great artist?"

"Yes, he was a great filmmaker, historian, writer, and intellectual."

"And he was your friend, so he must have been very nice."

"Yes, he was very nice and generous and we had many great discussions … and I miss him greatly."

"I'm sorry," she said as she ran her hand across the inscription and read the words out loud again, very slowly.

"And therefore I have sailed the seas and come to the holy city of Byzantium."

We sat down in our chairs and I read out loud, from an anthology of poetry, some of Simon's favorite poems, from T.S. Eliot, Blake, Byron, Shelley, Keats, Poe, Dante and of course Yeats. Bee interrupted me and asked if she could read one to Simon. I replied, "Of course, let me choose a poem that I'm sure Simon would love for a young, beautiful girl like you to recite to him."

I thought about it for a moment, turned to poems by Byron, and chose "She Walks in Beauty." I told Bee she had to read it slowly and she nodded approvingly. She stood up and began, reading:

She walks in beauty, like the night
Of cloudless climes and starry skies;
And all that's best of dark and bright
Meet in her aspect and her eyes…

Bee was reading slowly and softly, pausing at just the right parts, her voice oscillating beautifully. I closed my eyes and remembered back to the reading of Simon's last will and testament, and the last time I heard part of this poem read out loud, from Simon to Annie. Bee continued,

Where thoughts serenely sweet express
How pure, how dear their dwelling place…

I opened my eyes and looked at the child. Byron's words could easily have been describing Bee, whose ethereal beauty seemed to be on full display among the rolling green hills and the thousands of tombstones. She continued,

The smiles that win, the tints that glow,
But tell of days in goodness spent,
A mind at peace with all below,
A heart whose love is innocent!

She lowered the book and handed it to me with the page still open to the poem. Then she sat back down on her beach chair. I sat there, stunned by how naturally she had read these words, written some two hundred years earlier.

"You recited that beautifully, Bee."

"Thank you. Do you think Simon liked it?"

"Yes, I'm sure Simon *and all the angels in heaven above* loved it," I replied, and thought to myself, *and the demons under the sea.*

Just then, a black Jaguar rolled up quietly and parked behind my Volvo. I looked up and saw Annie step out of the sports car, dressed in a belted red dress and black flats. She stopped and looked at me from her car, then began walking over to us. As I watched her stride across the grass, all I could think about was that she *had* to be seeing someone else who was more suited to her station in life. I realized that I had been assuming this for a while now, especially when she stopped calling. Now the truth of the matter was hitting me in the face. No one could look this stunning or walk around dressed this way and not be courted and wooed by Mr. Perfect.

I looked down at Bee, and before I had time to get my bearings, the radiant lady in red had her arms wrapped around me and was nuzzling my neck and whimpering and repeating my name like a child. "Joe. Joe. You're here. I'm so glad. I can't tell you how glad I am." When I held onto her but didn't speak, she blurted out, "Please, tell me you still love me. Please, just say it."

If I said it was like a dream, I would by lying, because as we all know, my dreams are about dead relatives and friends and past mistakes. No, it was like a movie in which I had somehow been

166 THE NINTH SPHERE

miscast, or the makeup artists did the greatest makeover in the history of film. I grasped her arms and pulled back to look at her and said, "Why would you even ask such a question? Of course, I'm still in love with you. I'm terrified to ask this, but, are you still in love with me?"

She looked at me like I had said something that was too stupid to merit a reply. Then she pressed her soft lips against mine and we kissed for a long, blissful time. The world around us, including the child standing a few feet away from us, disappeared. I wasn't even sure Annie had seen her.

Annie's face brightened and she beamed at me from two inches away. "Everything was finalized yesterday. The bastard is no longer a part of my life, and Simon's company is all ours, just like he wanted. I came up here to ask Simon what I should do. I was so certain you had taken your money and moved on. Exchanged me for a couple of twenty-year-olds. After all, how long can a girl put a guy off?"

"Oh," I said, playing with her, "some girls can get away with a lot. I'm pretty sure I would have waited forever."

She giggled and flung her arms around my neck and held me, and we kissed again. Then she said, "Let's get married right away and go on a long, long honeymoon. I want to finally spend day and night in the hands of a man I'm certain loves me."

I chuckled and said, "I do love you, and we can get married, but I think the honeymoon might have to wait."

"I don't understand," she said, until I nodded in the direction of Bee. Annie turned and looked.

"Oh my God, has she been here the whole time?"

"Yes, the whole time. I hope you don't mind that I've added an additional piece to our happily ever after? I swear, once you get to know her, she's not nearly as bad as you might think." I winked at Bee when I said that.

Bee had her hands on her hips and was staring at us with an expression I hadn't seen before. She glared at me and a nervous little smile crept onto her lips.

Annie bent down to Bee's level and stared at her and then stuck out her hand.

"I'm Annie."

Bee looked at me, then back at Annie, and shook Annie's hand.

"I'm Bee."

"Bee? Like a bumblebee?"

"Beatrice, but yes, Bee like a bumblebee."

Annie, who was still staring, said, "My God, you have the most beautiful, heavenly face I have ever seen." Annie looked up at me and before she could ask, I said, "She sort of showed up on my doorstep, and now I'm in the process of becoming her foster parent."

Annie looked perplexed but not unhappy, and asked, "Where are your parents, Bee?"

Bee opened her mouth to speak but said nothing, so I took over, speaking softly. "Bee … was orphaned not too long ago. Her parents were killed in a car accident, from which she escaped unharmed."

Annie looked like she was about to cry. She looked over at Simon's headstone, as though he were there in person, then looked at me, then at Bee. "You were *in* the … oh my God. You poor, sweet angel. I'm so sorry."

Bee looked flustered as she tried to explain. "Thank you. I'm … okay. A lot has happened. But I'm very, very happy living with Joe."

Bee looked pointedly at Annie, then at me, and for the first time I saw how threatened she was by this strange new development. I was suddenly angry at myself for not telling Bee about Annie.

Annie, meanwhile, had jumped three steps ahead. She clapped her hands together and asked me, "Does that mean I could become her foster mother?" Then she looked at Bee and asked, "Could I? Would you let me?"

Bee looked utterly confused, but not obviously opposed to the idea, but she said nothing, and just looked up at me. I was almost as confused as Bee, but I tried to sound confident, as though I had already thought everything through.

"Yes, that is exactly what that means," I said, "and with your name attached to all the documents, it would make officially adopting Bee that much easier and quicker."

"Would that be okay with you, sweetheart?" Annie asked Bee.

Bee nodded her head shyly and Annie reached out her arms until Bee gave her a hug. "Two miracles in one day," Annie said, then looked to the sky and said, "Thank you, Simon. Thank you."

I looked down at Simon's tombstone and whispered, "Yes, Simon, thank you." It was like he had orchestrated everything before sailing off to the *holy city of Byzantium*.

Annie turned to Simon's gravesite and worked for a while, rearranging the flowers and then putting them back into their original position. She stood up straight as she looked across at the tombstone. She then bowed her head and whispered a few words as Bee walked over to me and took my hand and held it tightly.

Annie turned around, her eyes moist, and asked, "How about we all go over to the Smoke House for some lunch?"

"That sounds great," I said, as the three of us simply stood there as though frozen in time, and tears came gushing out from Annie's eyes and down her cheeks. Bee let go of my hand and walked over to Annie and hugged her tightly and said, "I'm sorry about Simon."

Annie wrapped her arms around Bee and kissed her repeatedly on the top of her head. "I'm okay now, angel. You made it better. Sometimes, my emotions just get the best of me." Annie then cupped her hand under Bee's chin and said, "My God, you are so adorable. I've just met you and already I'm in love with you."

Bee held herself a little stiffly throughout these shows of affection, but when it came time to drive to the restaurant, she agreed to drive with Annie. In the choice between my old wagon and her super cool Jaguar, the Jag won easily.

As I watched Annie settle Bee into the passenger's seat and make sure Bee was buckled up, then watched them drive slowly away from the gravesite, I was hit by the realization that in a short time I would go from a lifelong bachelor to a family man.

I shook my head in amazement as I folded up the beach chairs and stuffed them into the trunk of my car. I made the trip over to the Smoke House as if on autopilot, barely registering traffic lights and stop signs but still doing everything right. The whole way over, images flooded my head — scenes of Annie and Bee lounging by the pool and swimming together, of Annie playing basketball with Bee (I had no idea if Annie played basketball) while I refereed, and of Bee pulling on Annie's arm to get her out of bed to come with us on one of our walk-runs.

I may not have managed to work in the movie business, but I was making a movie in my head that day, and it was the best movie I had ever seen.

Chapter Twenty

I got to the restaurant first. The girls had told me they would be slow getting there because they planned to take the scenic route, but that I should go ahead and reserve a table.

It was already two o'clock and the lunch crowd was emptying out. I was seated immediately and told the hostess that I was expecting two young ladies. She said she would bring them right over when they arrived. After the hostess left, I realized that my description had probably been misleading. Annie was my age, even though she looked twenty years younger, but after spending so many years in the restaurant business I was in the habit of calling every lady, regardless of age, *young*. I found myself calling eighty-year-old grandmothers *young*, and whereas anywhere else in the country a grandmother might think you were trying to make fun of her or seriously needed a pair of glasses, here in Los Angeles they took it as a compliment. After all, it was Hollywood. I knew women who remained twenty-nine years of age for ten or more years, and with a compulsion for exercise, healthy eating and dressing correctly, and with a little plastic surgery here and there, many were able to pull it off.

I watched as the waiters and waitresses dropped checks and talked with customers and among themselves. It amazed me how disconnected I felt from the business side of things when I ate anywhere other than the restaurant where I had worked for twenty-five years. It was as though I had never worked in a restaurant. Freud might say I was repressing my guilt over never amounting to anything after so much faith and money were poured into my future … an extensive education that produced a big, fat, zero. If my life had ended a year and a half earlier and Heaven had rejected me, and I was sent down to Hell, I would have ended up in circle nine of Dante's *Inferno*, next to Lucifer. Circle nine was reserved for the treacherous, and according to my reading of Dante's masterpiece, I was guilty of the worst kind of treachery. I was given the tools to make a positive difference in the world, and I did nothing with those advantages, unless you count recommending weekly specials and wine choices to starlets and movie producers who spread money around like it was falling from the skies. Yes, I was in it for the money, so I was probably also a good candidate for the fourth circle of hell, which was reserved for the greedy.

Even so, I would be lying if I said that there weren't many times that I thoroughly enjoyed working in the restaurant. I loved conversing with fascinating customers and employees, and in the end, it was my willingness to sit with customers like Simon, long after my shift was over and I could easily have gone home, that would pay off in an unimaginable way. My conversations with Simon were undeniably the highlight of my career. Simon, in so many ways, was the embodiment of the type of people I thought I would be surrounded by when I first arrived in Los Angeles with grand plans to make my mark in the movie business.

Little did I know that Simon, like me, was the exception in his field. A towering intellect who excelled at both art and technique, Simon outpaced his colleagues and rose to the top of the film world. That is not to say that the people working in the business — the editors, cinematographers, directors, writers, actors, and location people — weren't great at their jobs. Many of them were very talented and accomplished, and some of them even managed to make good films. But their interests and knowledge were mostly confined to their jobs. And when it came to producers and executives, many of them were downright ignorant. Simon, on the other hand, could talk knowledgeably about physics, engineering, medicine, world history, current events, and of course literature. He was a true polymath who could synthesize knowledge and solve technical problems as readily as he solved creative ones. It might seem like hyperbole to call him a modern-day da Vinci, but the comparison fit him better than anyone I had ever met. If anyone could approach da Vinci's genius and versatility across multiple subjects and endeavors, it was Simon.

I wasn't sure what Simon saw in me at first, but over time, I came to accept that he saw a version of himself. His knowledge was clearly superior to mine, but I knew enough about all of the topics that interested him to be able to carry on intelligent conversations about Einstein's theories, medical advances in pediatric oncology, engineering masterpieces like the Brooklyn Bridge, and of course literature.

And my reward for sitting down and discussing these and other topics was half a million dollars, a fifteen percent share in a major film company worth nearly forty million dollars, and a chance to meet and fall in love with a beautiful, intelligent, and caring woman who was way out of my league. And if I was to believe her, she was in love with me too. It was unreal, and I didn't know if it would ever become real for me.

The waiter placed an iced tea in front of me, and as I took a sip I turned and looked over at the booth that Annie and I sat in for nearly six hours after Simon's funeral. Suddenly something Annie said that day came back to me. At the time I didn't think anything about it, but it was right after Simon's daughters left. She said in a near whisper, "My God, do they have a surprise coming their way." She had to be talking about Simon's will. Despite what she had said about knowing nothing of the contents of his will, she almost certainly knew enough to realize that his daughters would not be happy. And if she knew that much, then there was a good chance she knew what Simon had left me, and the implications that could arise from that. Maybe I wasn't as far out of Annie's league as I originally thought.

I looked up just as Annie and Bee were walking over to our table. I expected to see Bee bouncing around like a bumblebee, but for the first time since I had met her, she was walking in a straight line, looking up at Annie as they made their way across the dining room. I rose to my feet and greeted them and pulled out their chairs to seat them both, and for a second I felt as though I was working in the restaurant.

When they were seated, I winked at Bee and asked Annie, "Did she tire you out?"

Annie laughed and said, "Not so much. Besides, I am much too happy and excited to feel the least bit tired, and just knowing that this precious gem is going to be part of our life has added an inextinguishable spark of joy to this already amazing day." She ran her hand lovingly across Bee's face and reached over and kissed her on the cheek.

"She's a gift. Isn't that so, my beautiful child?"

Bee just smiled a shy smile and started rambling about how great Annie's Jaguar was and how it felt like being in a spaceship. Annie ordered a glass of white wine and I ordered a Coke for Bee and we started off with a basket of the restaurant's famous cheesy bread. Bee liked it so much that she devoured four pieces and was too full to order lunch.

Annie and I ordered steak salads with Italian dressing. We had a lot to talk about, but we couldn't do it in front of the child, and so we just talked idly and happily about a future I knew nothing about. Annie looked radiant, and if she could joke about me turning her in for a couple of twenty-year-old beauties, I could easily turn around and ask, "Why in the world would you choose me, when you could have any young stud you want? It might not be love, but it might be a whole lot more exciting."

The whole thing about Simon's will was starting to eat at me, but, of course, it was insane. If the reason Annie found me so attractive was because she knew I was set to inherit fifteen percent of a billion-dollar company, so be it. Annie already owned most of the company, and as far as I knew, she didn't really need my fifteen percent. If our marriage didn't work out, it wasn't like I was in a position to lose hundreds of millions of dollars. Annie had to be worth a billion dollars, whereas my new net worth was measured in mere millions. When I thought about it that way, it became even harder to understand why a woman so beautiful and successful found me attractive. This kind of thing had never happened to me before, and it wasn't like I had such high standards when it came to women. Yes, I loved looking at and conversing with beautiful women as much as the next guy, but I would never had married a woman for her looks alone ... empathy and intelligence definitely would have played a part. Luckily for me, Annie possessed all those traits and more.

Annie had to leave early, but not before ordering Bee a basket of cheesy bread to go, and giving me a passionate kiss. She was going to come over to the house after work and have dinner with us, and start planning our lives together.

A few minutes after Annie left, Bee and I also departed, and as I held Bee's hand on the way to picking up my old Volvo out front, I can honestly say that I felt like I was floating.

Chapter Twenty-One

After tipping the valet handsomely and making sure Bee was safely strapped into the passenger's seat, I drove out of the parking lot and stopped at the first red light before turning left onto Lakeside Drive across from Warner Bros. Studio.

I looked at Bee holding the bag with the cheesy bread and said, "I apologize for having to drive you around in such an old car, especially after Annie gave you a tour in her Jaguar."

"That's okay. She told me she owned a number of cool cars. Maybe, after you're married, she will let you borrow one."

"That would be nice."

"She said once I got my driver's license, she would buy me a really cool car. She's so sweet and beautiful."

"Yes, she is," I said as I looked at the beautiful little child tightly holding her bag of cheesy bread. I reached over and cleaned a speck of cheesy bread from her chin. I then turned onto Lakeside Drive and drove past the studio.

"Why didn't you tell me about Annie?" Bee asked as she looked out the window at the billboard for the Looney Tunes cartoons, "Why didn't you tell me…?"

I stopped at another red light and turned to her and was shocked to see her crying hysterically. "Bee what's wrong? Bee what's…"

"I love you more than anything in this world, Joe, more than…"

She started shaking and heaving as if she couldn't catch her breath. I turned the air conditioner on high and tilted her face toward the vent, but she just got worse. I made an illegal U-turn and headed toward Saint Joseph's Medical Center with police sirens blaring and two police cars speeding in my wake. I turned into the emergency room entrance and left the car there as I ran around to the passenger's side, pulled Bee out of her seat, and ran through the front doors with her cradled in my arms. She was turning blue from lack of oxygen as I stood in the foyer, looking around for help, and calling out, "My daughter can't breathe!" A nurse quickly approached me, put the child in a wheelchair and immediately rolled her into the emergency room, followed by two cops and me. They laid Bee down on a bed and put an oxygen mask over her face. A doctor immediately appeared beside Bee's bed as the nurse pulled closed the curtain around the bed. I yanked the curtain open and yelled, "Don't you want to know what happened?"

The doctor yelled at the nurse, "Get him out of here." The nurse ushered me away, and said I could tell her, but before I had a chance to speak, the doctor pulled the curtain aside and said, "She's stable now. I gave her two milligrams of lorazepam and she should rest peacefully for a while."

"She was perfectly fine a few minutes ago," I said helplessly. "What did she have, a panic attack? An asthma attack?"

"Probably both, or an allergic reaction, although she responded to the lorazepam without the need for epinephrine, so it may not be allergies. We'll know more after we do some tests," the doctor said as he walked away and the nurse took down all the relevant information I had and the two cops continued to look on. I took out my driver's license and handed it to the cops, saying, "I'm sorry, but I was too scared to stop."

The cops handed me back my license and one of them said, "We understand. We're not giving you a ticket, but if you don't mind, we would like to stop by later and check on her."

"Of course, that would be great," I replied.

"We both have children her age and we know how scary it can get."

"Thank you," I replied as the cops left. There was no doubt that Bee was my child, my responsibility, and I loved her as much as I imagined any biological father could love a child. The police officers had assumed that I was her father, and they were right, even though it wasn't official yet.

The nurse finished taking down all my information, and then she pulled the curtain aside, and said I could sit in the chair beside Bee's bed. She said she didn't expect her to wake up for several hours, and that she would be checking back every fifteen minutes or so. Bee was sleeping comfortably and all of her vital signs were back to normal. I thanked the nurse and sat down in the chair beside the bed.

Bee was receiving oxygen through her nose, and she was hooked up to electronic monitors that displayed her heart rate and blood oxygen levels. She was so tiny, and in that bed, surrounded by machines and monitors, she looked especially small. It was all so baffling … one moment she was talking like her usual self and the next moment she was crying so hard that she couldn't breathe.

Could she be having a delayed reaction to being in the cemetery? Was I wrong to bring her there? This looked like an extreme version of her reaction to being told that all of the books in my library would someday be hers. Did I say something in the car that reminded her of that subject? I didn't think we had gone anywhere near the topic, but what did I know anymore? Nothing, apparently.

Back at the house, before leaving for the cemetery, I was concerned that Bee might be clinging to me too much, as though it was the only way she could stop me from abandoning her like everyone else in her life. Despite everything I said and did to reassure her that she had found a stable home and a forever dad, she still had doubts.

Could it have to do with Annie? It was true that she had entered our lives very suddenly. For those first few moments at the cemetery, I had worried that Bee might view her as a threat. But then Annie and Bee connected so well, and I stopped worrying. If anything, the three of us being a family should have cemented the idea in Bee's mind that she would never be abandoned ever again. Annie and I would be the mother and father she never had — parents who loved and adored her and would always care for her. But maybe she saw Annie as the person who would come between her and me. Maybe she thought I would choose Annie over her.

I wasn't thinking rationally. How could I? Here I was looking down at the sweetest little wiseass and she looked utterly helpless — more pitiful than when I first met her on the park bench — cleaner and more angelic, but more pathetic.

The nurse re-entered through the curtain, looked at Bee's vital signs, and said, "She'll be fine. Again, she'll need to sleep for a while, but I don't expect her to have to spend the night."

"That would be great if she didn't," I replied as I looked at the nurse who was looking down at Bee.

"Your daughter has the face of an angel," she said, not taking her eyes off of her.

"Don't be fooled by her face. She can be quite the little wiseass at times."

"And yet, you wouldn't want her to be any different, would you?"

"No, I wouldn't," I replied. The nurse showed me the way to a café just outside the hospital. I ordered a coffee and sat down at a table away from everyone.

I called Annie and told her what had happened. She wanted to come right over, but I told her that Bee was sleeping, and that the doctor and nurse were fairly confident that once she woke-up and they ran a few tests, she would be allowed to go home.

I had to be honest with Annie, and she did not take it well. I told her there was a lot she didn't know about the child's history, and that before we got married she was entitled to know everything I knew, and that I would understand if she wanted to postpone the wedding or simply call it off because there was no way I could ever abandon Bee.

She remarked in no uncertain terms, "Seriously Joe, after everything you know about me, and about how I was raised, you think I would abandon an abused child because she suffers from asthma, or panic attacks, or whatever other illnesses might afflict her? My parents would turn over in their graves, as would Simon, and I would never be able to live with myself. My mother used her body to protect Simon from Hitler's bombs raining down on the city of London. Surely, you don't expect me to run away from you because that beautiful little child is sick. Seeing her and talking to her today was the greatest gift you could have given me. I have always wanted children, and she is perfect ... perfect, do you hear me?"

I heard my future wife loud and clear, and suddenly I felt guilty for even thinking that Annie had ulterior motives for wanting to marry me. Not only was Bee perfect, but so was Annie. I did have her agree to cancel our plans for dinner, and she asked if she could check in on Bee by phone later that night, and I readily agreed.

After hanging up the phone, I looked across at the large statue of Saint Joseph, holding the baby Jesus, that occupied the entrance to the hospital. Saint Joseph had always played a prominent role in my family. My aunt Angie, whom I never met, died at the age of thirteen from appendicitis. Back in the thirties it was not a rare thing to die from, whereas today it would be considered a tragedy. A few days later, my mother, age sixteen, was rushed to the hospital, also with an appendicitis, and the doctors told my grandmother that she would most likely die. My mother, who always prayed to Saint Joseph, swears that Saint Joseph came to her in the middle of the night and said she would be fine and would be going home to her family. The next morning, the doctors and the nurses found my mother out of bed, getting dressed. Her fever was gone and all her vital signs were perfectly normal. Everyone was bewildered, including my poor grandmother ... but in a good way, of course.

My mother made a promise to Saint Joseph that if she ever had a son, she would name her first son after him. Well, she had three sons, but she was forced by Italian tradition to name her first son after my father's dad, whose name was Salvatore. I, being the second son, was named after Saint Joseph, and, following in my mother's tradition, I always prayed to the caring and compassionate saint Joseph, despite what the Catholic Church preached about praying only to God.

And you can bet that as I sat there with my hands around a cup of coffee just outside Saint Joseph's Hospital, I was once again praying to my name saint, asking him to keep my daughter safe.

***

Back inside the hospital, I pulled the curtain aside and looked across at Bee. They had taken the nasal prongs out from her nose and she was breathing on her own. I gently ran my hand through her hair and reached down and kissed her on the forehead. She opened her eyes and said, "Hi Joe."

"Hello, my beautiful angel."

"Where am I?"

"In Saint Joseph's Hospital."

"Am I going to die?" she seriously asked with the type of fright you see in the eyes of children fleeing a war zone.

"No, you're not going to die. Don't you ever say such a thing."

"Is that a new rule?"

"Yes, that's a new rule. Hopefully, I will be taking you home shortly. You had a little panic attack, that's all."

"Are you sure?"

"Yes, I'm sure, you little wiseass."

She closed her eyes as tears rolled down her cheeks. I felt so helpless that I reached down and kissed her on her forehead again and began babbling.

"I love you so much … so much. Do you understand me? You are the most important thing in my life, and we are going home shortly, and if you behave, I might let you watch the Yankees play tonight."

She smiled and her dimples blossomed and for the first time since rushing her to the hospital I felt a certain amount of relief. The doctor entered, and asked, "And how is our patient doing?"

"Okay," she replied as the doctor listened to her heartbeat with his stethoscope and then told her to take deep breaths as he listened to her lungs. "You have a wonderful heartbeat and strong lungs. Are you by any chance a swimmer?"

Bee perked up right away and said, "Yes, I swim in our pool at home all the time, and I go running with my daddy every morning."

It was the first time she had called me 'daddy,' and if I hadn't had to hold myself together for Bee and the doctor, I would have been a puddle on the floor.

"Well, I wish every patient I had exercised like you." The doctor then had the nurse bring him a bronchoscope so he could look down her airways.

"Everything look okay down there, doctor?" I asked.

"Perfect, except that she now has me craving pizza. Is that what you had for lunch?"

"I had cheesy bread at the Smoke House."

"Oh, that's the best cheesy bread in town," the doctor said.

"Yes," Bee replied enthusiastically. "It's delicious."

The doctor laughed and then asked, "And now, I want you to answer me honestly. Have you had these attacks before?"

"Yes," Bee replied.

"How often, would you say?"

Bee didn't answer and then the doctor tried another approach and asked, "Is there a certain idea or something you fear that triggers these attacks?"

Bee reached up and whispered into the doctor's ear … just loud enough for the nurse and me to hear. "Yes, when I think they might be sending me to different foster parents."

"I see. Well, hopefully that is not going to happen anymore."

The doctor wrote out two prescriptions, one for a ProAir Inhaler, which asthma patients use when they feel short of breath, and another for a very mild tranquillizer for when one of these attacks might come on.

The nurse gave us a bag with a sample inhaler, which she showed Bee how to use, and a bottle with ten tranquillizers so we wouldn't have to run off to a pharmacy. I stepped outside the curtain with the doctor as the nurse helped Bee get dressed.

The doctor remarked, "She's had a tough life so far."

"Yes, but that is all over with. At the moment I'm her official/unofficial foster father, and in a few weeks, I'll be getting married, and my future wife and I are going to officially adopt her. Hopefully, that will relieve her anxieties."

"It certainly can't hurt, and it may just clear up a lot of her reasons for being anxious. She's in excellent physical health, and I didn't see any signs of childhood asthma, but always make sure she carries the inhaler with her just in case. It will definitely help if she has any more attacks. And now, I'm off to the Smoke House for some cheesy bread and a nice steak."

We both laughed as we shook hands.

Chapter Twenty-Two

An attendant wheeled Bee out in a wheelchair while I pulled up front in my car. I slipped the attendant a twenty-dollar bill and helped Bee into the car, then put on her seat belt and got back into the driver's seat. I drove out the exit and turned left on Riverside Drive and headed toward home.

"I'm sorry I got sick and caused so much trouble," Bee said with downcast eyes as I stopped at a red light.

"You never have to apologize for being sick," I replied as I reached across and lifted her chin up.

"Is that another new rule?" she asked.

"No, it's actually an old rule. My mother used to tell us that whenever we got sick."

"I bet she was kind and loving like you?"

"Yes, she was," I said gently. "Let me ask you, if I got sick, would you take care of me?"

"Of course, I would!"

"And why is that?" I asked.

"Because I love you!"

"Exactly. People who love each other take care of each other during good and bad times. And I love you so very much."

"And I love you more than anything in this world," she said.

"I know you do, my beautiful little angel," I replied as the light turned green and I started driving.

It didn't take a psychiatrist to know how very fragile this beautiful child was. When she was happy and bouncing all over the place like a beach ball, she glowed in a way that made you believe in the unbelievable. But there was a core of hurt under all that luminosity.

We rode in silence the rest of the way home, but it was an easy silence, not a worrisome one. I parked in the driveway and helped Bee out of the car. She still seemed a little fatigued from the mild tranquillizer they gave her at the hospital. But once in the house, she wanted to take a shower, and since she was bouncing around, I agreed, on the condition that she leave the bathroom door open. I wanted to be sure I could hear her if she fell. I picked up the house phone and was just about to order pizza for dinner when the child bounced back into the room and said, "We're supposed to have dinner with Annie."

"Annie called me while you were sleeping and I told her you weren't feeling well and so we decided to postpone until tomorrow. But I'm sure she would love to hear from you once you take a shower and we eat our pizza."

"You think so?"

"I know so. I think she is more excited about adopting you than she is about marrying me."

"No, she's not," she said with a smile, and then she ran into her bedroom and took a shower.

Twenty minutes later, Bee pranced into the kitchen, looking refreshed, and sat down at the table. Her hair was still wet and she was bundled up in comfy clothes. After she wolfed down two pieces of pizza and a piece of garlic bread she asked if it was okay to call Annie. I said yes and when I started to give her Annie's number she replied, "I already have it. We exchanged numbers when we were driving around before coming to the Smoke House."

"Great!" I said. She dialed the number on her cell phone and a second later she was talking to Annie. She told her everything that happened, even though she didn't remember much because she was asleep for most of the time. She apologized for getting sick and having to cancel dinner but said tomorrow they would have an even better time. She handed me the phone after she told Annie she loved her a bunch, and I told Annie that, yes, she was feeling much better ... just in case she couldn't tell from the way the child was talking. Annie laughed, and said that if it was all right, she wanted to spend the whole next day with both of us. I told her I couldn't think of anything the two of us would like better.

After hanging up, Bee looked at me and said, "I know I wasn't supposed to apologize for being sick, but I felt I had to. I'm sorry."

I took her by her hand and pulled her toward me and I said, "That only applies to you and me."

"But Annie told me the same thing. That there was no need to apologize for being sick."

"Well, I guess it is only right that Annie is included because she is going to be your mommy."

"And you're my daddy, the best daddy in the whole world." She hugged me tightly and then ran off to brush her teeth.

While she was doing that, I took the plasma TV from the guest room — the fourth bedroom — and moved it into Bee's room. I wanted her to have everything in her room that every other child seemed to have in their rooms these days. Also, I was told that if a plasma television sat unused for too long, it would stop working. Well, the living room TV was turned on all time, and the other television never. Thankfully, it still worked and we decided to watch the Yankees game in Bee's room.

Bee was already in her pajamas, and I had put on a pair of sweatpants and a sweatshirt. Bee didn't make it past the second inning before her arms were wrapped around my waist and her head resting on my chest. She was sleeping as peacefully as a newborn baby. I made it to the fourth inning before I fell asleep, and I suddenly found myself under the train station in the Bronx, next to the funeral home. A downtown train was passing by, and electrical sparks from the transformers were shooting aimlessly into the air.

I crossed the street and went into the grocery store and picked out the two coldest quart size bottles of Rheingold beer and a night owl edition of the *New York Daily News*. The grocery clerk said, "Let me put the beer and the paper in a shopping bag."

I replied, "That's not necessary, but thank you."

He insisted and put the beer and paper and two chilled mugs into the shopping bag.

I asked, "How much do I owe you for the mugs?"

"Nothing," he replied. "But please say hi to my old friend."

"I will," I said as I realized this was the grocery store my uncle Tony used to stop in after getting off the train from work and before walking home to my grandmother's house.

I walked across the street and opened the door to the funeral home and was greeted by the sound of The Cardigans singing, "Lead Me Into The Night." The lobby was decorated, and people were dancing and laughing and drinking cocktails.

Suddenly, my uncle Nick, who lived in Yorktown Heights and worked for the *New York Daily News*, grabbed my hand and called out, "Look, it's the California kid!" He hugged me and quickly dissolved, but before I had time to react, my aunt Rosie — my uncle's wife — gently touched my face and said, "You look just like your mom." I kissed her on the cheek and just like my uncle she quickly dissolved.

Before I was approached by anyone else, I took a quick glance around the room and realized that all of the guests at the party were deceased family members and close friends.

My cousin Johnny De Piro, a partner in a brokerage firm who also had a seat on the stock exchange, grabbed my hand and said, "You look great. Glad you could make it. I always told your mother you would turn out wonderful, and I was right." We kissed and like my aunt and uncle he simply dissolved.

I looked up and there was my mother. She smiled and her dimples glowed like my beautiful little Bee's. My heart was suddenly in my throat, and I looked at her, pained and excited to see her at the same time. I was overwhelmed by the need to apologize, and I launched right in, saying, "Mom, I'm so sorry. I know I should have done so much better. I know I should have took better care of the family." Even in the dream, a little piece of me knew that it should be "taken" and not "took" — Lord knows I had been corrected on my spoken grammar enough times since moving to LA — but I slipped back into my hometown speech the minute I laid eyes on my beautiful mom, and she smiled at me.

"Nonsense," she said, her eyes twinkling. "I am so proud of you, and your two brothers." We kissed and hugged tightly and I begged, "Please don't go. We have so much to talk about … so much." But like the others she quickly dissolved, and like in real life, she was gone much too soon.

But like in real life, there before me was my beautiful aunt Carmela … a mother to my two brothers and me in every way after our mother passed away. We kissed and we hugged and I whispered over and over again, "Thank you, thank you, thank you…" and after a few moments I was just left holding the shopping bag with the beer.

And then out of the crowd came three friends from the restaurant. The first was Anton, the chief chef who always wore a smile and who was always willing to help when a waiter got behind, and who one day came into work early on a Sunday, sat by his locker, put a gun to his head and killed himself. I hugged him tightly and said, "I never got to say good-bye. I never got…" and like that he was gone.

I then grabbed and hugged Brian, a waiter and bartender and aspiring comedian with an egg-shaped bald head. His biggest problem wasn't that he wasn't funny, because he was … his biggest problem was that he couldn't help laughing before delivering the punch line. He rented a room in a hotel in Hollywood, sat on the bed, put a gun to his head and killed himself. He whispered to me, "It simply got to the point where it was no longer any fun. Please, don't ever let it happen to you."

Carl, a dear, dear friend of mine, was the next to embrace me. He was a bartender at the restaurant, and we used to love to go to the movies together and talk about baseball, college basketball, and football. He was a huge Baltimore Orioles fan and I was a Yankee fan, and even though our teams had a big rivalry going we were gentlemanly enough never to let our arguments get out of control. In fact, Carl was way too nice to ever get angry with anyone for too long. He left the restaurant a number of years before me and started working at a bar at LAX. After not hearing from him for a while, I heard from my friend Vince on Christmas Eve that Carl had died. He was diagnosed with cancer a few months back and went to live with his family in Baltimore. Even though Carl was Jewish it was strangely fitting that such a good, kind, and gentle man would die on a holiday that celebrated the birth of a man who preached everything that Carl practiced. I said, "I miss our talks, but more than anything I miss you." He replied, "I know, Brother, I know, and I miss you."

Before I could wipe the tears from my eyes, my father came waltzing by with my aunt Jeannette on his arm. This made sense because my aunt Jeannette, although born with physical and mental disabilities, had a wonderful disposition and was always a bit in love with my father. My mother would joke with her sister that she was trying to steal her husband, and my grandmother would say, "Well, of course — she has wonderful taste."

Aunt Jeannette was one of the last of the Caggiano children, fifteen in all, to die. Years before she died, she was moved to an assisted living home in upstate New York where she flourished, sharing an apartment with another resident and eventually getting herself a boyfriend. I don't think she ever got over my father, because when family went to visit, she would always ask about my dad. The day she left for the assisted living home, I hid in the attic of my grandparents' home and cried. My grandparents, at the time, were in their eighties, and my aunt was in her forties. They couldn't care for her anymore, and even though it turned out to be the right decision, my poor grandmother never got over it. Italians, like my grandparents, didn't put their children in assisted living homes and have strangers take care of them. Children of all abilities are a precious gift from God and are never to be shut out … the door to their parents' home is always open to them.

My aunt Jeannette looked so lovely that I held out my hand and asked my father's permission to take her for a spin on the dance floor. With nothing to hinder her, she danced like Ginger Rogers. She spoke graciously, like a polished debutante, and said, "The days Mommy, you, and I spent in the kitchen were such happy times. The day they took me away you were hiding in the attic, crying, weren't you?"

"Yes, I'm sorry…" I said, but she put a finger to my mouth as we stopped dancing and we hugged tightly. She whispered, "I love you so much, Joseph," and before I could reply she was gone and I was standing beside my dad.

I looked at him and said, "Aunt Jeannette looks so lovely, and you always made her feel so special … but then you always made us all feel so special."

"It was easy, Son, because you were all very special," my father said as he wiped away the tears rolling down my face. I closed my eyes for a moment, and when I opened them everyone was gone, and I was left holding the shopping bag with the beer, chilled mugs, and the newspaper.

I walked into the viewing room where I knew my uncle Tony would be and walked up to his coffin. He opened his eyes as he climbed out of the coffin and sat down beside me. "Why did they all disappear like that?" I asked.

"I imagine because they had other engagements to get to. You know you're not the only Caggiano in the world, right?"

I laughed and asked, "How are you feeling?"

"A little stiff, but not bad for a dead person," he replied as he shook his head in disbelief.

"Well, I come bearing gifts," I said as I opened the shopping bag and poured my uncle and myself his favorite beer into two chilled mugs. We touched glasses and he made a toast, "To the Caggiano family."

"To the Caggiano family," I repeated as we drank up, and I refilled our glasses.

"So the little one had a tough day?" he asked.

"Yes, she sure did. There was a moment there when I thought I was going to lose her."

"But you didn't and that's all that matters."

"But I can't stop worrying."

He started laughing and then remarked, "Welcome to parenthood. It comes with constant worry, but the joy it will give you and your future wife will far outweigh all else. Your grandmother used to say that you can never shower a child with enough love, kisses, and support."

I looked at him, fifty years after he died on that fateful Valentine's Day, and he still looked as handsome as ever, with that twinkle in his eyes, and that infectious laugh that made everything seem so much better. I refilled our glasses and I made a toast, "To you, Uncle Tony, the most unforgettable person I have ever met."

He laughed, and then we drank up, and he winked at me and just like that I found myself back in the empty lobby, with the lights dim, and the silent whisper of ghosts forever ringing in my ears. I walked out the front door and watched as an uptown train rambled by, emitting electrical sparks into an ever-expanding universe.

***

I woke up and Bee still had her arms wrapped around my waist, asleep, and her head was resting peacefully on my chest. My precious little angel had given me a real scare that day, but the joy I felt at that moment as I felt her heart beating against my body far outweighed anything I had ever felt. She was my responsibility and I felt rejuvenated in a way I never again thought possible. Yes, I would shower her, like my family did for me, with love, kisses, and support.

Chapter Twenty-Three

The following morning as Bee was eating breakfast she asked, "Did the Yankees win last night?"

"No," I replied with a laugh and continued, "with you falling asleep during the second inning and me falling asleep during the third inning there was no one to cheer them on."

"Oh no!" she exclaimed.

"I don't really think that's why they lost. In a really good year, they'll lose sixty-two games."

"That many?"

"The baseball season is very long. They play one hundred and sixty-two games during the regular season. If they lose only sixty-two, that means they won a hundred games, which will almost always get you into the playoffs."

"Wow! That's a lot of games."

"Yeah, but it always goes by fast."

Bee asked if we were going for our walk-run, and instead of just saying 'no,' like I felt I should, especially after the previous day's trip to the hospital, I decided to act more parental and supportive, or so I thought.

"How about we just walk today?" I asked.

She looked taken aback. "Not even one little run?"

I stared at her disappointed face for a few moments, then caved in. "Okay, just one little run. I don't want you to overdo it."

She hugged and kissed me and then fished around in her pocket and pulled out her inhaler and held it up.

"See? I'll be fine. I promise to take it with me wherever I go."

"Good," I said.

We left the house, and before we even got to the street she was hopping back and forth like a bunny rabbit and talking incessantly. The child was full of energy and naturally when she asked if we could go for a second little run, after our first run, I caved — all the while telling myself that being a good, supportive parent means sometimes bending the rules.

When we got back home, she practiced dribbling the basketball for fifteen minutes. She was getting a lot better and was now dribbling softly with one hand. After she finished dribbling, I picked her up and let her drop the ball gently through the hoop. I was envisioning the day she would shoot the ball through the hoop on her own, but I figured we should take it one small step at a time. After all, she was only nine.

She then ran into the house and put on her bathing suit, handed me her inhaler, and jumped into the pool and swam for forty-five minutes. As I watched her cut through the water and refine her strokes by instinct, I couldn't help imagining her brilliant future. Just in case my dream of seeing her play for my New York Knicks didn't work out, I could definitely see her becoming an Olympic gold medalist in swimming.

Later, while Bee was taking a shower and cleaning up, I sat down at the kitchen table, opened my laptop, and started reading my emails. At the very top was a message from Lisa saying, "Congratulations! You are officially Bee's foster dad. Give me a call when you get in."

Just as I was ready to pick up the phone and call Lisa, Bee walked into the kitchen. She was all clean and looking like the most beautiful daughter in the universe ... or at least in my universe. I sat her down and showed her Lisa's email. She leaped out of the chair and into my arms, hugging and kissing me, and suddenly she became very quiet and I felt her tears soaking my shirt.

I lifted her head off my chest and said, "What's the matter?"

She shook her head and replied, "Nothing. It's just that I've never been so happy." She hugged me again, and just as suddenly she leaped backward and started jumping up and down like a happy kangaroo joey, saying, "Oh, oh, oh, I have to call Lisa. I have to call Lisa."

I tried to hand her the house phone, but she insisted she needed to call on her cell phone. She ran into her room, and a minute later she came out talking a mile a minute to Lisa. She was glowing, and I felt like the luckiest parent in the world.

When I finally got to talk to Lisa, she told me she would drop by after work because she just needed to get my signature on a few pieces of paper. I invited her to dinner and told her she could not say no because that would disappoint a certain little girl. I also told her I wanted her to meet my fiancée.

She went silent, then said, "Okay, now I am really intrigued." I was relieved to hear her response. Part of me worried that she would be angry, but she sounded fine.

I handed Bee back her phone and, once again, she started jumping up and down like a baby kangaroo, saying, "Oh, oh, oh, I have to call Annie. I have to call Annie."

She pressed the button beside Annie's name — no such thing as dialing for this generation of child geniuses — and she immediately started talking non-stop to Annie, telling her the great news that I was officially her daddy.

"We got home and the email was on his laptop and..."

As I listened to her and watched her hopping around, I suddenly understood my luck. No child came into this world with a guarantee of love from their parents. I had been so secure in my family's love that I had taken it for granted. People in my position basically won the lottery, and most of us didn't even know how good we had it. Bee had never known unconditional love, support or guidance from her family. She, like millions of other children, never received the emotional nourishment that every child needed and deserved. Annie and I had our work cut out for us, trying to make up for that hole in

Bee's life. But I had no doubt that we were off to a good start and that our love would never falter.

Bee hung up and said, "Annie said she'll be over in an hour and that she has a big day planned for us, and that she loves both of us a bunch."

I smiled as I took her by both her hands and said, "You're the best gift I have ever received, and I love you more than anything in this world." She hugged me tightly as I kissed her a bunch of times on the top of her head.

Almost exactly an hour later, a knock came at the door. Bee flung it open and found Annie standing there, peeking over an enormous bouquet of red roses. Being an intelligent lady, Annie had also brought along a beautiful crystal vase, figuring, correctly, that I did not have one in my home.

Annie put the vase and the bouquet down on a side table near the door and reached out to Bee, who hugged and kissed her.

"Can you believe it?" Annie asked Bee.

"I almost can't," Bee said, and hugged Annie again.

"I am so happy for you, my precious little angel."

"Thank you," Bee said, her face still smushed against Annie's light coat.

"Do you think you'll be almost as happy when I become your official mommy?"

Bee looked up at Annie's face and said, "Yes, I do," and Annie crouched down to be on Bee's level.

"And do you think you might be able to love me as much as your daddy?"

"Yes Annie, but I could never love anyone more than my daddy."

"I would hope not, but just knowing that you love me is all that I ask."

"I already love you a bunch," Bee replied as she, once again, hugged Annie who replied, "And I already love you a whole bunch."

Annie looked up at me and smiled. She held the child so tightly that I had an image of them united by an umbilical cord, which provided oxygen and nutrients to both mother and child. Annie glowed, and I was reminded, more forcefully than before, that not only had Annie not managed to marry the man she so loved, Simon, but she was also denied her wish to have children of her own.

I was not gullible enough to believe that Annie could ever love me like she did Simon. Truth be told, I wasn't even sure Annie really loved me, but with Bee it was a different story. At the cemetery, when Annie first saw Bee, it was like she was looking at the child she had hoped for her whole life.

I knew how she felt. From the moment I had looked at Bee — after she took a shower on that first night — I was mesmerized by her angelic (that word again) beauty. It was a beauty I had never seen before in any child, older or younger than her. She possessed a kind of purity — an ethereal, celestial quality — that one might find in a six-month-old baby, or in a da Vinci painting, or in the poetry of Dante. As I thought about that comparison, I remembered Dante's characterization of Beatrice, his guide through "Paradiso," the third and final part of *The Divine Comedy*. At the very end, in the Ninth Sphere, before Dante meets God, Beatrice becomes more beautiful than ever as a light encircles Dante, preparing him to meet God.

Beatrice then returns to her home in a large rose where all the other souls of Heaven live, as angels fly around the rose distributing love and peace.

I was dramatizing the current situation as though I was speaking to Simon. We used to do this all the time, taking real world events and finding the analogy to them in literature and art.

I finally got to kiss my lovely fiancée when she and Bee walked into the house holding the flowers and vase. She handed me a wrapped gift and said, "And this is for the new daddy." I looked down at the gift that I was quite certain was a book as Annie continued, "Go ahead, open it, but be careful."

I unwrapped the gift and looked down at a leather bound, first edition, first printing of Charles Dickens's masterpiece, *David Copperfield*.

I gasped and said, "Annie, you should not be spending this type of money on me."

"I'm sorry, I didn't realize I was on a budget. Would you like me to take it back?" she asked sarcastically.

I shook my head and laughed. The beautiful lady in front of me could easily afford a library full of first editions, even at five to ten thousand dollars a pop, which is about what I guessed this gift must have set her back. I reached over and kissed her for a long and passionate moment, then said, "Thank you very much. It's perfect, like you."

"Can I see?" Bee asked, and I handed the book to her. She turned the pages very slowly and said, "Wow! This book is really old."

"Yes, it is," I said. "This is a first edition, printed in 1850. Maybe, one day, you will read it." *Just not now*, I thought, *too many parallels to your old life.*

She handed me back the book as she and Annie went into the kitchen to arrange the roses in the vase. I walked into my study with my gift and stood there, staring down at the olive cloth binding. This was by far the most thoughtful — not to mention obviously expensive — gift that anyone had ever given to me, and I was still stunned by Annie's generosity.

I closed the door to the study and suddenly remembered the last time I was in there, when Bee had the first of her two panic attacks. I could feel my chest constricting and noticed that I was squeezing my new — old — copy of *David Copperfield* tightly enough to give an antiquarian book seller a coronary.

I relaxed my grip and set the book down on my desk, then started flipping back and forth through the pages until I found my favorite Dickens quote: "The most important thing in life is to stop saying 'I wish' and start saying 'I will.' Consider nothing impossible, then treat impossibilities as probabilities." Wise words that I would probably need for Bee at some point, likely when she was a teen. I found a few strands of silk thread that were pressed between two other pages and carefully moved them to that page for future reference.

As I continued to glance through the book, I remembered when one of my hobbies was collecting first editions from famous authors. The most I was able to afford back then was about five hundred dollars, and that was stretching it. Then one day I had this revelation that the words in the first editions were the same as the words in the modern-day publications I had of the same books that I bought for under ten dollars. So I gave up that costly hobby, and saved enough money for a down payment on my lovely house, all without having to sacrifice the luxury of having my favorite books readily available to me.

Of course, I would never tell my darling fiancée such a thing. First, I would never think of hurting her feelings. Secondly, it was because of her and Bee that what seemed like an impossibility was quickly becoming a probability: I was on the cusp of having a family of my own. I laid the book down next to my nine favorite books of all time and the large dictionary I always kept close by in honor of my uncle Al.

Suddenly, the whole idea of shutting myself off from my books seemed as obscure as paying five hundred dollars for the same book with the same words that I paid $3.99 for at Barnes and Noble. In a sense, it was all these books that had put me in the current, surreal state that I found myself in, and that I was afraid would turn out to be a dream. The knowledge I gained from these books allowed me to have magnificent, enthralling conversations with Simon, and in turn made me a very rich man, at the same time that it allowed me to meet Annie. I had said it before; it was as if Simon had orchestrated the whole scenario. He had given me a big enough share in his company to ensure that Annie and I would, at the very least, have to occasionally communicate. I was one of a handful of guests, along with Annie, invited to the burial, and had been asked to recite a poem of my choosing. At the reading of Simon's will, he mentioned Annie and me and the sharing of his library, and he had to know that his two daughters would offer no emotional help or support to Annie, but that I would come to her rescue. He trusted me, above all the employees at his company, to selflessly care for and fall genuinely in love with the one person he loved and cherished more than anyone.

I opened the door to the study and gently closed it behind me and stepped into the hallway ... so softly that the girls, who were in Bee's room, just a few feet away, did not hear me. I listened as Annie inspected Bee's woefully lacking closet that was only half full of clothes, shoes, and accessories.

"Surely, we have a lot of shopping to do. A girl's closet should never be only half full."

"But this is more clothes than I have ever had," Bee said. "And I don't have any money to buy more clothes."

"Hmm," Annie said sweetly. "I'm confused. Why would you need money?"

"To pay..."

"But that's what mommies and daddies are for," Annie said gently. "To buy you the necessities of life."

There was a long silence, and just as I was about to knock on the door, Annie said, "And since I am going to be your new mommy, I just want to make sure you have everything you need, because I love you so much."

"And I love you so much, Annie, but I don't want you to spend all your money on me."

Annie laughed and said, "You are so adorable and I cannot believe how lucky I am to be your mommy, and I don't want you ever to worry about money. Your daddy and I can afford to buy you whatever you need. Is that okay?"

"Yes, but I have to tell you about one thing you cannot buy me."

"And what might that be?" Annie asked.

"A two-piece bathing suit. My daddy only allows me to wear a one-piece, and I don't want to hurt his feelings."

"Well, you are a little young to be wearing a two-piece bathing suit. He's only trying to protect you."

"I know, and I like to joke about it with him but I would never wear one, even when I get really old."

I heard Annie chuckle and say, "Then we will definitely keep it off our list."

"Thank you," Bee replied, and I took the opportunity to knock on the door and poke my head inside her room.

"So what's on the schedule for today?" I asked, as innocently as I could manage.

"We're going shopping," Annie replied as Bee looked up at me and asked, "And you're going with us, right, Daddy?"

"Of course, he's going with us, sweetheart. We need someone to hold the shopping bags." Annie winked at me as Bee continued to look at me, anxiously, as though my response was a matter of great importance. I had to keep reminding myself that it had been less than a month since this child was homeless. Prior to that, she had lived with parents who blamed her — an innocent child — for their miserable lives. And here she was now, smiling brightly in the lead up to a shopping trip with two adults who had quickly grown to love her more than anything in the world.

I bent down and looked her in the eye. "I would have to be the stupidest guy in the world not to want to spend the entire day with the two most beautiful girls in the world. Of course, I'm going with you."

Bee hugged me and said, "Thank you, Daddy." I looked at Annie, who was smiling, and I winked. I had no doubt Annie understood the situation perfectly, and that it wouldn't be long until Bee put the same trust in her as she has in me.

Chapter Twenty-Four

The beautiful Brit was not only a big shot movie mogul, but also a superb shopper and personal stylist. By the time we finished, I was weighed down with ten bags full of clothes and accessories, all carefully chosen to mix and match and cover every situation that the child might encounter, and a few she might not (I wasn't sure she needed a floor-length gown, low heels, and a matching bolero, but what did I know?) As I carried the bags to Annie's Mercedes-Maybach GLS, I calculated that this haul must have cost about two hundred thousand dollars or more. But I wasn't about to complain. Not only did Bee's wardrobe increase tenfold, but she now had the most forward-looking fashions that any pint-sized nine-year-old could possess.

We then drove to Annie's studio, which was located in Burbank, directly across from Griffith Park. The name of the Studio was *S @ A*, which naturally stood for Simon and Annie. The studio took up an entire city block and the outside was beautifully manicured with signs advertising upcoming films and a number of currently running TV series. We entered the front entrance to the building, and the receptionists at the front desk greeted Annie by her first name, like they were greeting a friend. She had told me back at the Smoke House, after Simon's burial, how surprised she was when she first entered Simon's production company at how relaxed and carefree the atmosphere was. Forty years later, and with the company having grown a hundredfold in size, the atmosphere remained the same ... relaxed and inviting.

Annie showed us around the lot, introducing us to everyone we came across. She showed us the sound stages and interior sets, and Bee, who held tightly onto my hand, seemed to be overwhelmed and in awe. But it was not until we went into the animation building that the fun started. We sat down in front of a screen as the lights suddenly dimmed, and an animated rabbit named Jack, with the body of a human, suddenly appeared on screen, chewing on a carrot. He looked at us closely and motioned for Bee to come closer. Bee looked at Annie who told her to go and introduce herself to the rabbit. She assured her that he was very friendly.

"And what's your name?" the rabbit asked Bee.

"Bee," she replied.

"You don't look like any bumblebee I have ever seen, but you are very beautiful."

"Thank you, and you are very handsome," Bee replied.

Jack, still chomping on his carrot, said, "Since we both agree on how good-looking we are, how about we get married?"

Bee giggled and said, "I don't think I am old enough."

"How old are you?"

"Nine."

"Nine years old!" Jack repeated and continued, "That's plenty old. In rabbit years you would be like thirty years old. Surely old enough to get married?"

"But I don't think my daddy would allow me to get married," Bee replied as she looked back at me and I simply nodded.

"Oh, I get it. You already have a boyfriend. I should have figured a girl as beautiful as you probably has a thousand boyfriends. One doesn't happen to be a loud and obnoxious duck?"

"No! And I really don't have any boyfriends. I promise."

"Well, I believe you. But you have to promise me something. When your daddy gives you permission to get married, you won't forget me, will you? You can tell him that I'm rich, a star with my own dressing room, and quite good looking, as you know."

"I promise, when I get old enough and my daddy gives me permission, I will come to see you first. I promise."

"I believe you. It's just that you're so beautiful that all my dreams will forever be of you ... and a bushel of carrots. You understand, one has to keep one's strength up."

"I understand," Bee replied.

Jack pulled out a portable camera and aimed it at Bee and said, "Smile!" He took her picture, and put the camera against his chest, and looked at her tenderly. "I will keep this picture by my bedside, for I am sure that no girl in this world is more beautiful than you. My Bee, my beautiful, beautiful Bee ... not to be confused with a bumblebee."

Jack blew her a kiss and walked off the stage, chomping down on a carrot.

"Very nice meeting you," Bee called after him.

She then turned around and looked at Annie and me and said, "I think he's in love with me."

"Of course, he's in love with you," Annie said. "Who wouldn't be in love with a girl as terrific as you?"

"But I can't marry him. I really am too young. Maybe if he meets Lisa he will fall in love with her. She's very pretty and smart, and she wants to marry a movie star, and Jack is a big star. He has his own dressing room. And that super-hot guy she was dating has already dumped her. She told me he was only after one thing. Maybe we should never had bought her the TVs. He probably wanted one for himself."

"Who's Lisa?" Annie asked.

"She's Bee's social worker and she's very sweet. You will be meeting her tonight."

"Yes, and I think Jack would like her very much, don't you think so, Daddy?"

"Yes, but it won't be so easy for him to get over you. After all, you are one of a kind. Isn't that so, Annie?"

"Yes, you are ... my sweet, beautiful child," Annie said to Bee.

We got up and started to leave when a young intern named Bob came from behind the animation screen and ran toward us. "Oh, Bee, an admirer wanted you to take this with you." He handed her an envelope and Bee opened it and took out a publicity shot of Jack, looking quite sharp in a black and white tuxedo, and holding a carrot. He wrote, "To my lovely Bee, please do not let time get in the way of our future happiness. Keep my photo by your bedside as a reminder of my undying love for you, my beautiful, beautiful Bee ... not to be confused with a bumblebee. Love, Jack, your loving admirer."

Bee looked at all three of us as Bob asked, "Would you like to reply?"

"Yes," she said, and the intern handed her a pad, with a picture of the star at the top of the page, and a pen. She wrote, "I love you, Jack, and I will keep your picture right next to my bed and give it a kiss every night. I promise. Thank you for loving me."

She showed the short note to both Annie and me, and we both agreed it was perfect. She then handed the pad and pen back to Bob and said, "Thank you."

"Yes, thank you very much, Bob," Annie reiterated and graciously smiled.

***

After leaving the studio, we stopped off at a market and picked up a couple of bottles of Far Niente Chardonnay and Cabernet. Annie liked her wine, and since Bee moved in, except for that first night, I still had not had a beer. In fact, the two cases of beer I bought at the supermarket were still in the trunk of my Volvo. Who would have thought that after forty-five loyal, beer-drinking years, I would switch to wine? I guess anything is possible, and if the last year didn't prove that, nothing ever would.

After the market, we stopped off at Annie's home in Toluca Lake. Toluca Lake was only a few minutes by car away from my home in

204 THE NINTH SPHERE

Studio City, but the neighborhoods might have been on different planets. Annie's home was at least five times the size of mine, elegantly decorated, and overlooked the private natural lake fed by the Los Angeles River and maintained by the property owners.

Annie also had a house in Palm Springs, and had inherited Simon's home in Bel Air and his mansion in Malibu. I had occasionally been around extravagance and luxury through my work at the restaurant, when visiting rich customers' homes and places of employment, but Annie was making their possessions and hovels look meager.

She gave us a quick tour of the house, and the one consistent feature in every room of the house was that each one included framed pictures of Simon and Annie's parents dating back from before World War II and until they died in the early 2000s. If she had a trophy room, where she kept the many awards both she and Simon won, she left it off this tour. Annie was not the type to talk about her accomplishments; like Simon, she understood that nothing they had achieved would have been possible without the contributions of many talented individuals from the grips to the editors to location scouts.

They were not part of the 'me generation' of the last 40 years. In just the short time I'd known Annie, I had noticed a distinctive pattern: She rarely used the first-person singular — she rarely said 'I' — and she never spoke about 'singular' achievements, or implied that she deserved credit for anything to do with the studio's productions, or her home. In her tour of the house, she often stopped and explained certain unique architectural designs, and true to form, she always gave the credit to others for coming up with this or that magnificent motif or composition. She might be filthy rich, highly respected, and exceptionally creative, but from listening to her, one would never believe she had anything to do with it. That was my Annie, and by God she was going to make a great mommy ... even if she was going to spoil our little Bee beyond anyone's imagination.

President Lincoln said, "Nearly all people can stand adversity, but if you want to test a person's character, give them power." This might have been borrowed from Plato, who is said to have written, a few thousand years earlier, that "The measure of a person is what they do with power."

Walking through the studio with Annie, both quotations came to mind as I saw her interact with all of the workers that we ran across. Not one of them called her by her last name. It was always just Annie, and she stopped to introduce Bee and me to every person we came across. In every case, she gave us a brief description of their job and the marvelous work they were doing, and she asked about the health and well-being of family members, often by name. The workers were genuinely pleased to see her and talk to her, and she always gave her full attention to the person who was speaking. She held immense power, not only inside her studio, but also in the world of Hollywood and beyond, and I could already tell that she used that power for good, and to make the lives of her employees and all those she came in contact with better. President Lincoln and Plato would be proud.

Annie asked me if it was all right if she spent the night at my house, in the other guest bedroom. She wanted to spend as much time as possible with Bee and me, and to be a part of our family, even before we got married, which I was soon to find out she was planning on us doing immediately. Bee helped her pack a suitcase and just as we were leaving her house, she whirled around and exclaimed, "I feel like the luckiest girl in the whole world." She then kissed me and hugged Bee for what seemed like an eternity. Yes, I was living some type of dream. It might have taken forty years, but I would be foolish to say it wasn't worth the wait.

Chapter Twenty-Five

I sat at the kitchen table, drinking a wonderful glass of Far Niente chardonnay, as I listened to Bee and Annie laughing and joking while they unpacked Bee's new clothing and accessories and put everything away in our soon-to-be adopted daughter's bedroom.

We had made one stop after leaving Annie's house, and that was to pick up a lovely frame for the autographed picture of Jack, with its endearing inscription. No denying it, the rabbit was a romantic, and if not for the fact that Byron, Keats, and Shelley were dead, they would have a tough time keeping up with such artistry. Bee was still concerned that she might have offended Jack for not immediately accepting his marriage proposal, but I assured her that while he waited for her, he could find relief in pouring out his heart to Lisa. She agreed, and was quite sure that once he met Lisa, he would fall madly in love with her and that it would be super wonderful if they got married and lived happily ever after.

Moments like this filled me with delight while at the same time stoking my disgust for Bee's biological parents and wicked foster parents. For it was moments like this that defined my childhood. Kids were allowed to be kids in my family, even if that meant indulging a child's belief in a silly made-up story about an amorous rabbit. It is an unpardonable sin to purposefully deny any child the unrestrained imagination and fantasies that belong to this period of one's life, before our innocence is forever shattered.

It was while walking through the studio with Annie that I fully realized that my youthful dream of working in the film industry and writing great screenplays was truly dead, without a chance of resurrection. There was a time when walking through a movie studio would excite me. I would visualize one of my screenplays being directed by Martin Scorsese or Sidney Lumet, and imagine the thrill of hearing dialogue that I had written coming out of the mouths of Robert De Niro, Al Pacino, or Denzel Washington. But that excitement was no more … it was dead and buried, and I had long ago got over the mourning period. The dream began to die fifteen years ago while I was working at the restaurant, and slowly but surely the last shovel full of dirt was thrown over the remains.

My greatest regret would always be my failure to make a lasting and positive effect in the lives of the unfortunate … in the life of that handicapped child in the wheelchair passing by the basketball court every day with his mom while I was shooting by myself. I had a chance to reach out then and I didn't. I could see it in the child's eyes that he simply dreamed of shooting the ball through the hoop, but what did I do? I looked away.

Over and over again, my parents and loved ones stressed how lucky my two brothers and I were simply to be born healthy and with no physical handicaps. Anytime we complained about something stupid, such as not having a better and more expensive pair of sneakers, they would remind us how fortunate we were to be physically healthy and to have a loving family. And if we needed a reminder to use our God-given gifts of sight, hearing, and mobility to the full advantage that the good Lord intended, they would subtly allude to my uncle Tony's polio or my aunt Jeannette's multiple disabilities.

I took a large sip from my glass of wine and laughed, knowing full well that if my parents had the money, they would gladly have bought us the more expensive pair of sneakers.

It had never truly dawned on me exactly how much money I had and the possibilities and opportunities it opened before my very eyes. Maybe, it didn't truly register with me because I literally had no part in creating that wealth. Yes, Simon and I had the most amazing conversations and we shared similar ideas about the moral responsiblity all humans had toward each other, but it was not until after his death that I learned about Simon's early life and how much he worshipped his adopted parents and Annie.

I had told him numerous stories about my family and growing up in the Bronx. He always listened intently and told me that I should write down these stories because he had no doubt that they would make a wonderful collection of short stories, or a great novel.

I wrote quite a few screenplays, and on the rare occasion when someone actually read one, they would say, "You write like a novelist. Why are you wasting your talent on screenplays? If you really want to see your work on screen, write a novel, get it published, and try to sell it to a film producer." It was true; very few Hollywood movies were based on original screenplays. Most of the great movies, or shall we say moneymakers, were popular books made into movies, such as *Gone with the Wind*, *To Kill a Mockingbird*, *The Godfather* movies, *The Color Purple*, and *Field of Dreams*. And if not novels, characters and stories were lifted right out of comic books, for movies and TV shows featuring Superman, Batman, Spider Man, and The Avengers.

Yes, there were exceptions to this rule: Woody Allen, Spike Lee, Oliver Stone, Federico Fellini, and Ingmar Bergman all wrote their own screenplays and turned them into great movies. But Hollywood was much more likely to go with a proven commodity ... a best-selling novel, graphic novel, or a highly rated TV show that could be turned into a feature film. Simon was correct, the top executives and the production heads at the major studios were as sterile as castrated pigs and far less intelligent.

It is no surprise that Simon and Annie's company turned out so many award-winning movies and won Emmy after Emmy for best animated programing. Of course, it didn't hurt to have a superstar such as Jack on the payroll. Simon and Annie were exceptionally knowledgeable and learned. Simon easily could have taught literature, physics, chemistry, or history at the university of his choice ... MIT, Yale, Harvard, or Stanford. His curiosity, his desire to know all there was to know about the universe and the planet, was limitless. I would get to know this firsthand when Annie handed over volume after volume of his writings to me. His ideas and observations deserved to be in the Smithsonian, and it was this that made me excited about writing once again — not screenplays, but novels, biographies, and histories.

In never getting a screenplay sold and yet continuing to write them, I had become as sterile as the executives and production heads. I had refused to change, even though throughout the thirty or more years of writing screenplays I had never enjoyed the format and the limitations that went into writing scripts, and truth be told I found reading screenplays dull and boring. I got more excited from reading a single paragraph from a novel by Conrad, or Joyce, or the Brontë Sisters, or Toni Morrison, than I got out of reading *The Godfather* screenplays or an original Woody Allen script.

Without change, there is no hope. It is an idea that many of the great writers, from Gore Vidal to Tolstoy to Socrates, expressed. Change — and hope — are at the core of all scientific, medical, political, and educational advances, and yet here I was, for over thirty years, stubbornly sticking to one mode of expression, even though I basically disliked it and hadn't succeeded in making it work for me.

The same screenplays that were so easily dismissed or simply dumped into the trash without being read, I could produce quite easily now ... not only did I have the money but I had the backing of my future wife ... and yet I would get absolutely no satisfaction out of it. It would simply be a vanity project ... getting even with all those lying, conniving agents working for the major talent agencies and the sterile, castrated pigs heading up the production departments at the major studios. Not only would it be an affront to Simon's legacy and generosity, but it would morally bankrupt me ... making me no better than the agents and production heads ... and that was a road I had no intention of ever taking.

I had no intention of taking anything from Annie, and whereas we had not discussed signing prenuptial agreements, I would insist that Annie write up a prenuptial that gave me absolutely no rights to anything that she owned. I had absolutely no intention of ever divorcing her, but then one day she might wake up and come to her senses and ask herself, "What the hell have I done marrying this loser?" Of course, I was hoping that day would never come, especially since the little wiseass was such a major part of the equation.

Half of the fifteen percent share I had in Annie and Simon's company would go equally to my two brothers and Bee, which at its current value would add up to about five million each. The other half would go to my favorite charities ... research, care, and hopefully a cure for the many childhood diseases that kept children from enjoying the very special gift of participating in such activities as basketball, baseball, track, ballet, soccer, and the like. For all my moaning and complaining, I will forever be thankful for being able to simply go out early in the morning, as a child and teenager, and running up and down the basketball court outside our apartment and shooting, dribbling and pretending to be Walt Frazier on the floor of Madison Square Garden. I might never have amounted to much as a player, especially considering all the hours I put into practicing, but at least I had the opportunity, and that's something I would like every boy and girl to have.

I refilled my glass of wine, and when I looked up, the most beautiful sight in the world appeared before my eyes. Bee, dressed in a white, A-line scoop neck asymmetrical chiffon party dress with ruffles, twirled round and round, and came to a stop, bowed, and asked, "Do you like?"

"You look stunning. Is that the dress you are wearing to the wedding?"

"No, it's the dress I am wearing tomorrow night to the party."

"What party?"

Annie stepped forward, with an empty wine glass, and asked, "Would you kindly refill my glass?"

I refilled her glass and she replied, "Thank you, kind sir. The party you and I are throwing for our adorable daughter … a sort of coming out party. Please feel free to invite any respectable gentlemen you might know, but no ladies, please. Don't need any competition so close to our wedding day."

"That's one thing you don't have to worry about. Even the ladies I once knew, I wouldn't consider in the same league as you. The type of competition you could swat away like a fly."

Annie looked at Bee and said, "Isn't he simply the best?"

"Yes, yes, yes," Bee replied as she ran over and hugged me. "The best daddy ever."

Chapter Twenty-Six

It was a unanimous vote: four 'yeas,' one in absentia, but we counted Lisa as a 'yea' on Bee's reassurance that she would love Chinese food for dinner.

Lisa arrived shortly after the vote, looking exhausted, but after a hug from Bee and a glass of wine she began to perk up. I introduced the two ladies, and suddenly Lisa seemed perplexed and then asked, "You're not Annie…?"

"Yes, I'm sorry but I am."

"Oh, my God. You are one of my heroes," Lisa said.

"Really," Annie replied and continued, "I don't know why that would be, but I'm happy to take a compliment from someone so pretty, who is also doing such important work, finding homes for abused and orphaned children."

"Yes," Bee injected and continued, "I tell her all the time how beautiful she is, and that one day a movie star is going to come along and marry her. Oh, I almost forgot…" and Bee ran off to her room.

"I'm so sorry about your partner. My God, everything I read about him was simply amazing and everyone seemed to love and admire him."

"That doesn't surprise me," Annie replied as Lisa looked at Annie who looked like she was ready to burst into tears.

"You didn't read any of the articles?"

Annie simply nodded her head as I walked up behind her and started to rub her neck. Bee suddenly arrived, holding her framed picture of Jack.

"Look who I met today," Bee said as she handed the picture to Lisa.

"Oh, my God it's Jack the rabbit. I so love him."

"He's in love with me and wants to get married but I told him I was too young. But then I thought, if he met you, he would easily fall in love with you, and the both of you could get married. Maybe, if you ask Annie, she can introduce you. He has his own dressing room."

"But, he's in love with you," Lisa said. "I wouldn't want to take him away from his true love."

"But I can't get married for a very long time, and you could get married right away. I really don't want him to wait all those years for me. You think about it." Bee ran back to her room with the picture as Lisa dropped her head in dismay.

"Is my love life so pathetic, that a nine-year-old angel is trying to set me up with a rabbit? Is that what it has come to?"

Annie reached over and touched her hand and said, "But he has his own dressing room and he is well paid, in carrots, of course, but if the two of you do get married, I will see to it that some money comes your way."

"Thank you, Annie, that makes me feel so much better. I can't wait to tell my parents the great news that I might be marrying a well-off, famous … rodent? Are rabbits rodents?"

Annie and Lisa both started laughing hysterically at this, while I grabbed my phone and did a quick search.

"What do you know," I said. "Rabbits *used* to be considered rodents, but now they're lagomorphs." I read from a Wikipedia entry that said, "Lagomorphs diverged from their rodent cousins and have some traits that rodents lack, like two extra incisors."

"Thank you, sweetie," Annie laughed. "That should come in handy at the studio during my next round of contract negotiations with Jack."

Lisa, who was still giggling, sat down at the table and took stock of her surroundings as if for the first time. "I can't believe I'm sitting here with you," she said, smiling at Annie.

"Oh, gosh," Annie said, "what do you mean? The pleasure is all mine. I'll tell you what. You come down to the studio tomorrow and we'll have lunch. I can already think of five good-looking guys, handsomely paid and exceptionally talented, without cottontails or extra incisors, who would fall head over heels for you ... but unless I give them a little push from behind they would be to shy and intimidated to go near you, never mind ask you out on a date."

"You would do that for me?" Lisa asked.

"Of course, unless you want to take your chances with Jack?"

They both laughed as I refilled their glasses.

Chapter Twenty-Seven

The doorbell rang and Bee ran over and looked through the front window to make sure that it was Mr. Wang with our food. She opened the door and let him in. I took the packages from him and before I had a chance to introduce my friend to Annie, my lovely daughter started telling him all about the party we were throwing for her the next night, and telling him that he had to come. "Please, please, Mr. Wang you have to be there. You're my friend, and you must come."

Apparently, my daughter didn't think of the possibility that Mr. Wang might have to work that night. I addressed him and said, "We would love to have you come to the party, unless of course you have to work."

Mr. Wang bent down and took Bee's hand and replied, "Of course, I will come to your party. How could I resist an invitation from such a beautiful angel?"

"Would you like a drink, Wang?" I asked.

"Not tonight, Joe. But tomorrow night I will have a drink for sure," he replied as I introduced him to Annie, and Bee immediately added, "They're going to get married, and then they will officially be my mommy and daddy. I am so excited."

Wang looked at me and I said, "Yes, it's true."

Annie quickly added, "Very soon, and you and your family will definitely be invited to our wedding."

"Oh, thank you so much. No customer has ever invited me to a party or a wedding before. So very kind."

I paid Wang and handed him four fifty-dollar bills in a roll. He opened up the rolled cash, quickly counted it, and immediately tried to give it back, but I held up my hand and backed away smiling. I knew it was very likely that he would have to take tomorrow night off from work to come to the party, and I didn't want to deprive him of needed income.

"I'll see you tomorrow night?" I asked.

"Yes, Joe," he replied as Bee rushed toward him and hugged him tightly and repeated, "Thank you so much, Mr. Wang."

I opened the door and Wang left, waving good-bye to the ladies on his way out. As soon as he climbed into his car, Bee turned to us and started jumping up and down and clapping her hands as she exclaimed, "I am so excited. So excited!"

***

Bee set the table. She loved folding the napkins just so and placing the fork, knife and spoon in the proper order. I had taught her that little bit of social etiquette, and it was about the only thing I was willing to teach her from all my years in the restaurant business. I never wanted her to work in a restaurant. The restaurant I worked in was unique, a high-price speakeasy, as one customer had called it. It was loud and boisterous and famous people from around the world ate there, and it gave me an opportunity to converse with many amazing people, no more so than Simon. We made a lot of money, but the work was hard and stressful and the hours were exceptionally long. We were just starting our second shift of the day that usually lasted six to eight hours when most people were coming home from work. Occasionally, a customer would ask me, "Is it true that the waiters here make a hundred thousand dollars a year?" I would reply, "Some do."

"Wow!" the customer would exclaim. "That's amazing!"

And I would reply, "Well, the GM is taking applications, but you would have to probably start as a busboy and they only make about half of that."

"Oh no, I could never work in a restaurant. Way too hard."

They could never work in a restaurant because they had jobs making half-a-million with unlimited expense accounts and they had secretaries arranging their every move, and in some cases, doing their work for them. Yet, they found it unreal that a supposedly unskilled server could be making so much. It just didn't jive with the world they lived in.

After dinner, Bee and I cleared off the kitchen table, and after placing everything in the dishwasher and wiping down the table, we all sat down again. I opened our fourth bottle of wine and refilled all our glasses, and let me tell you, neither girl seemed to be slowing down. Lisa took out the papers I needed to sign to officially become Bee's foster parent. I had read all of the material that Lisa had provided me with, and so I simply signed, and just for fun I handed my copies over to my secretary, Bee, who was sitting right next to me … almost on top of me.

And from there, Annie took over, and when I say she took over, I mean she took over. It was like another person had inhabited her body. She turned to Lisa and spoke to her in a friendly but official tone. "I'm interested in the adoption and what we need to do to make it go as smoothly and quickly as possible."

"Getting married would be a first big step," Lisa replied.

"We'll be married by next weekend, won't we honey?"

"Yes," I replied like an unblinking robot.

Annie addressed Lisa again, saying, "I've talked to my lawyer and I sent him all the documents he requested to move ahead with the adoption." She looked at me and said, "I'll give you a list of the information he will need from you, and you can fax them over to him tomorrow. Then the only thing he will be missing is our marriage license and your report, Lisa. Hopefully, you can send that report right after we're married."

"Yes, of course. It usually takes at least a few months for an adoption to go through," Lisa said.

"It will take no longer than a week, I promise," Annie said defiantly as she looked across at Bee. "The child has waited long enough and so have I."

She raised her glass and said, "Cheers, to our lovely daughter." We all drank up as Bee went over and hugged her soon-to-be mom.

***

I walked Lisa to her apartment building. It was only a few blocks away, but Studio City was famous for its lack of streetlights, and with Lisa feeling no pain, I didn't feel comfortable leaving her on her own. A few times on the way to her building I had to grab her arm to stop her from falling. She stopped once, and while trying to keep her balance asked, "Just how did you two meet?"

"A mutual friend introduced us. Her business partner, Simon," I replied.

"And you knew Simon how?"

"Through the restaurant. What you really want to ask is, how did a one-time busboy, bartender, waiter, and manager of a restaurant end up engaged to the most successful woman in Hollywood?"

"Yes, that's it exactly."

"Luck, pure luck," I replied.

We got off the elevator at her floor and I watched as she wobbled down the hallway, turned to wave at me, and then let herself into her apartment. I waved back, then took the elevator back down and walked out of the building into a night so peaceful and quiet that I briefly forgot I was in Los Angeles. Standing in the parking lot of Lisa's building, I stared up at her apartment and watched as a form that looked like her walked through the living room. Then the light went out and was replaced by the pulsating glow of a TV screen. I started walking home and ended up taking the long way through the neighborhood, looping around to another residential street in order to add a few minutes of thinking time to my walk.

As I looked up at the stars, I mulled over Annie's sudden personality change when we were discussing the adoption and our impending marriage. The more I thought about it, the more unsettling it seemed. It was like she was five steps ahead of me, and she was ready to bulldoze her way through any obstacle to get what she wanted. I didn't really know her that well, and it was not that long since I had counted her out of my life altogether. Then came the scene at the cemetery, and her introduction to Bee. Was Bee the ultimate prize in this whole scenario? The abused, dirty child with the face of an angel that I picked up off the streets and took into my home? I could live with the possibility that Annie was more interested in Bee than in me. After all, Bee needed a mother, and I wanted her to have one. But I had no intention of taking a step back just because Annie was on the scene. I wasn't about to become a secondary figure in my daughter's life.

I walked into the house and into the living room where Annie was stretched across the couch, her head resting comfortably against pillows placed along the armrest, while Bee, dressed in her pajamas, slept peacefully on top of her. It was like a picture perfect, a loving scene of a mother and child, and yet I found it eerie and weird.

Annie asked, "Lisa get home okay, or did you have to carry her?"

I laughed and replied, "No, thankfully it didn't come to that. She stumbled a little here and there but she's home safe and sound. We've all been there."

"Can she be trusted?" Annie asked, and I thought to myself, This coming from a woman who wanted to take me to bed after spending one drunken day together.

"Of course, she can be trusted," I replied.

"Great, because I really like her and I would love for us to become friends."

"I think that would be wonderful. She's a really nice kid, and she helped me out quite a bit with Bee."

Annie looked down at the sleeping child and gently rearranged a section of Bee's hair.

"Do you want me to carry her into her bedroom?" I asked.

"No, I don't want to disturb her, and I'm quite comfortable just lying here with her. She's so adorable. It's as though she was dropped from Heaven into our lives."

"Well then, with everything okay with you two beautiful ladies I shall go off to bed," I said as I started walking toward my bedroom.

"What, not even a good night kiss? Has the romance already gone out of our relationship?"

I turned back around, and replied, "Of course not." I bent down and kissed her and before I knew it the kiss became very passionate and she wouldn't let go. I finally pulled away and she asked, "What's wrong?"

I looked down at Bee and Annie simply said, "Oh."

I kissed Annie on the forehead and said, "Love you."

I walked toward my bedroom as she remarked, "I wonder if you would have pulled away so quickly if it was Lisa you were kissing?"

I pretended not to hear her remark and walked into my bedroom and quietly closed the door. I sat down on the bed and tried to think rationally. Lisa, Annie and I had finished off four bottles of wine, and whereas Annie and I weren't stumbling all over the place, it didn't mean we were less drunk. Actually, there were times I did not know what was going on in Annie's mind. She was in a tremendous hurry to get married, and she had made plans without even consulting me.

It amazed me how little I really knew about Annie, but I was certain she knew everything there was to know about me. She probably knew what kindergarten I attended. I took it for granted that her marriage failed because her husband was a cheating, unloving bastard, but for all I know it was maybe because she was borderline crazy.

But no, it couldn't be. I was convinced that Annie and I getting together was Simon's clever handiwork, and Simon would never do that to me. He would never put me in a situation that would make my life miserable. But he *would* put me in a situation in which he trusted that I, and only I, would take care of Annie, at any cost. What if Simon felt so responsible for Annie that he needed to find someone — a nice dupe like me — to keep her on an even keel after he was gone? Could Simon have left me in his will in a desperate, last-minute bid to keep Annie from going off the rails and ruining his legacy?

I laid my head down on the pillow. It was going to be a long, restless night. Suddenly, I did not trust my fiancée with Bee. For all I knew, she could be planning to bundle Bee up and take her God knows where. She had enough money that she could convince or buy any judge she wanted and take that child away from me, and have Lisa, who was star struck, testifying against me. I started opening my door every fifteen minutes and making sure the British chick and my daughter were still on the couch. This went on for over two hours. Finally, I walked out of my bedroom and into the living room, pretending to go to the kitchen, and looked down at the couch. They were still there, but now Annie was passed out like Bee, with one arm draped over the child. Bee had slid a little further down between Annie and the back of the couch. They looked like a couple of entangled, co-sleeping puppies.

I shook my head and walked back into my bedroom, wondering if I had lost my mind. I lay down on the bed and stared at the ceiling a while longer. My thoughts were a jumble. One minute I was chastising myself for being paranoid and the next minute I was congratulating myself for being cautious of this woman whom I really didn't know. A good father checks out everyone who will have anything to do with his child, I told myself. No exceptions.

I finally fell into a deep, blank and mostly dreamless sleep, during which the only thing I could remember was a single image, like a movie still, of a female dragon flying low over a brilliant green pasture with a sheep between its jaws.

Chapter Twenty-Eight

I woke up at my usual time, a little groggier than usual, and changed into my running gear, then walked into the living room and found an empty couch with the pillows put back in place and a blanket neatly folded.

"Good morning, Daddy," I heard Bee say from the kitchen as I walked toward her.

"Good morning, beautiful," I replied as I looked at Bee eating a bowl of cereal. "Did you sleep well?"

"Yes, I don't remember much, except for falling asleep on the couch and waking up this morning in bed with Annie. She's still asleep."

"Are we going to go for our run?" I asked.

"Of course," she said as she finished her cereal and wrote Annie a note saying we were going for our run. She put the note beside Annie on the bed, then picked up her inhaler and made sure that I saw that she had it before putting it into her pocket. She didn't go anywhere without it, and always made sure that I saw that she was carrying it with her. She didn't want to worry me.

We walked outside just as it was getting light out, and immediately Bee started jumping around like a bumblebee. She was talking non-stop about her party, about how no one had ever thrown her a party before, and about how excited she was to wear her dress and talk to people and have Mr. Wang there and eat appetizers.

All thoughts of needing to baby my new hip were long gone. We had worked ourselves up to about three miles of running alternating with three or four miles of walking. At about the halfway mark, I stopped and bent down and caught the bumblebee with both my hands. She laughed and said, "What are you doing?" and I said, "I just wanted to hug you and tell you how much I love you. You are the best gift I have ever received." I held her tightly, a little longer than usual, because I didn't want her to see me crying and needlessly worrying on her big day.

Once I was fully composed, I let go, and I held her hand as she walked beside me.

"How about we walk the rest of the way?" I suggested. "It's such a beautiful morning and I have the honor of holding the hand of the most beautiful girl in the world. I'm in no rush."

She looked up at me and smiled. Her face was aglow, and her dimples were like magical orbs emitting warmth and solace. Yes, it might sound like a cliché, but she was angelic.

⁕⁕

Back at the house, I stood by the sliding glass door and watched Bee as she practiced dribbling the basketball. Suddenly, Annie came up from behind and hugged me tightly. I jumped briefly and then relaxed into her embrace and grasped her arms as they crossed my stomach.

"I could get used to this," I said.

Annie chuckled and said, "Well, I hope so because there is going to be plenty of it coming your way." She went silent for a long moment before letting out a sigh.

"You okay?" I asked.

"I'm fine. Just a little embarrassed."

"Why?" I asked, though I already knew.

"That's very kind, but I owe you an apology. I said some stupid and hurtful things last night, and I'm not proud of myself."

"I did wonder what might be going on," I said gently, and Annie hurried to explain.

"I admit it, I do get jealous. I was never like this, but after being married to a man who showed me no affection at all, I guess I've become more sensitive. I don't want to lose the man who makes me feel like a queen."

"Well," I said slowly, "I treat you like a queen because you are one, and the only way you are going to get rid of me is if you open your beautiful eyes and realize you can do so much better."

"My eyes are wide open, and from where I am standing, I know there is no way I could ever do better. I am so happy, Joe."

I turned around and kissed her. When we came up for air, she whispered, "Does this mean we're okay?"

"Honey, we are better than okay. We're perfect," I replied as we looked out at our child dribbling the ball. Seconds after we started watching her, Bee lost control of the ball and nearly flattened herself chasing after it. It looked like she might have tripped over one of her shoes. Annie's arm flung out at the sliding door as though she was trying to catch Bee from forty feet away. We watched as Bee skip hopped across the court and lost the ball again, then ran onto the grass to retrieve it. Annie laughed, once she knew Bee was fine, and said, "Basketball lessons going well?"

"Believe it or not, she is getting a lot better." We had a quiet chuckle over that, and I added, "Wait until you see her in the pool. She's like a female Phelps." Annie raised her eyebrows with respect and said, "I look forward to that."

Then she looked at me and said, "I want to tell you something, but first you have to swear you won't be disappointed."

"Of course," I replied.

"She told me yesterday that she was practicing really hard, and she didn't want to disappoint you, but she didn't think she would ever be good enough to play for the Knicks."

I laughed and said, "She's probably already good enough to play for that team. They are that bad."

Chapter Twenty-Nine

Annie was getting ready to leave for work at about nine o'clock when she asked Bee if she wanted to come along. Bee said she would love to, but that she "didn't want to leave Daddy by himself."

Before Annie left the house, she and Bee had a short conversation about the party. Annie asked a bunch of questions about Bee's favorite colors and music and food. She told us both that she had some expert party planners at work who were going to make all of the arrangements, which included caterers, waiters, a bartender, and party decorators. It was all coming together at the last minute, but these employees specialized in coordinating launches and other events for the studio, and Annie assured us that if anyone could pull together an impressive fête on a day's notice, it was her team.

When Bee squealed and said she couldn't wait, Annie just about cried. But she recovered quickly and wrapped Bee in her arms and said, "I'll see you tonight. It'll be a blast."

After seeing Annie off, I walked into my study and found on my desk a list of everything I had to send to the lawyer. It was more or less the same paperwork that I had to provide Lisa with to become a foster dad, so that made it easy. I immediately started faxing everything to the lawyer and as I was doing that, Bee walked into the study and stood beside me. She asked, "What are you doing?"

"Sending Annie's lawyer all the documents he needs to make you officially our daughter."

She hugged me and didn't let go and then asked, "Do you think Jack is coming to my party tonight?"

I thought about it a moment, not remembering who Jack was, and then it hit me like a jackhammer. It was the rabbit. I replied, "I'm sure he would love to come, but Annie told me that he was working very late tonight because he just started shooting a new movie. He's a very busy guy. I'm sorry, sweetheart."

"Oh, that's okay," she replied as she let go of me. I could see that she was not very upset as she continued saying, "It's probably better because I know how upset it makes him that he has to wait so long to marry me. I hate to see him sad."

"That's very kind of you. We're going to have a great party tonight, aren't we?"

"Yes, Daddy, and I'm so excited that Mr. Wang is going to come and I also get to wear my beautiful new dress. I am so happy!"

The rest of the day went from odd, to strange, to bizarre. Thankfully, I got most of my information second-hand. It all started with Lisa calling up Bee at about ten-thirty and asking the nine-year-old child what she thought she should wear to lunch with Annie at the studio. They couldn't decide, so Lisa decided that she would try on as many outfits as she could and hopefully they could decide which one looked the best. They carried out this fashion show over Zoom. From what I could hear and understand, Lisa changed into about ten different outfits before both girls decided on a black wrap-around dress with a modestly plunging V-neck. Bee assured Lisa that it was the most glamorous outfit that she had tried on and told her that "every guy would fall in love with her." Lisa replied, "I'm just hoping for one guy, but thanks … I have to run or I will be late. Love you a bunch."

At one o'clock Bee's phone rang, and it was Lisa commiserating about how terrible she was doing. Annie had introduced her to four eligible, attractive young men, and they all seemed interested in her. In fact, she thought they couldn't take their eyes off of her, but when Annie mentioned the party and told them that Lisa didn't have a date, not one took the bait.

"It was like I suddenly became the creature from the black lagoon. I swear, my grandma was right. I should have become a nun."

I could hear her crying over the phone and Bee said, "Why don't you go see Jack? I know he will fall in love with you and he's a big star."

I know my lovely daughter was only trying to be helpful, but I could swear that I heard such a mournful screech from Lisa that I had to cover my ears.

The decorators came at two o'clock and did a wonderful job of sprucing up the pool area and the living room. They put up several arches in the backyard and decorated them with gauzy material and fresh flowers, then strung fairy lights everywhere. Then they added some tall torches around the pool and created some extra seating areas with comfortable chairs and love seats borrowed from the studio. Bee was so excited that she went from being a bumblebee to a hummingbird. She was running and hopping all over the place, and I didn't have the heart to tell her to calm down. She was having so much fun, and the decorators were enjoying her antics.

At three-thirty in the afternoon, Bee's phone rang. It was Lisa again, but this time she was over the moon with excitement. Ed Monroe, a rising, young movie star who had been in a number of big hits, had stopped by Annie's table in the studio cafeteria while they were eating lunch, and they had hit it off immediately. Like Lisa, he was from Brooklyn, and they started naming a whole bunch of places they both used to visit, including pizzerias, bakeries, movie theaters, bars, and restaurants. Like Lisa's parents, his still lived in Brooklyn. And he, like Lisa, was a Mets fan — which was a big *ugh* for me, but I decided I wouldn't hold it against them because they were also both long-suffering Knicks fans like me. Best of all, Ed Monroe was single, and when Annie brought up the party, he wasted no time asking Lisa to be his date. She agreed right away, and they made plans for him to pick her up at her apartment at six-thirty. As he was getting up to leave he whispered to Annie, "My God, she's beautiful. I can't believe she's single, and from Brooklyn, and has a real job, helping abused and abandoned children. My parents would love her."

Lisa told Bee she had to rush home to get ready for the party. Even though she loved the outfit she had on and was certain that was one of many reasons that she had caught Ed's attention, it wouldn't be proper for a woman to wear the same outfit at lunch and then to a party. She emailed Bee a bunch of photos of Ed that she got off the internet, and said that she would definitely need Bee's help in picking out a new outfit for that evening. She had total faith in the nine-year-old's judgment and fashion sense. After all, she had already helped her choose one winning outfit. Lisa needed her to work her magic one more time.

A few minutes later Annie called, sounding quite excited, and filled me in on the same scenario that I had just heard over Bee's speakerphone. I wasn't quite sure if she was excited for Lisa, a beautiful young lady who finally managed to get a date, or for herself, given that, at least for now, Lisa would no longer be a threat to her happily ever after with Bee and me. But it didn't matter. She was bubbling over with enthusiasm for Lisa and Ed, and happy with her new role as matchmaker to displaced Brooklynites.

"That's a pretty specific skill," I said. "You should probably keep your day job."

"Oh, I could do both," she laughed. "It could be a side gig."

"Okay, Yentl. Shalom."

"Ha ha."

At five o'clock the caterers showed up, and I didn't even have to give them any directions. Apparently, my fiancée and her helpers had drawn a diagram, telling them exactly where to set everything up ... seven tables with three chairs at each table, twenty feet apart, and thirty feet away from the pool, a tent where the food would be served, appetizers, hot and cold dishes for dinner, and of course a variety of desserts, and a separate bar area, fully stocked with only the best in alcoholic beverages and plenty of soda and juice for Bee and any other kids.

Twenty-five years in the restaurant business, and I have to admit that I was impressed. There was no denying it — Annie was efficient, and an incredible leader. She knew how to get the best out of people, but she could also be firm, sometimes to the point of being intimidating. I would hate to be the one who crossed her, which made me wonder even more how such a woman stayed over twenty years in a loveless, emotionally frustrating marriage. In truth, I knew, but I wasn't about to go there ... sometimes knowledge could be a deadly thing, a hurtful exercise, and when one allows it to become weaponized it is very likely to turn on you and leave you with a lifetime of regrets and missed opportunities.

At five-thirty, Bee and Lisa were back on Zoom. Lisa tried on one outfit after another and Bee gave her professional feedback. Lisa was telling the child that she was looking for just the right outfit — something sexy enough that Ed couldn't take his eyes off of her, but not so sexy that he had thoughts of hitting a homerun on his first date. She was not that type of girl, and if she ever did something like that her grandma would turn over in her grave or come and haunt her in her apartment.

Bee said, "I didn't know Ed played baseball. Do you know for what team?"

"He's an actor, not a baseball player. Why would you think that?"

"Because you said you weren't going to allow him to hit a homerun."

"Oh, that. I'm so nervous I don't know what I'm talking about."

After standing at the door and listening to that insanity for a few minutes, I decided to go outside and sit by the makeshift bar. I asked the bartender, a gentleman in his mid-thirties, if it would be too much trouble to get a double shot of the Macallan 25, one of the best scotches in the world at about two thousand dollars a bottle.

"Absolutely. Would you like a little ice with that?" he asked.

"Absolutely not. Not at a hundred dollars a shot. That would be like taking a prime porterhouse steak and slathering it with barbecue sauce. A crime against nature."

He chuckled and poured me a double shot in what is known as a Library hand-cut double old-fashioned shot glass. The type of shot glass that rich people might bring out to impress a certain select type of clientele. Not the type you would normally see at a nine-year-old's party.

"Wow! Annie goes all out," I remarked.

"Annie's the best, and let me tell you, our whole staff was genuinely shocked and saddened when we heard about Simon's death."

"So you guys have worked for Annie and Simon before?"

"Oh yeah, for many years. Our regular staff is about ten times this size, and I would say we do at least ten banquets a year for Simon and Annie's studio, usually for groups of around two to three hundred. In many ways, they keep us afloat. They do not cut corners." He reached over the bar and whispered, "Simon left each member of our staff twenty thousand dollars in his will. You tell me, who does that?"

"Simon, that's who," I replied, being a major recipient of his generosity.

"Simon actually spent more time talking to the staff at these events than he did the guests, and it wasn't because he was shy, because he wasn't."

My beautiful daughter came out and joined us, dressed in her lovely party dress. I picked her up and sat her on a barstool. "And this is Bee, tonight's guest of honor, and the whole reason for this party."

"Wow, you are one beautiful young lady."

"Thank you," she said shyly.

"Are you looking forward to tonight?"

"Yes! This is the first party anyone has ever given for me."

"No, I can't believe that."

"It's true! I'm so excited."

"Are you an actress?" the bartender asked.

"No, but one day I hope to play for the New York Knicks. I need to practice a lot more and grow a whole bunch."

The bartender suppressed a smile and said, "So you want to be a basketball player. That's really exciting!"

"Thank you, I think so, too. What's your name?"

"Mike, and it's a pleasure to meet you." He reached out and shook her hand.

"It's very nice to meet you, Mike."

"You want something to drink, sweetheart?" I asked.

"No, thank you, Daddy."

"Did you and Lisa decide on an outfit for her to wear?"

"Yes," she replied and then she whispered in my ear, "But then she got so excited that she peed her pants. So we had to start all over again, after she stopped crying. But the outfit she has on now is great, and I told her it looked even better than the one she had the accident in."

"That was very thoughtful of you, sweetheart."

"Thank you. She's having a glass of wine to calm down before Ed picks her up."

At that moment I could not tell you how happy I was that my lovely future wife, the tough-as-nails Brit who might as well have been trained by MI6, had taken the lead with the adoption, rather than leaving everything to Lisa. Usually, a couple waits until they are in a relationship for either the man or woman to crack up, but Lisa had apparently decided to get a head start and crack up before even exchanging a good night kiss. I could only hope that the worse she might do that night would be to pee her pants, or dress, again.

I looked up from my beautiful daughter just in time to see Annie striding over in a gorgeous little black dress — a body-hugging number with a tastefully plunging neckline. She came straight for us and kissed me, then studied my face and asked, "What's that look about?"

"Just total amazement that my date is the hottest woman at this party," I replied.

"Is that so? And did you pick up that lingo from Byron, Keats, or Yeats?"

"Actually, I think I picked it up on a Bronx basketball court. You know, there were a lot of good-looking girls back home, but none of them could compete with you."

"Is that so?" she repeated as she looked down at Bee and asked, "Do you believe this nonsense your daddy is throwing at me?"

"I think what he *means* to say is that you're very beautiful, Annie." Annie laughed as she hugged and kissed Bee and said, "I've missed you so much, my little angel."

"Would you like a glass of white wine, Annie?" Mike asked.

"Yes, Michael, that would be wonderful. I gather you have met my fiancé and my lovely daughter?"

"Yes, but I never knew you had a daughter or were engaged."

"Oh yes, it all happened kind of suddenly, but I could not be happier." She pointed to Bee and said, "In a little over a week or so, this lovely creature will be officially adopted by both Joe and me, and we could not be more proud and thankful."

"And it could not happen to a more deserving and loving lady than you," Mike graciously added.

"Thank you, Michael." She looked at me and said, "We have known each other for a long time. What is it Michael, fifteen years?"

"Exactly," Michael replied as Annie smiled at him and then suddenly turned away to admire the room. She fought back tears and chokingly commented, "Everything looks so lovely." She then turned to Bee and lifted her off the chair and gently lowered her to the floor before taking her hand. "Let's go introduce you to the rest of my friends." They started to walk toward the other caterers and I asked, "How about me?"

"You can stay here and keep Michael company. I'm sure the two of you have plenty of hot chicks you would love to reminisce about." She winked at me, and then walked off with our daughter.

I shrugged in Michael's direction and said, "On that note, how about another double Macallan?"

He poured as I looked across at the two lovely girls in my life. It was becoming crystal clear to me that the little wiseass might very likely follow in Annie's footsteps. Like Annie, she was a social creature, and a real charmer. As Annie introduced her to the other caterers, she greeted each one with a smile and looked directly into their eyes as though that person, at that moment, was the most important person in the world. It was like she had been practicing for this role her whole life, a diamond in the rough, whose exceptional potential and qualities were quickly being refined and polished right before my eyes and in a very short amount of time. Yet, to forget that she was just a child, whose fragile nature was on full display just a short time ago with our trip to the emergency room, would be a great mistake with long-lasting effects.

I picked up the glass of Macallan and took a sip as I looked over the pool area and surrounding landscape. Like everything else in my life, it looked and felt completely different and I was, once again, reminded of the saying, that "Without change, there is no hope." And at this moment in my life, I felt as hopeful as I had in many years.

I took another sip and said, "You can get really used to drinking such a smooth and refined whiskey."

"Yeah, it's hard to go back to the regular stuff after tasting the best."

After being introduced to all the caterers, Annie took Bee to the guest room. They were gone for about ten minutes, and when they emerged, Annie was wearing a simple, comfortable summer dress. That's when I realized that the black dress had been her work attire, and that this was what she planned to wear to the party. When she and Bee reached the bar, Annie looked at my face, laughed, and twirled around, and asked, "What, no more hot chick comments?"

"Oh, you're as hot as ever, but now you have left a little something to the imagination."

She whispered, "Are you trying to say that I was showing a little too much?"

"It really depended on the angle one was looking at you from. Believe me, you have nothing to be embarrassed about and I had a great view."

"You pig, and here all along I thought you were a gentleman!"

"I'm only joking with you Annie," I said.

"Seriously," she replied with a bit of disappointment.

"You really liked that I called you a hot chick, didn't you?"

"Maybe, a little. It's kind of nice to know that my body has retained its girlish curves."

"Oh, it's retained a lot more than just that, and you don't hear me complaining."

She whispered, "Think we are going to make it to our wedding night?"

"Yes, I'm very traditional when it comes to things like that, but then again you can be quite persuasive. Would you like another glass of wine?"

"Yes, please." Mike handed Annie another glass of wine.

"You're quite the party planner," I remarked.

"Well, thank you, but all of the credit goes to my incredible team."

"Who's on the guest list?" I asked.

"A couple of lawyers, family court judges, a politician or two."

"A Tammany Hall type meeting. I'm quite impressed. Anyone a distant relative of Boss Tweed?"

"Possibly, I don't really get into their genealogy, unless they offer it up."

"You don't take chances?"

"Oh, I take chances, but not with our daughter's future. I'm sure being of Italian descent you totally understand my position?"

"Totally! In fact, until you entered the picture I was prepared to move to Canada if they didn't give me total custody of the little angel."

"Well, now you won't have to worry about the snow and cold. Bee will be officially ours sooner than you ever could have imagined."

"You know, for a hot chick you really are quite a calculating and resourceful babe."

"Wow! Being called a babe and a hot chick all in one day. I'm warming to this lingo, especially from a guy who I thought would only be reciting Byron to me in praise of my celestial beauty."

"One has to mix it up. I would hate to bore a celestial beauty such as you."

"How thoughtful, and while I am sitting around eating up all these compliments, is there anything expected of me in return?"

"Just the promise that you will keep me around and let me feed you peeled grapes and compliment you for the rest of our lives."

"I think I can handle that."

"Perfect."

I reached over and kissed the hot chick, and our hands found each other as we grabbed this small moment of passion before the rest of the guests arrived.

Chapter Thirty

The party was a big success. The bumblebee, slash, wiseass, slash, jumping jack, slash hummingbird, slash darling angel was a superb hostess and guest of honor, along with her divine mother.

Lisa and Ed were the first to arrive. Bee greeted them at the front door and let out a little gasp when she saw her fashion choices manifested in person. Lisa looked beautiful — but then, apart from Lisa herself, almost any person with half-decent eyesight would think that she was lovely. Ed had been around plenty of actresses, like I had at the restaurant, and Lisa, with her luminous olive skin, smooth dark hair and near-perfect oval face, could compete with any of them, even if she, charmingly, had no idea that was the case. Ed could not take his eyes off of her, and had his hand around Lisa's waist from the moment they came inside the house. It felt strange to watch them, but I was happy for her.

I shook Ed's hand when we were introduced, and although I had seen him and talked to him a few times at the restaurant, I realized quickly that he had no idea who I was, and I didn't bother to remind him. You can often take a restaurant employee and put them into a different context and there is a good chance that a regular customer — even one the employee has talked to dozens of times at work — will not even recognize them. Most people don't actually *see* the people who serve them, and stars, even nice ones, are no exception.

Lisa showed up with a gift bag for Bee and handed it over proudly. Bee pulled out the colorful tissue paper that was sprouting from the top, looked inside, and gave a little shriek.

"These are some of my favorites," Lisa told Bee. "Save a couple of them for us to play together, okay?"

Bee ran back over to Lisa and gave her a big hug and said, "I will. Thank you so much." Bee then ran over to me and opened the bag. Inside was a stack of video games.

"Ahhh," I said, finally understanding. "Those should keep you busy."

Lisa looked at Ed, as if to say, "You're on your own for a few minutes," then grabbed Bee's hand and said, "Come with me, munchkin." Then they ran into the child's bedroom with the bag swinging from Bee's hand. Watching all of this, my first guess was that Lisa had peed her pants again, but thankfully I was wrong. It turned out that she just wanted Bee's expert opinion about Ed. My daughter reported that she gave him two enthusiastic thumbs up, and told Lisa that apart from Jack the Rabbit, she did not see how Lisa could have done any better.

After Lisa rejoined Ed, Bee stationed herself back in the foyer next to Annie. A few lawyers arrived, and whereas it was difficult keeping Bee from opening the door to greet them, Annie adroitly stepped in front of her and greeted them first and then introduced them to the lovely child, who politely shook each of their hands ... wondering, I am quite certain, why they hadn't come bearing gifts.

Then came the judges. One of them, a tough-as-nails circuit court judge in her late fifties, who was known for her stern rulings and her burning hatred of drunk drivers and deadbeat dads, stepped two feet into the foyer, took one look at Bee, and melted into a puddle. She dropped down to Bee's level and said, "Sweetheart, you look just like my granddaughter." The woman looked up at her husband, a well-known law professor at one of the local universities, and said, "Honey, doesn't she look like Tasha?" Her husband nodded and tilted his head as if to give Bee the advantage.

"I think Tasha would be very flattered by the comparison," he said dryly.

The judge rose up and swatted her husband's arm gently and smiled and said, "You are terrible." Then she rested her hand gently on Bee's forearm and said, "I look forward to getting to know you, Bee, and someday I hope to introduce you to our granddaughter."

"I would love to meet Tasha," Bee said with a big smile.

Other local luminaries followed — several more judges, a congresswoman and a state senator — and whereas they brought gifts, they were more of the grown-up variety, including several bottles of superb champagne, wine, and liquor. Like a true champion, Bee let slide the snub, and simply took in the adulation that flowed from all sides.

When Wang arrived, Bee threw out the rules and flew past Annie to give her special guest a big hug. He was wearing a stylish sports coat, black slacks, and spiffy black shoes, and looked more like a movie star than Ed. Bee kept repeating, "You came, you came! I'm so happy!" When she had let go of his neck, Wang bent down and presented the young princess with a lovely bouquet of white lotus flowers, and explained that for the Chinese, the lotus flower symbolizes exquisite beauty, perfection and purity of mind and heart. Bee started to sniffle and then cry, and Mr. Wang, like a true gentleman, took out a handkerchief and wiped away her tears and said, "Please, no crying."

"I'm just so happy," Bee said.

Annie was watching all of this with both hands raised to her mouth as her own eyes filled with tears. She finally took the flowers from Bee, smiled at Mr. Wang, and walked into the kitchen to look for another vase that she had brought from her house. I followed her and asked, "You okay?"

"They're so lovely," she said as she found a pair of shears and got to work snipping the ends off the flowers. "And she's so lovely. And everything else Mr. Wang said." She put the vase down on the table, turned, and put her head down on my shoulder and cried uncontrollably. "I'm just so happy, Joe."

"That makes three of us," I replied as she raised her head from my shoulder and smiled. I might have been misting up a little too, but I wasn't about to go down that road, with a couple dozen people in the house.

"Come on, now," I said. "Let's pull ourselves together and get back to our guests." Annie nodded bravely and wiped her eyes one more time before putting some finishing touches on the flower arrangement and taking my hand.

As we walked back into the living room, we saw Bee take Mr. Wang by the hand and start to lead him outside. They stopped by the bar, where Lisa and Ed were hanging out, gazing into each other's eyes like two star struck lovers. Ed had planted one hand on Lisa's lower, *lower* back and was pulling her hips close to him. As I took all of this in, I thought, *Uh-oh. This guy looks like he intends to score on the first date.*

The electricity was momentarily put on hold as Bee moved toward them and tugged at Lisa's arm. Lisa immediately jumped out of Ed's clutches and greeted Mr. Wang with a big hug and then introduced him to her date.

I crossed the room and joined this group, with a half-formed plan to intervene. I threw my arm around Wang's shoulder as I tugged at my little princess, who seemed transfixed by the two lovebirds and the freedom with which Ed seemed to be, again, running his hands all over Lisa's body. The scene was quickly moving from PG to R, and if it kept up like this, Mr. Ed just might be hitting a grand slam sooner than later ... but I was determined that it was not going to happen in my house. Lisa occasionally slapped at Ed, but in a joking manner... not in a way that said, "You keep it up like this and I will send you and your barely concealed woody packing."

"What would you like to drink, Wang?" I asked.

"A beer, Joe, like always." I ordered two cold Budweiser beers from Mike who poured them perfectly into two chilled mugs. It was the first beer I'd had since going shopping that first day with Bee, and my God, did it taste good.

Bee was staring at the lovebirds, who now had their hands on each other's backs as they stared in each other's eyes, looking very much like two people who thought they might be alone in a hotel room. I tried to distract Bee by pointing to something outside, but she kept looking at Lisa and Ed and asked, "Are they going to wrestle?"

"I hope not," I replied. I swear, I was ready to dump a bucket of ice water over both of their heads.

I suddenly saw Annie walking toward them like a woman on a mission. In a controlled but deadly declaration, she hissed, "If you two don't cut it out right now, I will be kicking both your butts the hell out of here." Never in my life did I see two people separate so quickly. I could only imagine what was going through Ed's mind — something along the lines of, "And there goes my budding career." As for Lisa, God only knows what she was thinking. Annie kept her gaze on Ed for a long time, and all he could do was lower his eyes and say, "Sorry."

She then turned her gaze on Lisa, and if ever the girl from Brooklyn was going to pee her pants, I thought it would be that moment. Annie continued, "And if anyone should know better, it is you." Lisa stepped back and almost tripped over herself, but was saved by Wang, who caught her.

Annie then turned toward us and smiled as if nothing happened. She said, "I cannot tell you how happy I am that you were able to come, Mr. Wang. The lotus flower is my favorite, and it is so appropriate that you gave that bouquet to our little angel."

"You are so welcome, and I am so happy that you and Joe and beautiful Bee are going to be a family," Mr. Wang replied.

"Thank you so kindly, Mr. Wang."

Bee looked up at Annie and asked, "You didn't want them to wrestle?"

"No, sweetheart, they can wrestle in the dirt or go somewhere else, but not at my baby's party."

Annie excused herself, and all I could think of was that if she wasn't an MI6 operative in this life, she definitely was in a past life.

The lovebirds were now sitting at a table across from each other, and they could just as well have been an ocean apart. Annie formally introduced me to the LA version of the Tammany Hall crowd, and I recognized a number of them from the restaurant, but in a setting like this, and in the presence of Annie, they had no idea who I was. I couldn't help feeling my fiancée was a queen, engaged to a pauper, and let me tell you, I found her so hot and sexy I felt like I was twenty years old.

Halfway through the evening, Bee went into the living room and turned on the stereo and the Beach Boys came blasting through the outside speakers, drowning out a small jazz quartet that had been playing to the guests sitting around the pool and the grounds. The musicians took this in stride; they were due for a break anyway, so they put down their instruments and went to fill their glasses. When Bee realized what she had done she said, "Oops, sorry about that!" But they just smiled broadly at her and raised their glasses in a little toast to the girl who had, in a fit of enthusiasm, changed the channel.

Bee and Mr. Wang looked at each other and he raised his hand with an invitation to dance. Bee took his hand and together they walked over to the basketball court, which immediately became a dance floor. As a crowd gathered around the court, Mr. Wang and Bee launched into a wild dance, twirling, twisting, flipping, lifting and laughing the whole time. They danced through three Beach Boys songs, and when they finished and took a bow everyone started clapping wildly. All Annie and I could do was watch from the sidelines in amazement as we saw another whole side of our beautiful daughter. For the second time that night, Annie buried her face in my shoulder and said, "I am just so happy, Joe."

With the court cleared of the main event, other guests started dancing, and when Annie invited the catering crew to join in, a number of them started dancing, too. It was a real party, except for Lisa, who was sitting by herself. Apparently, her date had dumped her, giving her the lame excuse that the sound director on his latest film had texted him and asked if he could drop by the studio and loop a few more lines. I knew from Annie that she ordered all studio operations closed down by eight o'clock, and it was past ten.

I walked over to Mike and handed him a couple of hundred dollars, and whispered to him, "Please, ask Lisa to dance?" He replied, "Why would she dance with me? She's with that actor."

"The son-of-a-bitch ditched her. Give me a moment with her, and as soon as I get up to leave, you come over. I'll take care of things here. I've tended bar a few thousand times in my life."

I walked over to Lisa and sat down. She looked at me forlornly and I took her hand. "No one is mad at you. We love you, especially my little girl."

"I am so stupid, Joe. He just wanted to get me into bed, and I was more than willing to go along with it. That's how desperate I am."

"Please don't say that. How about I get you a glass of wine?"

"That would be great, thank you."

I got up and walked over to the bar, where I had Mike pour her a glass of wine and bring it to her. He chatted her up, and within a few minutes, he extended his hand, she took it, and they ended up on the dance floor. Not for nothing, Mike was better looking than Ed, and I was quite sure that he possessed a stronger moral compass. I stepped behind the bar and looked out at the guests having a good time and watched Mr. Wang and Bee as they prepared for an encore.

Annie took a seat at the bar and said, "I saw what you did. It was very nice of you. I don't think I could be so forgiving."

"I know what it's like, being the only guy at a gathering without a date and no girl the least bit interested in dancing with me. Please, for Bee's sake, make up with her. If not for her, we wouldn't have Bee."

Annie smiled a non-committal smile and said, "Would the bartender be so kind as to pour the lady a glass of wine?"

"The bartender would be honored." I poured Annie a glass of wine, and one for myself, and we clinked glasses and shared a kiss across the bar.

"You're more like Simon than you will ever know, Joe," she said. "I'm a lucky girl to be engaged to a man who possesses the character and moral fiber of not only Simon, but my own father. Of course, I will forgive her."

We looked out at Mike and Lisa dancing. They were definitely having a good time, and I was pretty sure I would be taking over bartending duties for the rest of the night and was glad to do so. Annie remarked, "They make a lovely couple, and unlike Ed he doesn't look like the only thing he's interested in is getting her into bed."

"No, he's a class above your actor," I remarked.

Annie smiled, and if I could read her mind, I would say that it was the type of smile that did not foreshadow much of a future for Ed at her studio.

The party ended a little before midnight, and the caterers cleaned up quickly. Mike escorted Lisa home, and, as we would later learn, he left her at her door with a good-night kiss and the promise of a future date. That information was provided to us courtesy of the nine-year-old, who received a call from Lisa the moment she entered her apartment.

Almost as soon as she hung up the phone, Bee sunk onto the couch and fell asleep. I carried her into her bedroom, and when Annie tried to take off her party dress and put on her pajamas, Bee woke up just enough to sleepily ask if she could stay in her dress because she never wanted the night to end. Annie chuckled and looked at me and we both shrugged, and Bee smiled with her eyes closed. Annie pulled a blanket over her and kissed her gently on the forehead, then sat down on the bed beside her. She held my hand loosely off to the side and watched the sleeping child, the way only a loving mother can.

As I gazed down on this scene, it occurred to me that the abused and berated child finally had what every child needed and deserved: a loving mother. Annie, meanwhile, an accomplished and brilliant lady, had finally received the gift of maternity she so desired.

Chapter Thirty-One

Back in the living room, I turned off the Beach Boys — who were still playing in a loop long after the party ended — and put on Sinatra singing "Strangers in the Night." I reached out to Annie, who was standing beside me, and asked, "May I have this dance?"

"You may indeed, kind sir."

We slow danced around the pool area that was still lit up with festive lights. She was so beautiful and graceful, and I was so happy in her arms that I had the feeling that the past didn't exist — that there was only tonight, and a future resplendent with joy and happiness.

"Did I tell you what a wonderful hostess you were tonight?"

"Yes, but let's not forget I did have help."

"What a show Bee and Wang put on. Fred and Ginger, move over."

Annie laughed at this and said, "You know, I haven't said this, but you finding her and taking her in is one of the most generous and caring acts I have ever heard of."

"I guess I haven't told you the whole story. She found me! Like a stray cat picking out a new owner. I was sitting in the park watching some kids play basketball and she sat down on the bench next to me and started up a conversation. Then she waited for me for hours while I sat in a bar drinking, hoping she would be gone once I left. But she wasn't. She followed me home and I tried to get rid of her by offering her hundreds of dollars just to go away. And then I asked her what she wanted and she said, 'I don't won't any money Joe. I just want to take a bath and clean up and not have to sleep on the streets another night.'"

Annie gasped and listened for more as I held her tight. I smiled and stopped talking for a moment as Sinatra's buttery voice loosened up my memories.

"So I let her come home with me. And when she came out after taking a shower, dressed in my clothes that were ten sizes too big, I honestly didn't recognize her. Her face literally glowed, and like the lotus flowers that Wang gave her tonight, she looked like the essence of beauty, perfection and purity, of the mind and heart. The only thing missing was a halo around her head. And maybe it was there all along. Maybe it's still there and we can't see it because we're earthbound and she's not."

"Ha! That's an interesting idea. Maybe all this time we've been calling her an angel she's actually been one."

"Stranger things have happened," I said, and took her for another twirl around the dance court.

I paused for another moment as Sinatra started singing, "Bewitched." Like a trillion other fans, I felt like he was singing to me, and recapping different parts of my life. Yes, it was like a spell had been cast over me as I danced with this beautiful lady, and we talked about our child, who seemed to be a gift from providence. I continued, "When I looked at her that first night after she cleaned up it was like looking into the face of divinity."

"Divinity or not, she is undeniably divine," Annie remarked.

As Ol' Blue Eyes transitioned to "Moonlight Serenade," I reached in and kissed my lovely fiancée. I thought of Byron and wholeheartedly agreed that my Annie "walks in beauty, like the night of cloudless climes and starry skies," and that "all that's best of dark and bright, meet in her aspect and her eyes."

We danced and danced, kissed and kissed some more, and laughed like teenagers in love.

When it started to get chilly, we decided to go back inside, and I asked Annie if she would like a nightcap.

"Only if you'll be joining me," she laughingly replied, adding, "it's not like I have any intentions of going into work tomorrow."

It was almost three in the morning — the latest I had been up since working in the restaurant, when getting home before two a.m. was an accomplishment. I poured two glasses of white wine and handed one to Annie and sat down beside her on the couch. In truth, I didn't know how this night was going to end. We might have kissed twenty times while dancing outside, but we had never been intimate, beyond that, and I had this crazy idea that I wanted to wait until we were married. Even while dancing, I never once let my hands stray into uncharted territories.

"A toast," I said as we raised our glasses, "to a wonderful party and the beautiful lady who arranged it." We clinked our glasses and drank up, and Annie smiled at me expectantly. A silence followed, which I finally broke.

"I seriously hope our daughter doesn't expect her aging father to get up in a few hours and go running."

Annie laughed and said, "I think there's a good chance that our lovely daughter might not be getting up early either. She was so tired that she couldn't even manage to brush her teeth, and you know how she feels about dental hygiene."

"Ha ha, yes, just one of her many heavenly qualities," I said. "And now, on a more serious note, when exactly are we getting married?"

Annie's eyes widened and a smile overtook her face. "Wow! Finally. I was wondering when you were going to get around to asking that question."

"Since you seemed to have everything under control, I didn't want to interfere and get in the way of your creative process."

"How thoughtful of you," she said with a laugh. "Next Saturday at Simon's house in Malibu. I'm not what you would call very religious, so having a Justice of the Peace perform the ceremony would be fine with me. But if you would prefer to be married by a priest, I have no problem with that."

"A Justice of the Peace sounds wonderful. How many guests are we planning on?"

"Well, how many friends and family would you like to invite?"

"I'm not inviting anyone, except for Fred Astaire, aka Wang, and I would like for us to invite Lisa."

"So, you are only going to invite two people, who I was also going to invite. No other friends? Your brothers in New York? Ex-lovers…?"

I laughed and replied, "No that's it, and of course if it's okay with you, Ginger Rogers, aka Bee?"

"Well, you can't invite one half of the dance duo without inviting the other half. It just wouldn't be right."

"I totally agree, so that makes three for me. How about you?"

"Well, the lawyer who will be handling the adoption. As soon as we get married, he will get a copy of our marriage license, and thank you, by the way, for sending all the documents he requested to him so quickly. So, with the license he will have everything he needs. The two judges and their spouses, who you met tonight. One of them will be finalizing the adoption for us a couple of days after we are married."

"We need a judge to finalize the adoption?"

"It was a personal favor."

"Nice. How much did it cost?"

"Wow! I can't believe you asked such a thing. Do I actually look like the type who would offer a bribe to a judge or two?"

"You look like the type of woman who loves that nine-year-old girl so much that you would do anything to assure her safety and wellbeing. So how much?"

"Two internships at the studio, one for a daughter of one of the judges and another for a son of the other judge."

"Wow! You got away cheap," I replied.

"And the promise that I would love to contribute to any future political offices that either might seek in the future. Both are considering runs for Congress in two years from their respective districts."

"I see. Any other guests?"

"Just my assistant who has been with me nearly twenty-five years. She's a real doll. She has a special needs child and it has not been easy on her. Her family, for the last fifteen years, has been begging her to put the child in a home but she refuses. It's her child and she's not giving him up."

"And the father?"

"He skipped town once the child was properly diagnosed at two years old. She hasn't heard from him since. Have you been around many children or adults with disabilities?"

"I was actually raised by one. My aunt Jeannette. She was both physically and mentally challenged — that's what we used to call it at the time — and she spent almost every day in a specially designed chair in the kitchen of my grandparents' home, entertaining guests all day long with my grandma. They used to take care of me when both my parents were working during the day, and I used to sit with them and do my homework and listen to a whole bunch of wonderful stories."

"Oh, she sounds so lovely. I wish I could have known her."

"Me too. She was such a doll, and she was in love with my father. He would come downstairs after work and talk to her for hours. My grandparents had to eventually put her in a home. Not one of these pits you see on TV, but a really nice one where they taught her to be independent and she eventually got herself a boyfriend, the little flirt that she was."

Annie laughed and I kept going. I was on a roll now, remembering the old days and suddenly wanting to share every detail with my bride-to-be.

"My grandparents were almost eighty when they finally had to put her in the home. She was in her mid-forties at the time, and there was just no one around anymore that could help them with her. My parents were working ten-to-twelve-hour days. My grandparents' house was just too big, with too many stairs. The day they took her away, I hid in the attic and cried and cried. Strange, outside of my aunt Rena, my aunt Jeannette was the last one to die out of fifteen children."

Annie caressed my hand as I continued, "It was a very long time ago."

"Not by the way you tell it," Annie said. "It still feels like yesterday, doesn't it?"

"Sometimes it feels like I never stopped living it. Like those two weeks I went every night to see Simon in the hospital before he died. It's like everything we talked about, every thought that went through my mind, our joking around with each other and the nurses, my somber drives back home through the deserted streets of West Hollywood, over Laurel Canyon, and back into Studio City. It's like I'm sitting in a movie theater, watching the same movie over and over again."

"Hmm," Annie said. "That's pretty deep." She took a sip of her wine and we sat in silence for a few moments. Then she looked at me and asked a question that must have been on her mind for a year.

"Did Simon ever receive any chemo or radiation treatments, or did he just go there to die?"

I lowered my eyes and realized for the first time that she didn't know, and I replied, "I'm sorry, Annie, but I can't answer that."

She smiled knowingly and said, "You just did. It's what I always suspected."

She got up from the couch and walked into the kitchen, then came back with the bottle of wine and refilled my glass and her glass, finishing off the bottle. She sat down next to me and took a sip.

"It feels strange to know something so important about Simon that he didn't share with you," I said.

"It does feel strange, but it's not your fault."

I felt compelled to say more about my relationship with Simon, even though Annie was in no way pressuring me. I guess I felt a little guilty.

"It might sound odd, but I never knew what Simon did for a living, and I never asked," I explained, without being prompted. "I mean, I heard something about his being a big movie producer, but I hope you understand that our friendship had nothing to do with that. We talked about everything from medicine to politics, history, and especially literature, and we loved to talk about the specific careers of brilliant scientists, thinkers and artists like Aristotle, Galileo, da Vinci, Newton, and Einstein, but we literally never talked about movies. It was off limits, a taboo subject. Apparently, Lisa knew more about your movie empire and your accolades and awards than I did. Was it just with me, that he never wanted to discuss movies?"

"I'm not sure," she said. "You don't become as successful as Simon did in this industry without having an intense love for movies, and the process of making movies. But in the end, it all became make believe to him, and he was searching for the truth. Not an abbreviated or packaged version of the truth, but truth itself. He talked about that toward the end with unabashed sincerity, and I think he saw you as someone who could help him reach the truth, because you were outside the industry and could discuss so many other things besides movies."

She took a sip of her wine, looked at me, and shook her head. "You know, when my mother got sick, Simon immediately flew to England to be with her. He left me in charge of the studio. He didn't even ask me if I wanted to go. He stayed with her over three months. He took care of her in every way possible. There was not one thing he would not do for her, anything to make her feel more comfortable, and to ease the pain. I told him that I thought we should move her out here ... that she could live with me or with him. I argued that the warm, ocean air would be good for her. But she just refused. She didn't leave her beloved England during the war, and she 'wasn't about to leave it now.' I started flying out every weekend to see her. She was deteriorating quickly, and Simon was frantic. He started bringing in one specialist after another to see what they could do. In those few moments I was alone with my mother, I would hold her hands and look into her eyes and I just knew that she was ready to die, and that Simon's search for a miracle was preventing her from going peacefully. I couldn't even talk to him about it. The most rational man I knew was being totally irrational.

"Simon was so obsessed with my mother's wellbeing that he never once asked me how I was holding up. She was my birth mother, but to Simon she was so much more. He had put her on a pedestal. She was Beatrice in Dante's trilogy. She was perfect. Pure. An angel bejeweled in the giant petals of a red rose."

"She was buried next to your father?" I asked.

"Yes, in a cemetery bombed by the Germans during the war."

"How long ago was this?" I asked.

"Twelve years ago. Simon died on the same day as my mom eleven years later. All day, I was expecting the call, and at night when the phone rang, I didn't even have to answer it because I knew he was gone."

Annie finished off the wine in her glass in one big gulp and asked, "Would you be so kind as to open another bottle?"

"Of course," I replied as I walked back to the kitchen and took out a chilled bottle from the refrigerator. I took down two clean glasses, opened the bottle, and walked back over to the couch. Annie was fairly drunk, and under any other circumstance I would have tried to persuade her not to drink any more, but it was apparent she needed to talk to me about this, and I needed to know. I put aside the glasses we'd been using and filled the two clean glasses and handed her one as I sat down beside her. "Such a gentleman, you are, my sweet and caring fiancé."

"Thank you..." I replied as I asked her, "so after the two of you got back from the funeral, did things go back to normal?"

"Not so much. For the longest time I blamed him for allowing my mother to suffer unnecessarily when there was no more hope." She paused and took a sip of her wine before continuing. "But then how long can you stay mad at someone for loving someone too much? About six months later, he called me into his office and apologized for the way he behaved during my mother's illness. The pain he still felt was as strong as it was in the days leading up to her death. I so badly wanted to let loose on him and tell him how difficult he made things for me. He made me, her biological child, feel like I wasn't doing enough to help our mother. But his pain was so intense that I couldn't make it worse. So I accepted his apology and told him I understood how difficult it was on him and kept my mouth closed about the rest. After all, what good would it do? It was time to heal."

I nodded my understanding and agreement and took another sip as she kept going.

"That night he took me to the same restaurant in Malibu that we went to the first day I arrived in Los Angeles. It was still there, some thirty years later. Over dinner we talked about a few projects that were just starting up, and then suddenly he remarked that I should immediately file for divorce from my 'philandering, womanizing piece of shit' husband. At first, I thought this was his way of telling me that he wanted to marry me, but no. He said, 'the possibility of him physically hurting me was driving him insane,' and that 'no man was worthy of me,' especially not the 'dehumanizing beast' that I chose to marry. He would take care of everything, and make sure that that beast was never within a hundred miles of me. It would be a gift to our mother, who was constantly worrying that my husband was going to physically hurt her little girl."

"I always knew Simon was smart," I said.

"Yes, well, at the time I was speechless. I had talked to him numerous times about my failing marriage, and he was always very supportive and would tell me that whatever I decided to do he would support me one hundred percent. So I asked him point blank, 'And once I'm divorced, are you going to marry me?'

"He looked at me as though I had gone off the deep end and replied, 'You know we can't do that Annie. We've discussed this before.'

"And I said, 'That was before my mother passed away. Now the circumstances have totally changed. You're in love with me, or I believe you are, and I have always been in love with you. What's stopping us, Simon?' And of course, I succumbed to vanity and insecurity and asked him whether it was because he 'just didn't find me as attractive as he did when I was twenty-five.'"

"Oh, boy," I said. "What did he say to that?"

"He said, 'Don't be silly. You're the most perfect, the most beautiful woman I have ever seen, etcetera, etcetera ... at twenty-five, at any age — it was all very flattering, and he made me believe him — but he said it wouldn't feel right sharing the same bed with the woman who he had thought of as his sister his whole life. He said it would feel 'dirty, perverted.' And he said, 'Surely, you must feel the same way?'"

"Ouch."

"Yes. That question was like a knife to the heart. Here he was, thinking it would be 'dirty and perverted' for us to be together, and he couldn't imagine that I would feel any other way. That was easily the most mortifying and painful moment of my life. I got up from the table and went into the ladies room and cried. I couldn't help but feel that the smartest person I had ever known was captive, a prisoner to a fable.

"He insisted that I stay overnight at the house in Malibu. I slept in the same room I always slept in when staying overnight. The princess room, the bedroom specially designed for me. I pulled the covers back on the bed, lay down, and lifted the covers up to my chin. I had always felt like a princess in that room. The only problem was that the prince had left the castle."

"Did it ever get back to normal between you two?"

"Eventually, but the hole my mother's death left in Simon could never be filled by any woman. It was like every day of his life was a return to his first memory of my mother reading a fairy tale to him, or her using her body as a shield against the German bombs that were raining down night after night on them, or the two of them walking through the shattered streets of London searching for food, standing for hours on food lines, the agonizing screams of wounded soldiers flooding into the makeshift hospitals throughout the city that my mother volunteered at, with Simon by her side."

"It sounds like your mother was an extraordinary person. It's no wonder Simon idolized her."

"My mother *was* an extraordinary person, like the tens of thousands of other mothers living in the city at that time who also shielded their children with their bodies ... but it was as if Simon only saw *her*, which was kind of strange for a man who, more than anyone I have ever known, was a genius at seeing the whole picture."

"He was only a child. It would be only natural for him to see her as his savior, especially under the circumstances."

"I know that, Joe. It's like with Bee. She sees you as her savior. Nearly every time I looked at her tonight, she seemed to have an eye on you."

"She's quickly coming around to you, Annie, and I have no doubts about that."

"And I agree, but would it be the case if I came into her life six months from now, a year from now?"

"I don't know, I just thank God that you are in her life now, in my life, and that we are going to be a family."

"Yes, we are," Annie agreed and happily smiled for the first time in what seemed like hours.

"Question: When do I get to buy my lovely fiancée a wedding ring?"

"Answer: At this very moment, I am adding a tiny red diamond to my mother's wedding ring. That will be my wedding ring, but thank you for asking."

"The same ring you wore as a wedding ring with your former husband?"

"Yes, the same ring I wore with that philandering, womanizing piece of shit, but with the addition of the diamond."

"The tiny red diamond which, if am not mistaken, symbolizes passion, and a degree of flexibility."

"You're so smart," she said with a smirk and a sip of wine.

I said, "I'll use my father's wedding ring, but with no additions, if that's okay?"

"But of course."

"One other issue, if you have not already taken care of it already. In the prenuptial agreement I will be signing, please make it clear that I agree that I have no right to anything you own, including homes, the studio, bank accounts, stocks, lingerie, new or old toothbrushes — anything. The only thing I ask is that if one day you wake up and realize that you have made a terrible mistake in marrying such a loser and you decide you want a divorce, that you have no claim to this house, my bank account, or my fifteen percent share in your company."

Annie looked at me with surprise and I continued with my terms.

"In my will, I want to leave twenty percent of the stock value to each of my brothers and twenty percent to our daughter. It would also mean an awful lot to me to leave forty percent to a number of charities that are very dear to me. In all honesty, I have never felt entirely comfortable with all the money or the fifteen percent share I hold in a company that I had nothing to do with, and which Simon nevertheless left to me."

"He wouldn't have left it to you if he didn't believe in you and love you like a brother. He must have seen all of the same wonderful character traits I have seen in you since the moment we met."

"Well, I don't know if I deserve that, but I'll take the compliment all the same. Thank you. One other thing: When Lisa was behaving relatively normally, we discussed the possibility of me homeschooling Bee for at least a couple of years."

"I think that is a great idea. School can be tough on children, and she has already been knocked about far too much. And how lucky is she to have you as a teacher. I have no doubt that you will be as great a teacher to Bee as Simon was to me."

"I can only hope so. Have you made honeymoon plans?"

"No, that is something I would not do without consulting you," she replied with a slightly embarrassed expression as she sipped her wine.

"I think it might be best to just stay around here, like at your Malibu house overlooking the ocean? It's not like we can go anywhere without taking Bee. Her sense of security is still very fragile, as I found out when I had to rush her to the emergency room."

"I completely agree, and the house in Malibu is beautiful," she said, as she took another sip of wine, lowered her eyes, and suddenly she seemed deflated and uncomfortable.

"What is it, Annie?" I asked.

She sighed and said, "I have not been intimate with another human being in so long that in some cultures I might be considered a born-again virgin."

"And do you think I've been some type of Don Juan? I might not be considered a born-again virgin, but I'm not far behind."

"I just thought after that night in the limo after Simon's funeral that you might have thought I was some type of pro when it came to sex..."

"I never once thought that. We can take it as slow as you want. Just having you in my orbit is more than I could ever have dreamed of."

She reached over and we kissed, and just at that moment a sleepy-eyed nine-year-old walked into the living room wearing a slightly rumpled party dress.

"What are you doing up, angel?" Annie asked.

"This is the time daddy and I go for our run," she said as she sat between the two of us, barely able to keep her head up.

"We're going to skip our run today. After all, you got all that exercise dancing with Mr. Wang. You were the life of the party; everyone fell in love with you. Isn't that so, Annie?"

"Absolutely true," Annie said.

"It was the best day of my life," she said as she placed her lagging head on Annie's shoulder.

"And there are going to be many, many more days like that," Annie said as the bumblebee fell asleep. I picked her up and carried her into her bedroom, with Annie following. Annie took over from there but not before I got a good-night/good-morning kiss from my lovely fiancée.

I walked back into the living room and looked out the sliding glass door as it started to get light outside. I picked up the empty wine glasses and the empty bottle of wine and brought them into the kitchen.

I opened the refrigerator and took out an ice-cold Budweiser left over from the party. I stood by the sliding door and cracked it open just enough to hear the birds chirping and the rustle of a morning breeze. It is so strange how in one life, we live many lives. This time of the morning had always been my favorite part of the day. Back when I was just a teenager, during the summer months when we were out of school and living in our humble apartment in Parkchester, I used to go out about this time and buy a six-pack of beer. I was never questioned, or asked for proof of age, by the grocery owner because it was so early in the morning that he never suspected a teenager would be up at that hour. Occasionally I would drop a line and mention that my father worked nights and had just got home.

I would then take the beer, and with my basketball under my arm, I would take the elevator up to the roof of my favorite building in the development ... a building overlooking the basketball court on one side and on the other side a supermarket getting ready to open up. I used to sit down on the gravel roof, my back against the wall of the roof facing the courts, and drink my beers. It was so peaceful, and it was here that I would fantasize about hitting game-winning shots or about marrying this beautiful girl in our building whom I never had the courage to talk to, but whom I have never forgotten. Until this very day, forty-five years later, I still think of her at least a couple of times every week. She was not very big, maybe five foot three, and she had this beautiful, straight, glistening dark hair that she parted down the middle, and wore down to her shoulders. She had a perfect oval face, golden, radiant skin, with dark brown eyes and a small mouth that curled just perfectly whenever she smiled. I still dream of her, but like in real life I never end up with her ... she always goes off with someone else ... so much for Freud's theory that dreams are a form of wish fulfillment.

After I would finish my beer, I used to take the elevator back down and go play basketball for hours, shooting and practicing alone, until I got tired and went back to the apartment we lived in and took a nap for an hour. The real games didn't start until five o'clock in the evening, when the great players came out after work ... Jerry, Charlie, Clarence, Pete, Kevin and the rest...

Throughout the years, especially when I had the next day off from work, I would still start drinking at this time, not having gone to bed because I didn't get home from work until three in the morning. I would sit outside by the pool, listening to the birds singing, fantasizing like always, and reading my beloved *New York Times* ... the printed edition, not the digitized, web edition. The paper would be folded every which way, and after I was finished reading it my hands would be as black as dirt from the print. It was truly wonderful, the only way a newspaper should be read, and naturally the beers went down smoothly.

A lot of time had passed since I was a teenager drinking beer early in the morning on a roof in the Bronx, and as I went back and forth to the refrigerator for another ice-cold Budweiser, the sun started rising, and the reflection off the water in the pool was luminous and radiating like the sublime illumination at the end of Dante's *Paradiso* in the Ninth Sphere. And in the middle of this splendid illumination, I could see a large, red rose and the pure, exquisite beauty of the child, Beatrice, sleeping on a petal while a bumblebee danced around her, sprinkling the splendid blessings of our Lord onto the sleeping angel.

Chapter Thirty-Two

The Justice of the Peace declared us husband and wife and gave me permission to kiss the bride, who of course looked divine. I reached in and we kissed, and whereas my sleeping dreams never seem to have a happy ending, the real-time, conscious dream I was experiencing at this moment was more miraculous than anything I could have imagined.

Bee bounced up and down in her flouncy new gown — a Catrin creation, "in ecru," she and Annie informed me — and clapped excitedly after the ceremony, along with all the other guests. She then stood between us and I reached down and picked her up and gave her a big kiss, and then literally flipped her around, so her mother could hug and kiss her.

Naturally, my ever-efficient wife took the Justice of the Peace aside, before he could even have a congratulatory drink, and had him fill out the marriage certificates. Then she made scanned copies of the certificates and handed them to her lawyer, along with the glowing recommendation from Lisa. While she talked to the lawyer, I walked over to Lisa and her date, Mike the bartender, and she hugged and kissed me and I whispered, "Are you happy?"

"Never more so in my entire life," she said. Then she stuck out her hand and showed me the gorgeous engagement ring that Mike had given her, and I asked them when they were getting married and they said in unison, "Very soon." Of course, I knew all this because she had been in constant contact with her nine-year-old therapist and fashion consultant, who spoke just loudly enough during their frequent phone calls so I could hear her entire conversations.

As I started walking away Lisa called out to me. I turned around and she said, "Hey Joe, if I didn't believe in fairy tales before, I do now," and she looked in the direction of Bee and then lifted her ring finger up and pointed happily at her engagement ring.

⁎⁎

Simon's Malibu house was spacious and stunning, unlike so many of the tacky monstrosities along the coast of California. Everywhere you looked, inside and outside, you could not help but feel the care and the artistry that went into the creation of this gorgeous home. Simon had put his mark on every inch of the property, in a way that only reinforced my impression of him as a modern-day Renaissance man — the Michelangelo of Malibu. From the lemonade berry trees and the tall grasses at the front of the home to the breathtaking views of the ocean from the open living areas on the ground floor, the entire property was an elegant testament to the possibilities of good design.

Annie and I had decided to keep the reception simple, except for a bartender and a couple of waiters who passed around hors d'oeuvres and took drink orders. The main course was served buffet style, with a choice of steamed Maine lobster, Maryland crab, sliced roast beef, porterhouse steak, or lamb chops, and plenty of side dishes, and to satisfy Bee's unique tastes, we included pan fried dumplings direct from Wang's place of business, as well as pizza. Annie could not resist. Cristal Champagne flowed generously and the bar was fully stocked.

Even though I had been around lavish displays of wealth for a long time at the restaurant, I was always seeing it from the other side, from the vantage point of a busboy, a bartender, a waiter, or a manager. At the restaurant it never failed to amaze me how stark the gap was between the rich and the working class. On one side, separated by a wall, you had the kitchen staff who were working their butts off — the chef, the broiler men, the pantry men, and the dishwashers — and besides the chef, not one of them was making more than thirty-five thousand dollars a year. On the other end you had children younger than Bee — children who were already millionaires, thanks to their families, and who would never have to work at a strenuous job — dining with their parents, grandparents, relatives and friends, all of whom earned in one hour what the dishwashers made in a year. And I knew from experience that the super-rich were not always smarter than those on the other side of the rich-poor divide.

I could not help but think of Bee, and how she would eventually turn out. She might not realize it now, but she was soon to be a very privileged child with exceptionally rich parents — one of them so rich and connected that she could get a judge to approve an adoption, that would usually take at least six months, in a couple of days.

Bee's first nine years had been a living hell, and whereas I desperately wished I could erase that time from her memory, I also knew that her experiences would make her better and stronger than she would have been otherwise. I hoped that she would never forget how tough times can really be, and that she would choose to take that experience and make it a better world for other children who suffer similar abuse. The biggest problem, or shall we say obstacle, might be her two parents, who were very willing and able to spoil the child beyond anyone's imagination.

But I could not help but believe that my little girl was different. Despite the difficult circumstances she lived through, there was something enchanting, life-affirming, and joyous about her that was unlike any other child I had ever known, either back home in the Bronx or through the restaurant.

After dinner, I was given the honor of the first dance with my lovely wife. We danced to the sound of the Beach Boys, another little whim that my Annie could not deny herself or our daughter. Once we stopped dancing, the floor was opened up to all who wanted to participate, and before we could wander away to refill our glasses, Bee and Mr. Wang took over, creating a spectacle that would have stirred envy in the real Fred Astaire and Ginger Rogers. There was no artifice in their dancing. They were making it up as they went along. But it was wild and heartfelt, and Bee's uncontrolled laughter cast a spell over the entire house. Her squeals mingled with the far-off sound of the crashing waves and mixed with the music of the Beach Boys. It was a sound so pure and joyful that it seemed to reach the Heavens, and everyone who heard it felt renewed.

***

By the time evening arrived, only a handful of guests were still there. Lisa and Mike were sitting inside talking to the bride and the daughter. The three adults were drinking Cristal out of champagne flutes and the daughter, not to be left out, was drinking a Coke out of a flute.

Wang and I were sitting outside on the patio, overlooking the beautiful Pacific Ocean, enjoying ice-cold Budweiser beers next to a fountain with two Cupids spouting water.

We got to talking politics, which you're not supposed to do at a wedding, but we did it anyway. Wang, who was originally from Hong Kong, spoke about his cousins and his sister back home. He was worried about them. They ran businesses, and the Chinese government had been cracking down on their freedoms more and more in recent years, gradually taking away the freedoms that Hong Kong citizens enjoyed until 1997, when the Brits gave the former colony back to China.

"Hong Kong ... it was a democracy," he said at one point. Then he raised his hands in a kind of frustrated way and tried to explain the impact on his family. "To be free and to lose that freedom is worse than never being free at all. My cousins and sister remember what it was like before. They feel bad every day, losing their freedom."

I raised my beer high in the air and shook my head in sympathy. "I hear you, buddy," I said. "Damn bullies. And the current occupants of the White House are not helping."

We talked about the lukewarm American response to Chinese domination of the region, and about how the social conscience of the sports world, the National Basketball Association, has decided to remain quiet about the repressive and deadly force used against the protestors because, after all, when billions of dollars are at stake one does not want to rock the boat of such a rich source of revenue as the Chinese Communist Party, or The Republic of China.

I turned to Wang and said, "It's nice to see how the one percent live."

Wang laughed out loud and said, "But now you are part of the one percent. Looks to me like you might be rich like Bill Gates. Will you be living here all the time?"

I laughed and said, "No, we'll be living in my same house, at least during the week. Annie's company is very close, and Bee would not be able to live without the pan-fried dumplings your restaurant makes. Also, we would never want to be far away from her dance partner."

Wang laughed again and said, "That's good. I like that." Then he paused and said, "She is like sunshine, Joe. A gift from Tianzhu, the Chinese name for Lord of Heaven."

"I have been very blessed to have her in my life. She is very much a gift from Tianzhu. I'm sure she has told you her story."

"Oh yes, and you are her hero, Joe. I doubt a child could love a father any more than she loves you."

"Thank you, Wang. I've always meant to ask you if you have always worked at the restaurant you are at now?"

"Oh no, Joe, unlike most of my relatives I came to the United States through New York, not California. I worked for my uncle who had a restaurant on Fordham Road, not far from the university and the Bronx Zoo. We did wonderful business, but we got robbed at least once a week and the police couldn't do much to help us."

"That's a tough neighborhood. I was raised in the Bronx, but to the east of Fordham. It was a nice neighborhood when I was growing up in the 70s and 80s but it changed drastically and now there is like a murder a week around where I used to live."

"Yes, it is a real shame because our customers were wonderful. They used to eat in and take out two or three times a week. But during one robbery my uncle was badly hurt and we had to take him to the hospital. After he recovered, we decided to move out to California and be with our other relatives. We gave them the money we had and they enlarged the restaurant that my uncle and I work in now, and like in the Bronx we have many loyal customers and we do great business, and we have never been robbed."

"Well, that's a good thing. Your restaurant is in a nice neighborhood, and there are always police cars patrolling around the area."

"Yes, we like it very much, and the weather is much nicer than in the Bronx. Do you go back to the Bronx to visit relatives and friends?"

"Not so much anymore, so many have passed away and the younger ones have moved away from the Bronx and into the suburbs. The neighborhoods and schools are much better and safer there."

"I was so happy to see Lisa with that very nice man who was the bartender at Bee's first party. I could see that they are truly in love. That other one she came with at Bee's party had rabbit eyes. It was disgusting the way he was looking at her and touching her all over. He was just going to use her, but this new gentleman will take care of her. I used to feel so sorry for Lisa when I would deliver her food. She always seemed unhappy and alone, but she pretended not to be. One night, she asked me if I thought she was ugly. Ugly, I thought, she is so beautiful and I told her so. People must have really hurt her when she was young like they did Bee. But this new gentleman is no rabbit, and I am so happy for her."

Suddenly, the strangest thought went through my mind. Jack, the one madly in love with my daughter, is a rabbit. If that little sucker ever tries anything with my daughter, I will end his career and life. I looked over the ocean, seriously contemplating that rabbit's real motives. Wang suddenly touched my shoulder and asked, "Are you okay, Joe?"

I shook my head and replied, "Just some very strange thought ... nothing that another ice-cold beer can't fix. I reached into the cooler by my side that was filled with ice and pulled out two beers. I handed one to Wang and opened one for myself. I made a toast, "To our long friendship." We drank up as my lovely little bumblebee, dressed in her beautiful ecru dress, came bouncing down the steps and landed on my lap. She said, "I am so happy you came, Mr. Wang. It means so much to me. My mommy said that sometime this week my adoption will be finalized, and that we are going to have another party. You and Lisa have to come. It is going to be at this house, but my mommy said she would have a limousine pick you and Lisa and her boyfriend up and then drive you back. She said she would make it all right with the restaurant you work at and that she didn't see a problem. What do you think?"

"I think, how could I say no. I'm your dance partner, and I don't want anyone taking my place," Wang replied as she jumped off of me and hugged and kissed him and remarked, "I love you so much, Mr. Wang, and thank you."

She ran up the stairs to tell Annie, and Wang looked at me and we both said, "A gift from Tianzhu."

I could only imagine what my lovely wife had in mind when she said she would take care of everything with the restaurant ... a five-, ten-, or twenty-thousand-dollar donation, or a contract for a year's worth of catering? It would be something substantial, for sure. My wife could compete with the biggest of the big shots, but then again, my beautiful Annie was probably the biggest of all the big shots.

At about nine o'clock, Lisa, Mike, and Wang got into the limousine that Annie provided them with and a chauffeur drove them home. We watched as the limo drove down the driveway, and toward the Pacific Coast Highway. I put my arm around my lovely wife as we walked back toward the house and jokingly asked, "And

266 THE NINTH SPHERE

should I even ask how much you plan on paying Wang's restaurant so that he can have off another night to celebrate the adoption of our beautiful daughter?"

"No, you shouldn't ask, that would not be very gentlemanly. Besides, it's a gift."

"Okay, would you like to place a little wager on whether our daughter sleeps in her dress tonight or not?"

"No, because I already know. Of course, she is going to sleep in her dress tonight."

"At least you're honest, besides being the most beautiful bride ever."

Chapter Thirty-Three

I sat up in bed re-reading Hemingway's *The Sun Also Rises* for the thirtieth time. Or maybe it was the thirty-first. It was probably the book I have read the most in my life, and it was certainly one of my favorite books of all time. I had to say "one of my favorites" because the idea of choosing one favorite book always seemed like asking a parent to choose their favorite child.

Annie was in the bathroom getting ready and had been in there a long time. She was nervous, and to be honest, so was I. She had put a bucket beside our bed with a bottle of Cristal Champagne, and two chilled flutes, but I was not to touch it until she came out. And really, what kind of a monster would I be to start in on our champagne while my bride was in the bathroom getting ready for our wedding night?

Annie finally did come out, dressed in a red silk mini slip. She looked stunning, sexy, and above all else as nervous as a basketball player at the foul line with the championship on the line.

"Wow," I said. "Wow."

"Is that good?"

"Um, yes," I answered, unable to get a full thought out.

"Thank you," she said in an anxious voice I was not accustomed to. She simply stood in place for what seemed like an eternity and then I got the bright idea of offering her a glass of champagne, which she gladly accepted. She sat down on her side of the bed with her eyes lowered, sipping at the champagne. I offered to give her a neck massage that she eagerly agreed to as she turned her back to me. I started rubbing her shoulders and neck, and they were as tight as a drum.

I started to tell her a story about when I was five years old and living in my grandmother's house with my parents, my aunt Jeannette and my aunt Carmela, who was still living at home and sleeping in one of the many bedrooms on the middle floor of the house. My aunt Carmela who became our mother when our biological mother passed away.

"Well, I was very close to my aunt Carmela," I continued, "and whenever she went shopping, I would go with her. She always found money because she used to walk with her head down, and I was always the lucky recipient of her good fortune. Sometimes, she might find as much as fifty cents and give it all to me. It was like hitting the lottery for me. My aunt was very pretty and I'm not exaggerating when I say she looked like Sophia Loren. We were very close, and when she got engaged to my uncle Al she promised me that I could go on the honeymoon with them when they got married." Annie started laughing and I could feel the muscles in her neck and shoulders loosen up.

"Well, I told my mother all about my plan to go on their honeymoon with them, and my mother simply went along with the whole thing. Well, the night before the wedding I took down one of the suitcases that were stored up in the attic and packed everything I thought I would need on the trip. I hid the suitcase under my bed and by the time the wedding and reception were over the next night, I had fallen asleep. But I had reminded my mother and the bride throughout the reception that I was all packed and ready to go in the morning. I was so excited because this was also going to be the first time for me on an airplane. They were going on their honeymoon to Puerto Rico, like fifty million other newlyweds from New York."

The muscles in Annie's neck were just about fully relaxed as she continued to laugh, and I continued to tell the story.

"The next morning when I got up, I immediately reached under my bed and pulled out my suitcase. I was fully prepared as I walked into the kitchen, with suitcase in hand, and sat down at the breakfast table with my mom and dad. I asked my mom, 'What time is Aunt Carmela coming to pick me up?' She replied, 'Oh, sweetheart, they had to leave last night right after the reception because their flight this morning was cancelled but the airline got in touch with them and told them if they wanted to, they could get on a flight an hour after the reception ended. We tried to wake you up, but you were so tired you wouldn't budge. I told them to go on without you, that you would understand, because it was after all their honeymoon.'

"'You mean, I'm not going?' I asked.

"And my mom said, 'I'm sorry sweetheart, but next trip they go on they promised to take you with them no matter what.'

"I picked up my suitcase and walked back into my bedroom and I didn't even bother to have breakfast, which was my favorite meal, because I was so sad."

"Oh, poor baby," Annie remarked, turning around to stroke my cheek.

"Yes, it was truly terrible, but when they finally came back from their honeymoon, my aunt brought me back a whole bunch of gifts, and the promise I would go on their next trip, and all was forgiven. My aunt was a real saint."

"Did you get to go on their next trip?"

"Yes, but it was more a family trip and my parents, two brothers and I went along with them, but it was to a resort in New York so I still didn't get to ride on an airplane."

She turned toward me and asked, "How many times do you think we have kissed?"

"Hundreds upon hundreds," I replied as she put her champagne flute down on a side table.

"Well, since we have got the kissing down, I think it's time to move on," she said as she lowered her slip and we started to kiss passionately. The rest was pure magic — the love making, yes, but even more so the holding her tightly all night long.

Chapter Thirty-Four

The only room in the house I had not entered was the library, and I thought it was only right to enter it for the first time with Annie. I took her hand as we passed through the wide double doors, and it felt like crossing the threshold with my bride for the first time.

It was a purely magical place, and to reach at least half of the many thousands of books, one had to use a ladder. There were four ladders on rollers, and each of them could easily be moved to the location of the books you were looking for. I told Annie that we had to come up with a new rule for the bumblebee and that she was not allowed in the library unless accompanied by an adult. I could already see her rolling around the library, at the very top of the ladders, just for the adventure of it all. The top shelves nearly touched the domed skylight that looked like it was at least one hundred feet high.

In the middle of the room was a long mahogany desk with a computer on each side. It was similar to how Annie had described it to me that day at the Smoke House after Simon's funeral. My eyes were immediately drawn to a stack of leather-bound notebooks that one would associate with writers and artists from centuries back, certainly not used by many writers of today, since the advent of computers. I asked, "Are they like the original sketches, formulas, and theories of da Vinci?"

"No, those are Simon's memoirs, or I guess one could call them his diary. He kept them throughout his lifetime."

"Has there ever been a biography written about Simon?"

"Not that I know of, and certainly not one that had his blessing."

"And no autobiography?"

"Only what you see there."

"Can I take a look?" I asked hesitantly.

"Of course," she replied as I picked up the top notebook and immediately an envelope fell out of the book and down onto the floor. I picked it up and looked at the name printed on the envelope. "It's addressed to a Joe. I'll just leave it here and when I'm finished going over the notebook, I will put it back."

"Why not just open it?" Annie asked.

"It could be personal," I replied.

"Or it could just as likely be intended for you. The last time I checked you were named Joe."

"Are you sure?" I asked and Annie nodded her head.

I opened the envelope and started reading it to myself. Simon wrote, 'Hi Joe. If you are reading this letter, I am fairly sure that my lovely Annie has allowed you to visit my library, or even better, that the two of you have gotten along so well after meeting that you have fallen in love and are now married. If that is so, my sincere congratulations to both of you. I cannot think of a couple more suited for each other. She is the most amazing woman I have ever known, and besides our parents, the only other person I can say I loved unconditionally. I have told her all about you.

'In a city filled with pseudo-intellectuals and geniuses, you and my Annie, in my opinion, are the only two whom I would certify as true intellectuals and geniuses. I have never given permission to any writer to write a biography on me, and I have never been so arrogant to write an autobiography. My life and ideas are on full display in the various notebooks I have filled over my lifetime. If you would like, I give you the permission I have denied myself, and many famous historians, to write my biography.

'Please, do not consider yourself unworthy of such an assignment. And do not try to encourage Annie to get a famous historian to write it. I have told her numerous times that once I have passed away, the only person I give her permission to allow to write my authorized biography is you, and only you, if you so choose. You, I trust, and any additional information you might need you can get from Annie, who has a mind like an Encyclopedia.

'I cannot begin to tell you how much I enjoyed our conversations over the years. After I lost my mother, I was as close as ever to taking my own life, and during this time I drove my undeserving Annie crazy. It was our conversations as much as anything about family and the inevitable grief that accompanies a strong and caring family that helped me get through this tough period, and I will always be eternally thankful.

'I wish you only the best, and please take care of my precious and beautiful Annie. Also, if she is standing beside you while you are reading this letter I give you full permission to hand it over to her … otherwise she won't be able to sleep trying to figure out what was in the letter and won't stop nagging you to let her read it.

'Love to you both,

Simon.'

I looked up at Annie and said, "He said to let you read it if you so wanted." I handed the letter to Annie who sat down at the desk and read every word. After she was finished, she gave it back to me, as she laid her head down on the desk and cried.

With quite a bit of hesitation and anxiety I took on the assignment. It would take me over three years to complete the biography. It was an instant best seller, and made the *New York Times* top-ten lists for best books written and published that year. But what I learned about the man was more important to me than any recognition. He was truly a Renaissance man, like one of his heroes and mine, the great da Vinci.

Yet, it was the opening line in his diary, which I used as an opening line in the book, that had the most impact on me. He said, 'In the United States they like to argue about when life begins, in the mother's womb, as a fetus, or after the baby has been born? But for me, life began with my first memory, and that was as a two-year-old looking into the beautiful and loving face of my mother as she read me a fairy tale. She was my protector against the bombs the Germans dropped indiscriminatingly down upon the city of London. The one who saw that I always had enough to eat when she went hungry, and the one who held the dying hands of soldiers who were brought in off the battlefield and into the makeshift hospitals set up throughout the city. She was my hero then, and shall remain so until my dying day.'

Chapter Thirty-Five

As my lovely wife predicted, three days after our wedding our little bumblebee became legally ours. She finally had what one would hope that every child had, loving and caring parents who loved her unconditionally. And yes, we had another party, and she danced with Mr. Wang, and she insisted on wearing her new dress, her third in little over a week, to bed. After all, it was the best day of her life.

We stayed at the Malibu house for the two weeks following our wedding, and since I immediately started working on Simon's book, I came to appreciate even more the precious bond between mother and daughter. From the patio, during my afternoon breaks, I watched the two of them as they splashed around in the ocean and the laughter from both mother and child filled me with a sense of well-being I had been searching for since I arrived in Los Angeles.

One afternoon while watching them I fell asleep and I found myself suddenly back in the Bronx at the funeral home. It was nighttime and it was quiet and very dark. I went to open the front door of the funeral home, but to my surprise it was locked. It had a large chain around the entrance and it was dark inside. I banged on the door and shook the chain. I simply had to get inside to see my uncle Tony.

Suddenly, I felt a police club rubbing against my back and I turned around and there was a uniformed cop, a hulk of a man, looking down at me. He asked, "What do you think you are doing?"

"I need to get in to see my uncle who has died and is laid out inside."

"Are you crazy? This place hasn't been a funeral home in over forty years," he replied as he shined his flashlight down on me. "Let me see some identification."

I pulled out my wallet and handed him my driver's license. He looked down at it and said, "It says you live in Studio City, California. What are you even doing in this part of the Bronx? You can get killed." He looked at my name and said out loud, "Joseph Caggiano. I knew a Joseph Caggiano back in the days when I was living in Parkchester. We used to play ball together."

I looked more closely at the police officer and said, "My God, it's you, Jerry. The greatest half-court ballplayer I have ever seen. I could have sworn that I heard that you retired years ago from the force."

"I did, but they asked me back because of all the rioting and killing that's been going on."

"Wow! Your children must all be grown up. Do they play ball?"

"What in God's creation are you talking about? One son is a doctor and the other is a professor at an upstate university. They barely know how to dribble a ball. I have grandchildren in their twenties. Are you sure you're not on drugs, or at the very least drunk?"

"No, I swear. You can give me one of those tests if you like."

"I'm not giving you any tests."

"I need to get to Parkchester, do you think you can take me?"

"Holy shit, you really are crazy ... too much sun out there in California. Parkchester is nothing like it was when we lived there. There's like a murder a day there."

"Please take me, it is very important."

"Okay, but are you on some kind of suicide mission?"

"No, Jerry, but I need to go there. Please."

"Get in the car."

"Is it all right if I sit up front?"

"I don't know why not, it's not like anyone else is sitting there."

I sat up front, and before I knew it, I was in Parkchester where the old Cornel's used to be and I asked Jerry to pull over. He stopped the car and said, "Are you going back to the basketball court we used to play on? Because if you are it is no longer there. They tore it down."

"I know, but I have to see it for myself," I replied as I got out of the patrol car just as Jerry was getting a call about a robbery about a mile away. "I need to go. Please, Joe, be careful."

"Thank you, Jerry. Those days back here playing ball were the happiest days of my life."

He smiled as he pulled away and I walked through the pathway to the basketball court. It suddenly became light outside, the morning light that I have always loved. Todd Rundgren's "I Saw the Light" was playing on a large portable radio that was on a bench, inside the court, next to a basketball, my basketball. The court was as it always was. The nets were a little tattered and were gently blowing in the wind. I picked up the ball, and it was like I was sixteen again. I was dribbling like Pistol Pete and shooting like the great Walt Frazier.

I suddenly noticed the mother wheeling her disabled son past the court. They looked at me, the desire in the young boy's eyes piercing right through to my very heart. I ran toward them, and asked the mother, "Do you think your son might want to take a few shots?" She looked at me as though she was uncertain and then looked down at her son who eagerly nodded. "That would be great," she replied and she wheeled her son onto the court.

I said, "I am going to pick him up so he will be closer to the rim and it will be easier for him. Believe me, I am an old hand at this."

I could see the worry on her face grow, as I bent down and picked the boy up. He was as light as my lovely Bee. She handed him the ball and he threw it right up and through the hoop. She started to cry, as she handed him the ball over and over again and like the great Walt Frazier he hit shot after shot as her tears disappeared and the smile of a proud and grateful mother was written all over her face. I told them that I play here every morning and that whenever they passed by to drop in. "I see great potential in your son," I remarked as I shook the boy's hand. "You did great," I said to him and he smiled.

She wheeled her son off the court, but before disappearing through the pathway she turned and smiled at me and I waved back at her. I then bent down on my knees, as I tightly grasped the ball, and kissed the court that was so much a part of my life.

I suddenly woke up as my beautiful daughter's face appeared directly in front of me. She kissed me on the cheek, and then as an added benefit my lovely wife reached down and kissed me on the lips. They warned me not to stay out too long in the sun. They walked into the house, laughing and laughing.

As to that second epiphany I spoke of earlier, it was quite simple: Don't let past regrets dictate the rest of your life. Or as my uncle Tony used to say, "The past can be either your tutor or your poison," and in honor of him I chose to make it my tutor.

CPSIA information can be obtained
at www.ICGtesting.com
Printed in the USA
FSHW010948070621
82161FS